COLD CUSTOMER

By

MYRA McFARLAND

COLD CUSTOMER by Myra McFarland
Title ID: 8575766

Copyright 2018 Myra McFarland

ISBN 13 – 978-1720685838
ISBN 10 -- 1720685835

This work is in memory of:

George Tetherley, a city editor of the old school,
who once told me a story;

and LauraBelle Hibbetts McCaffrey,
an inspiring librarian and sharp-penciled first reader.

CHAPTER 1

Monday, July 3, 1933

Knowing things is dangerous. I know things. It's my job.

Right at this moment, I knew one thing with absolute certainty: it was hot -- ninety-six degrees at five minutes before noon. That was outside. Inside, the temperature was at least ten degrees higher. I would swear on my grandmother's grave that the news office of The Telegraph-Register had metamorphosed into the front porch of Hell.

Come to think of it, if anyone deserved to be in Hell, it was Grandmama. I can just see the old bat. She would be wearing one of her interchangeable starched black dresses accessorized by the *pince nez* balanced on the tip of her nose and the frown fixed on her stingy lips. Lack of self-assurance was never among the old lady's shortcomings. She could be counted on to slap away the flames and correct the Devil's grammar with never a by-your-leave. Give her a couple of millennia, and she would be running the joint.

Scrub that thought. Too hot.

I unbuttoned the second button on my shirt. I had discarded my suit coat at nine o'clock, ripped off my tie fifteen minutes later and sweated through my shirt by ten. Only the flies, the drifting cigar smoke and the ceiling fan stirred in the newsroom at 318 East Main Street, which was two blocks from the county courthouse, three blocks from my favorite diner, across the street from what passed for home and next door to the B&O railroad tracks.

I'm a newsman, a damn good one, if I say so myself. Call me what you want. A reporter. A typewriter jockey. A nosy-parker. A pain in the ass. A stiff finger in the eye of big shots, self-important do-gooders, the high and mighty, the lowest of the lowlifes, and all thugs hidden out of view and operating in plain sight. I like to think of myself as a friend to all who love a good story told true, gotten first and written tight.

The scarred Underwood on my desk contained a story for today's edition, Monday afternoon, July 3, 1933. This one was a front-pager about an abandoned vacant lot on the margin of the downtown business district. The town council had performed its hocus-pocus and called it a park.

The politicians named the park after Col. Thomas B. Wentner, a hometown hero from the Great War who had died in the trenches on the plains of France. Rumor had it that the bullet with Wentner's name on it had come from his own troops. But that was only a rumor. The council somehow conveniently forgot Wentner had been the mayor's brother-in-law and a first-class horse's patoot. The so-called park was a public-relations swindle pure and simple. Thanks to that little economic hiccup people called the Great Depression, it would be years, if ever, before the town could afford to seed it with grass and add benches, swings, a fountain and all the other grandiose accoutrements so lavishly promised. Until then, the lot would attract little more than wind-blown rubbish and civic contempt, even if it did sport a pretty plaque.

My story was done. It could use another polish, but I was so numbed by the heat that I could not move one more brain cell or tap one more typewriter key. Instead, I propped my feet up on my desk and day-dreamed air so cold the wind was a blue norther that turned milk into ice cream before it left the cow's teat. Take last December, when a Christmas blizzard brought everything in Paradise, Indiana, to a standstill.

The clipped story from December 27, 1932, usually gave me a chuckle. Today, I read it in a futile effort to cool off by way of verbal association.

STORM GENERATES FREAKISH MIRACLE IN CHICKEN COOP

By Walter G. Pratt

Here's what happened in a nutshell. For thirty-two days straight, the temperature never rose above freezing. At the worst of the early winter chill, Mrs. Roberta Hansen, wife of Joseph P. Hansen of Boundary Pike northeast of town, telephoned to inform me a hen had frozen solid outside her chicken coop. The hen miraculously revived when brought inside the warm barn. Mrs. Hansen reported the chicken laid two eggs before being paired with noodles for supper. The eggs were frozen, too, she said, through and through.

This story had Paradise readers talking for a week. It would never have played in Chicago. If I had turned that story into the city desk when I was a cub reporter in the big city, I would have been laughed out of the newsroom. I sometimes missed those days of chasing news, the competition with other reporters, the sense of being a small part of something big and important. I did not miss the sweaty crowds, the haste, the noise, the dirt, or the stink. I have to admit, though, I long for the gangsters. They were one of the twin holy grails of Chicago journalism – gangsters and rotten politics. There has never been politics like Chicago politics. We do have politics in Paradise, of course, just not to the same degree of colorful venality. No gangsters, though. Damn.

Voices in the corridor broke into this woolgathering. I identified the genial baritone as belonging to Ed Jones, the printer. Someone told a joke.

Hahahahahaha. High-pitched. Hollow. Phony. That laugh belonged only to one man.

I would rather offer myself as a snack for a starving tiger than traffic with Francis Rumsey. I didn't like him, and he didn't like me. I knew where he went and what he did on his trips to Chicago. He was a simple man given to complex and expensive pleasures. And he knew I knew.

"Where's Delores? I've got her birthday present."

Rumsey didn't waste time on social niceties like a handshake, hello, how are you, nice day. Instead, he fiddled with the carnation that always sprouted from his lapel. He wore a natty brown suit today, one suitably austere as befitted his profession. Rumsey's wardrobe had improved lately. The suit must have been hand-tailored because it managed to conceal most of the gut that threatened to spill over the waistband of his trousers.

"Guess you'll have to deal with me, Frankie," I said. "Delores is in Muncie helping her sister with a new baby. She'll be back next week."

"That's Francis to my friends. Mr. Rumsey to you, Pratt."

"Aww. Why, Frankie, what a thing to say. And we're relations – sort of."

"You can't choose your family."

"More's the pity, I always say."

"Huh?" Rumsey chewed that one over. No one ever accused him of being fast on his feet. He clenched and unclenched his fists, shifted his weight from foot to foot and stared at the ceiling, as if to pull divine guidance from the embossed tin that covered the plaster above his balding head.

The nicest thing I could say about Francis Tolliver Rumsey was that he was a snake dressed in human skin. But that description did a disserve to reptiles. Superficial sympathy kept his business going. The big laugh and the traveling-salesman jokes made the Rotary regulars, the Elks, the Moose, the Odd Fellows and the Masons split the seams of their blue serge suits. Hard, button-brown eyes and a miserly smile never warmed his doughy face. He was a cousin of sorts. His mother was my grandmother's brother's niece by marriage. All that meant was we kept our dying in the family, so to speak, and the Pratts went to Rumsey's establishment instead of Miller's Funeral Parlor in our time of need. I've left instructions to take me to Miller's or let me rot.

I enjoyed Rumsey's discomfort but I couldn't stand the silence. I also couldn't curb my curiosity. That trait has gotten me in trouble a time or two.

"What's this year's birthday present?" I nodded toward the small box poking out of his breast pocket. "Two tickets to the Primrose Theater? No, that was last year. Two hams? No, too big for your pocket, and that was the year before last, if I recollect."

"Just spit it out, Pratt. I've never seen you at a loss for words."

"Let's see." I pretended to think about it for a moment. "Uh-huh. You like to do things in twos, don't you, Frankie? Like twins – say, red-headed twins?"

His cheeks burned at that one, a darker red under the crimson brought on by a short walk in the sun and the rosy glow left over from the bootlegged Canadian whiskey in the bottom drawer of his office filing cabinet.

He slammed the gift box on my desk scattering dust, cigar ashes and erasers. "Cards," he finally sputtered. "They're playing cards. Fancy ones with gold letters on 'em. Two decks."

I laughed so hard even Hattie Webster, who was hard of hearing on the best of days, looked up from her desk outside the editor's private office. The newspaper's secretary and bookkeeper was skinny as a wire, and her sense of public propriety was as stiff and unforgiving as her corset.

"What's the matter?" Rumsey shouted. "Not good enough?"

"No, no." I reined in the guffaw to a chortle. "I guess you don't know Delores as well as you think. Delores Mackey is strict Evangelical Brethren. She'd no more be caught dead playing cards than wearing yesterday's underwear."

Rumsey pulled himself up to his full five-foot-seven and looked as though he was about to blow a fuse. I laughed again. I couldn't help it.

"You damn Pratts! You're all a pack of liars and cheats. You failed in Chicago, that's why you slunk home like a rat looking for a hidey-hole. You call yourself a newsman?" I could almost hear the gears grinding in his brain as he searched for the words. "You'd – you'd – you'd sell your own mother for a story."

"Difficult to do, Frankie. Mother's priceless."

That one went over his head, too.

"I'll show you, Pratt. What if I told you that you've got the biggest story of your life sitting right under your nose, and you don't even see it?"

"See it? Don't you mean smell it? When you're around, there's a big stink, that's for sure. Damn straight, pal." I was shouting now, too.

Hattie Webster grunted and fled into the inner office. There went another ten cents out of my pay envelope. A discreet *gosh darn* would set her thin lips into a hard line. She might shake her head in disapproval, but she usually wouldn't complain. That was about as far as I could go in her hearing without incurring her wrath. *Damn*, however, was over the top. Hattie, the agent of Mrs. Arletha Heston, my publisher, enforced unbendable rules about swearing on the premises.

Rumsey didn't notice Hattie's shock. He groped in his inside breast pocket and pulled out a thin blue envelope. He flipped the envelope at me, just missing my face. I picked it up off my lap and opened it. I recognized the format. I contained funeral information for Mrs. Ruby (Craig) Bailey, late of Green Township.

"Enjoy the cards. You'll have lots of time to play patience when you're on the dole and sucking off the county's tit." Rumsey nodded toward the office. "That's if I have anything to do with it."

Now it was his turn to laugh. *Hahahahahaha* followed him all the way out the door.

The gift was an advertising giveaway emblazoned with RUMSEY FUNERAL PARLOR AND MORTUARY in sparkling gold on a tasteful dark blue background. I tossed it onto my desk next to the 1933 calendar from Cooper's Service Station featuring ladies displaying more goosebumps than clothes. The date of Saturday, July 22, 1933, was circled in red. My wedding day was less than three weeks away.

Jefferson T. Heston's head appeared from the inner sanctum, his office, otherwise known as the place where he hid from his mother and Hattie. He walked to my desk, parted the clutter like Moses at the Red Sea and perched his substantial haunch on the vacated real estate.

I had known Jeff to take a small drink and cuss a little, that is when his mama wasn't looking. But he had a business to run and Hattie Webster was the glue that had cemented Lincoln County's one remaining newspaper together for nearly thirty years. Francis Rumsey was one of the paper's biggest advertisers and Rumsey paid his bills on time, a trait to be worshipped in the middle of the nation's worst Depression. I was eminently useful but ultimately expendable.

He must have seen the wince I tried to conceal because he patted me on the shoulder and said, "Don't worry, kid, I'll make sure there's a little something extra in your Christmas bonus."

Kid. I hated that.

Jeff Heston, at a still-boyish-but-running-to-fat thirty years old, was scarcely four years older than me. Physically, we could not have been more different. Jeff had thinning blond hair, a chunky physique and stretched to a little over average height. Like all the Pratts, I stood out in a crowd. I was tall, topping out at six-foot-three, thin to the point of skeletal, and dark, with an untamable shock of black hair that fell over my forehead, and brown eyes with strange golden flecks. Adele Atkinson, my fiancée, said I reminded her of a solitary crow, one of those perched on the telephone wires observing the comings and goings about town. I like to think I looked like a young Abe Lincoln.

But Jeff and I were completely alike in that we loved Paradise, and we loved newspapering. I have caught him, more than once, standing alone on the catwalk over the press, leaning on the railing, just staring into space. No one else was there. The press was still, and the paper long since put to bed. I knew exactly what he was doing. He was inhaling the intoxicating perfume of ink and machine grease and dreams. I have done the same myself.

"What's this?" Jeff hefted Rumsey's gift.

"Delores's birthday present. Rumsey was just here, but you already know that. Ruby Bailey died."

"Which Bailey is that?"

I consulted my mental map of the county.

"Ruby is – was – the wife of old Jed Bailey. They have a little farm, maybe eighty acres, in Green Township about three miles from town. You know the place. They painted the house red back a few years before the '29 Crash because they had left-over barn paint. People talked about it for months. It's on Winchester Pike past the gravel pit, next to the Country Club. Can't miss it. She was a Craig. Her brother's Delmer Craig on Fourth Street, used to own a little butcher shop before he retired."

"You never fail to amaze me, Walt. You're a regular walking encyclopedia of Lincoln County. What you don't know isn't worth knowing. That's why you have a job here." Jeff thought a moment. "Let's look into this."

"C'mon, Jeff, Ruby Bailey was a nice lady, but it's just another obit." Scoffing, along with sarcasm and ambition, was among my better qualities, or lesser qualities if you listened to Adele tell the story.

"You never know. Where's Rumsey's funeral information? Does it list a time and date for the service?" Jeff pulled reading glasses out of the pocket of his white shirt, so white and starched to the nth degree that it nearly shone, propped them on his nose and pawed through the layers of paper cluttering my scarred and wounded oak desk. He frowned when he found drafts of a couple of short stories I was working on. "More stories? When are you going to write that novel you're always talking about?"

"I need something big to write about. I haven't found it, yet."

Jeff dug deeper and found a half-smoked cigar and a copy of The Chicago Tribune. "Job hunting?" He asked that with a smile, thank God.

"Nah. Adele likes small-town life. So do I. I buy it to keep up to date on the gangsters, and Adele reads it to keep up to date on the latest hat fashions."

"Here it is!" Jeff waved the blue envelope in the air. He quickly scanned the single sheet of paper inside. "Yep. Chapel closed Thursday for Independence Day. Visitation Wednesday. Eastern Star service Wednesday night. Chapel service Friday at 2:30 p.m. Burial in Greenlawn Memorial Cemetery. Services set and paid for."

"So?"

"So – you know Rumsey's policy. No credit. Cash on the barrel head. No money, no service, no embalming, no burial. The question to ask is – ?"

"Where did Jed Bailey get the money?" I turned the possibilities over in my mind. "I'd be willing to bet this week's pay – what's left of it – that Jed Bailey doesn't have a spare nickel to his name. All he has that's worth anything is that little farm. He sold his dairy herd a couple of years back. Couldn't sell the milk. Couldn't afford to feed the cows. They were probably hanging on by their fingernails waiting for the county to seize their land for back taxes. Right?"

"Right!"

For all Jeff Heston's mild-mannered, mama's-boy exterior, there beat the heart of a newsman under his tightly buttoned, Presbyterian vest.

"Remember Laird Johnson around Decoration Day and the Thompson baby a couple of months before that?"

I nodded. "Vaguely."

"Well, there's been some talk – soft, but talk. Both times it was two weeks or so before the funeral took place. Johnson sold his house in a hurry. Ted Thompson sold his farm. Nothing unusual there, except both times the buyer was a Chicago corporation, according to our often drunk and talkative County Clerk. Now, why on earth would a big-city company want eighty acres in little ol' Lincoln County? Unless – ?" Jeff quirked an eyebrow like the dashing hero in a vaudeville skit.

"Unless – that Chicago company was a front for someone here? Someone like – let me guess – Francis Rumsey?"

"Yep, you got it in one try. Can't prove it, but it's certainly possible. Nothing illegal about it, probably, but it smacks of something funny going on."

"But Rumsey doesn't look like he's swimming in money," I said. "Yeah, he's wearing good suits these days, all spiffed up, but his funeral parlor could stand a new coat of paint. I hear he had to borrow Miller's hearse for a funeral a couple of weeks ago because his was broken down. It's this," I glanced in Hattie Webster's direction, "this *gosh darn* Depression. How many businesses have we lost in Lincoln County? Rumsey's wouldn't be the first or the last to go belly-up."

Jeff slid that around in his noggin. "Really? He's a little behind in paying for his ads, but I let him slide. He always catches up. Don't tell anybody about that, especially my mother. She'd have a conniption."

"Not a problem, but the Bailey property could be a money maker. It's decent farm land, but good dirt's a dime a dozen. It's the location. Think about it. The Bailey place is right next to the Country Club, which, according to usually reliable gossip at Smoke Truby's barber shop, would like to expand from nine holes to eighteen, maybe add a swimming pool and tennis courts."

"You know about that? It's supposed to be a secret."

I nodded with all the modesty I could muster.

Jeff sighed and rolled his eyes. "So, Rumsey, or whoever is behind that Chicago company, stands to have a ready buyer and possibly make a substantial profit. Maybe all that isn't illegal, but it sure is damn – *darn* – close to extortion. Folks around here would rather sell their souls to the devil than have to beg the county to bury their loved ones."

"I have a couple of connections in Chicago. Let me poke around, see what turns up."

"OK, Walt, but let's keep this between the two of us. I think I'll take Rosemary out to dinner at the Country Club tonight. Never know what you might hear at the bar. I'll ask around."

"Adele and I are heading to Chicago for wedding shopping and a little outing this weekend. Remember, you promised me a couple of days off – *with pay?* The T-R still owes me for all that extra time I put in during the blizzard last winter."

13

Jeff acknowledged that, if a little reluctantly.

"I'll snoop around a little while I'm there, OK?"

"Alright, but carefully. By the way, what's with you and Francis Rumsey? I could hear the two of you in my office with the door closed."

"Old story. Old history. Nothing to do with this," I said. There was more, but that was not any of Jeff's business. "Let's just say I like to keep him on his toes."

"There's more to it than that."

"A lot more," I finally admitted. "I know things about Rumsey."

"That's all you're going to tell me?"

"Yeah. Like I said – ancient history." I changed the subject. "What about Rumsey's scheme to extract money for funerals? It's a good story, if we can figure out how to prove it."

"Look into it but keep it quiet. For God's sake, don't spread this all over town. We don't want to ruffle too many feathers. Rumsey has friends and most of them advertise in the paper. Paying customers, you know. And reputation is everything in business. Rumsey could ruin you and me and the paper with a couple of well-placed rumors. I wouldn't put it past him."

"I'm not afraid of Francis Rumsey." I stood, puffed out my chest and organized my body into something resembling a boxer's pose.

My editor and my friend gave me a long, thoughtful look. "Maybe you should be. Rumsey has a temper, so I've heard, and he's not a forgiving man. Be careful. Take it slow. Don't tip your hand. That's a long-term story, yes sir. It'll take a lot of leg work. But the daily stuff comes first."

Jeff clapped me on the shoulder. He ripped my story about the ersatz city park out of the typewriter, gave it a once-over, then disappeared toward the back of the building where the typesetter and the press were located.

"By the way," Jeff tossed the words over his shoulder, "remind me not to play poker with you. You've got a real cold deck there, don't you? Probably need a stiff one before you sit down to play."

Hahahahahaha. Jeff's warm chuckle echoed Francis Rumsey's cold snigger. I might have been imagining it, but I would swear I still inhaled the scent of Rumsey's dead, hot-house flowers.

CHAPTER 2

Tuesday, July 4, 1933

"Walt, get your lazy ass out of bed."

Bill Andrews, the dyspeptic desk clerk at the Travelers Hotel, woke me at 9:30 a.m. I had overslept. I thought I was hearing thunder, but that turned out to be Bill pounding on my door. The noise at the door broke through a dream that had something to do with a summer meadow and butterflies flitting about in the sunshine. My fiancée, Adele Atkinson but soon to be Mrs. Walter G. Pratt, also was there, I think.

"Jesus, Bill," I yelled at the door. "It's the Fourth of July. Go away. I don't have to go to work today."

"Hoyt Peterson says get out to the City Dump pronto," Bill said. "I'll be glad when you finally get married and move out of here. I'm sick and fucking tired of being your goddamn secretary. Walter Pratt, newspaperman, la dee fucking da. Go, don't go. I don't give a shit."

I considered rolling over and going back to sleep. I considered calling my editor, Jeff Heston, and letting him handle it. I hesitated with one leg in my trousers. Hoyt Peterson was the Lincoln County Sheriff. If Hoyt said be there *pronto*, it had to be important.

One call I absolutely had to make was to Adele. She had planned a picnic. We were going to visit the old Indian reservation outside Prattsburg, tramp around a little, maybe hunt for arrowheads, get away from the pre-wedding madness for a few hours, and carve out a little time for ourselves.

"I'll come along," Adele said.

"No. God only knows what's out there."

Stern silence bristled along the telephone wire.

"Do you think I'm some timid maiden who has to be protected from the ugly realities of life? I have been to the dump, you know. Besides, we can have our picnic later. Everything's ready. Pick me up on your way."

"Yes, dear." I had the uneasy feeling I would be saying those two words a lot in the next fifty years.

The Paradise City Dump was two miles east of town. It sat in the middle of a large wooded area, so its neighbors, mostly chipmunks and raccoons, did not complain about the stink.

The trip there gave us time to talk. Adele did most of the talking.

"Walter, I love you, but you must give up this knight-in-shining-armor fixation you seem to have. If I had been a boy, I'd be in place to take over from father at the steering wheel factory. But father – well, you know father's opinions about *a woman's place*. He can scarcely abide the fact that I'm a teacher. Making my own money? Scandalous! All one-thousand, two-hundred and sixty-five dollars a year. Gasp! Choke! 'No daughter of mine,' *et cetera, et cetera*. Mother just wrings her hands, but I know she's proud of me. What father won't admit, ever, is that I ran that factory for five months last year after he had his heart attack. And did a darn good job of it, too, if I say so myself."

"Do you wish you'd been born a boy?" We had never discussed this before.

She thought for a long moment. "Yes and no. I'd like the freedom, certainly. I'd like never wearing stockings and a girdle ever again. I'd like all the choices I would have available to me. But, no, I want babies." She pondered that for maybe half a second. "Three babies, possibly four. At least."

I gulped. We had never discussed that either. In general terms, yes, but not the specific number. I was having a difficult enough time imagining myself a husband. Being a father was beyond my reckoning.

"Yes, dear."

"Good Lord, Walter. *Yes, dear.* You sound just like my mother."

Marcus "Snooky" Slack, one of Paradise's three city cops, rescued me from discussion of names for our imaginary children, interfering parents, the proper role of women, and my future.

Slack slouched sideways in the driver's seat of his patrol car. Snooky was not my friend, not even friendly. He had parked at the entrance to the dump, directly under the metal sign where the rules for using the dump were posted. *Open Monday-Saturday. 7 a.m. to 9 p.m. Closed Sunday. No burning. No hunting.* Everybody ignored the rules. You could not read them, anyway. The sign looked like Swiss cheese thanks to dozens of bullet holes. Snooky did not look particularly happy.

"What're you doing here, Pratt?" Snooky leaned a beefy forearm on the ledge of my open car window. He recovered enough of his forgotten good manners to tip his hat when he saw Adele. "Miss Atkinson."

"The sheriff called. Said to get out here right away."

"Peterson, huh?"

"Yep."

"You won't get in so easy after I'm elected sheriff. There's an election next year, you know."

"I'm sure Hoyt's shaking in his boots. Don't count your chickens before they're hatched."

"I've got friends."

All three of them, I thought. And two of those were near cousins.

"What's going on in there?"

"You're the reporter, find out for yourself."

I threw a sloppy salute in his direction, and he glowered back as we drove in. The actual dump began a hundred yards or so from the road, screened from passersby by thick brush and trees. I swerved my almost-new Buick around a wringer washer some lazy fool had dropped off just far enough from the road not to be caught in the act. Maybe I could get a story out of how people used, or misused, the dump.

It was just past ten o'clock, and the temperature already had to be in the low nineties. I wiped sweat off the back of my neck. The trash piles ranged from low mounds to teetering skyscrapers. Car paths wound haphazardly between the piles of trash. There was no plan and no order to what was dumped where. On my left, some nonchalant soul had heaped car parts on a stack of mattresses. Thousands of tin cans topped every pile like sprinkles atop the icing on a particularly filthy birthday cake. Tree trimmings. Old window screens. Chairs and davenports. Scrapped tools. Clothing. Lamps. Garbage wrapped in newspaper. Wire. A tall grandfather's clock with its guts eviscerated. You name it, it was there – somewhere.

"Uh, oh," I said aloud.

I steered toward the group huddled near a smashed, rusted-out Model T Ford. Sheriff Hoyt Peterson was impossible to miss at six-foot-five and three hundred pounds. The polished brass buttons of his well-pressed uniform sparkled in the sun, the only remotely cheerful object in a fifty-yard radius. The sheriff's patrol car parked next to a hearse marked the locus of the activity. Two private vehicles sat a little distance away. Two boys wriggled next to what appeared to be their parents. Johnnie Porter sat a distance away next to his beloved bicycle. Francis Rumsey and his assistant Ralph Gardner keep to themselves next to the hearse. To my way of thinking, the posy in Rumsey's lapel was too cheery for this temple dedicated to the discarded and forgotten. I parked behind the sheriff.

"It's the boy wonder," Peterson said.

"Exactly."

"You're full of yourself, son. Ain't befitting."

"What happened here? Why'd you call me?"

"Take a look. Uh, Miss Atkinson, you might want to stay back. This ain't pretty."

The sheriff walked me ahead about twenty feet. He pointed to the ground at the base of an eight-foot-tall mass of soggy, crumbling cardboard boxes. I looked.

"A pile of junk and an old sheet? This is what you brought me out here for on my day off?"

"Take another look-see. Hope you brought your hanky. This ain't no perfume store."

"Oh, it's perfume – just the rotten cabbage, skunk, out-house variety. Typical dump. I've smelled – Oh, my God!"

"Yeah."

There was a sad tinge in the sheriff's voice. I immediately understood why.

Flies buzzed around the lovely face of a young woman in her twenties. She was wound into a white sheet that was tucked neatly under her feet and covered her to her waist. It was obvious she was dead. Part of the back of her head was missing.

"It's her," I said. I choked back the bile crawling up my throat.

"You know her? You got a name, family?" the sheriff asked. "I never seen her before. And I know most everybody in Lincoln County. Her, I'd remember, for certain sure."

"I can't say I *know* her, not exactly. I saw her yesterday at the Daisy Diner. Suppertime." I stared. "Didn't talk to her, really. Maybe said hello."

I pulled a notebook from my breast pocket and unscrewed the cap on my second-best pen. The notebook was limp from humidity and sweat.

"Murder?"

"Ain't no suicide. You don't kill yourself, then wrap yourself in a sheet and fly like an angel to curl up under some boxes at the City Dump."

"How'd she get here. Any clues?"

"Nope. Car, truck, buggy, farm wagon, magic – your guess is as good as mine."

I knelt beside her and waved the flies away. He eyes were partially open. They were green but filmed over in death. Her hair, although disarranged and matted with blood, fell in bright, blonde waves to just below her ears. I could not see any other obvious wounds. She still wore the distinctive yellow dress I had seen her in the day before. There was a brown smear on the fabric under her breasts that might have been a bloody handprint. The expression on her face revealed nothing about her death or her killer – no shock, no surprise, no pain, nothing.

"This is pretty much how she looked when we got here," Peterson said.

"How'd you know she was here?" I started scribbling. "You patrolling the dump these days?"

"Them two boys." Peterson jerked his head toward the pair of ten-year-olds fidgeting next to their parents. "They was camping out in the woods, playing at cowboys and Indians. They come over here exploring. Like I said, playing, looking for junk. Doing boy stuff. They was going to move some of them boxes to make a fort, found her and lit out for home on their bikes. That's when I got called. I told Bill Andrews to get you out here."

"Thanks." I touched the hem of the sheet. "May I?"

"Snooky already took pictures. Knowing him, they might or might not turn out. Yeah, go ahead."

"Oh, Walter! She's so young."

I had not heard Adele join us.

"Miss Atkinson, this really ain't no place for a nice lady like you," the sheriff said.

"Sheriff, I've seen worse. Accidents at the factory. People mauled in machinery, screaming in pain, an arm or leg a bloody mess."

Peterson let out a grunt that was more acknowledgement than approval.

I pulled back the sheet. I stood, removed my hat and bowed my head. She was utterly exposed, swathed in secrets and embraced by the ultimate loneliness of death. Whoever did this to her deserved a terminal punishment. I was not an avenger. I believed in justice, not revenge. I could not help her in that fashion, that was the job of someone else – the sheriff, a judge, somebody – but there was something I could do. I offered up a little prayer. *Young lady, whoever you are and wherever you came from,* I promised her silently, *I will give you a name.*

"Any suspects?" I spoke after I could find my voice again.

"Not yet. Too early for that. Probably another stranger," the sheriff said. "Hope it's a stranger. Don't want to think one of us done that."

I heard a rustle beside me. Adele bent over the body.

"They're not here," she said.

The sheriff and I looked at one another.

"What's not here, Miss Atkinson?" the sheriff asked.

"You know, things – women's things, personal things. You might not notice, but a woman would. Her purse. She had to have had a purse. Maybe jewelry. You can see here." Adele held up the woman's left hand. "She had a ring here, see how white the skin is? Maybe a wedding ring, do you think?"

"That's mighty fine detective work. If you'd been a man, you would've made a good policeman."

Adele gave me a look of disgust that she carefully hid from the well-intentioned, but decidedly old-fashioned sheriff.

"Maybe we got a motive, at least – a robbery gone bad," he said.

I looked around. "And where's her other stuff?

"*Other* stuff?" Adele and the sheriff responded in one breath.

"I remember, now. She had a large suitcase. Couldn't miss it. Brown with tan stripes."

"If she's a stranger in town, that means she was traveling. She would've had a hat and gloves, too. Maybe a small case with lingerie, cosmetics, toiletries, items of that type. I don't see them, either," Adele said.

"Good point. I'll check into that," the sheriff said, scratching notes on what appeared to be the back of an old dry-cleaning bill.

"Ask Herb Daishell, he might remember something," I said.

"Look here," the sheriff said. "One shoe's missing, too."

"What's this?" I grasped her ankle and turned up the bare foot. It was cold despite the heat, like dead meat.

Peterson leaned over to get a closer look. "Dirt?"

"Yes, but what's this?" I scraped a bit of the material into the palm of my hand and held it out to the big man making shade over me. "I'm not certain, but it looks like flower petals."

"For sure it does. Could be something, could be a whole lot of nothing. Christ Almighty! I hate this. Pretty young thing like her. What we got here is a real mystery. Ain't that the truth? And I hate mysteries."

I turned to the spectators. The two boys turned out to be Jeffrey Packard, Jr., and Dwight Huff. They found the body about 8 a.m., they guessed.

"We found a silver dollar once," said young Huff, "but nothing like this. At first, we reckoned it was just some old store dummy that got junked."

"Yeah, we were building a fort," chimed in Junior Packard. "We pulled off some boxes. There she was. We didn't do nothing wrong. We were just playing, you know."

"Either of you touch anything else? Take anything?"

Both boys shook their heads in the negative.

"Ask the moron." Packard pointed to Johnnie Porter.

"Don't point, Junior. That's not nice," Mrs. Packard said. "That Porter boy can't help the way he is. He's just a little slow, that's all."

Mr. Packard puffed himself up. "Slow, my ass, Velma. He's a retard and a bastard. You can't trust somebody from that kind of family. Probably inbreeding. They're not our kind of people, and I don't want my son associated with moral degenerates like that."

"Sorry I'm late." A familiar voice interrupted. "Broken leg. Farm tractor turned over in a ditch out in Jefferson Township. What's going on here?" Dr. Wilson P. Joplin, Lincoln County Coroner, elbowed his way through the bystanders. The body brought him up short. "I guess I won't need this." He set his leather doctor's satchel at his feet.

"What do you think, Doc?" the sheriff asked.

"Hocine tibi habeas locum?"

"Speak American," growled the sheriff.

"She's dead." You could always count on Doc Joplin to not mince words.

Doc knelt beside the corpse and spent a long moment observing. When he turned her head to the side, brain matter fell out onto the sheet from the gaping cavity in her skull. Adele gasped.

"Take notes, Walt," Doc said. "Powder burns surrounding wound. Gunshot, definitely. Close range. Bruise on left side of the face. Could be from a punch, maybe a fall." He manipulated the arms. "Time of death? Hard to tell in this heat. Just guessing, let's say last night, sometime around midnight."

"What kind of gun?"

"I'd like to know that, too," said the sheriff.

"Can't tell definitively. It wasn't a big hunting rifle or a shotgun. There wouldn't be anything left of her in that case. Something smaller, probably a sidearm." Doc dusted his hands on his trouser legs and stood. "Sorry, sheriff, I can't give you any more information right now. I'll have to perform an autopsy. Maybe I'll have more for you, then. If we're lucky, the bullet's still in there. That might tell us something."

"How long is this going to take? I've got a business to take care of. I can't wait out here all day." Francis Rumsey stepped next to the sheriff. He paled noticeably when he got a good look at the dead woman in the yellow dress. He picked nervously at a small plaster on his cheek.

"Nick yourself shaving, Frank?" I asked.

"Shut up, Pratt."

"Keep your shirt on, Francis. She ain't going nowhere. And neither are you," the sheriff said.

A buzzard, more brazen than most of his kind, flapped his wide wings and settled on a heap of cast-off tires just ten feet away. He had a bone in one claw. The sheriff picked up a tin can and threw it at the bird. I had heard that Hoyt Peterson had been quite a pitcher in his day. He hit the bird square on the breast. The bird let out a squawk and sullenly flapped twenty feet away, unwilling to relinquish an easy meal. A half dozen of his brothers circled high overhead.

The sheriff turned back to me. "Anything else, Walt?"

"I'd sure like to know what happened to her belongings." I scanned the mountain range of trash surrounding us. "Maybe they're here someplace."

"I'll call Rollie, have him bring out his dogs."

Rollie Parker, although reputed to have a comfortable livelihood, lived like a pauper outside of town near the Ohio state line with his crippled wife and a pack of prize bloodhounds. The puppies, alone, were worth their weight in gold. There was a waiting list for each litter, with police departments and dog fanciers from as far away as Boston and Albuquerque willing to pay a pretty penny for one of the justly famous tracking dogs.

"I ain't hoping for much. Too many smells out here, even for Rollie's dogs," the sheriff said. "Way too much stuff."

"While you're making chit-chat, I've got work to do," Rumsey said. "Can we get on with this? I don't know why you called me, anyway. It was Miller's turn."

The sheriff looked at Doc. "You done here?"

"For now."

"Okay, she's all yours, Rumsey." The sheriff waved to the spectators. "You folks can go home, now. We'll be in touch. Oh, and thanks, boys. You done the right thing telling your parents about finding her."

Rumsey motioned his assistant, Ralph Gardner, to the body. Gardner wasn't from around Paradise. He was late-twenties, slim, dark, with an expressionless face and downcast eyes. He was the kind of man who faded into the woodwork without even trying. He kept himself to himself. No one would have noticed him if he had settled in amongst the buzzards. Like them, he was always dressed in black, with the same long neck, prematurely balding head, eyes shielded and averted. Nobody knew anything about him or his relations, except that he came from somewhere in The Region – Gary, East Chicago, Whiting – on the Hoosier side of the Illinois state line. The only words I could remember Gardner speak were yes, no, come this way, and may I help you.

"You take the body. I'll get the stretcher," Rumsey ordered.

Sheriff Peterson guffawed and slapped his thighs. "What's the matter, Francis, you afraid of dead people? Don't you worry none, she won't bite."

That comment was crass but funny. Rumsey did not see the humor. His face resembled an overripe tomato about to burst.

"Don't spread that around, Hoyt. I'll blackball you in every lodge in Lincoln County. Forget re-election."

"Crikes! Can't you take a joke, Francis?"

"I told you, it's not my turn. I shouldn't even be out here." Rumsey swiped at the sweat dripping from his forehead. "This damn heat. It's not my turn, damn it."

The sheriff sighed. "Look, goldangit, Miller's out of town, so you're up to bat. And the county pays you seven dollars and fifty cents to transport the corpse, ain't that right?

"Yeah, so?"

"One thing's for sure true about you, Rumsey. I ain't never seen you turn down cash money."

Rumsey grumbled to himself, but removed his suit jacket, carefully folding the boutonniere to the inside to protect it. He let out an exaggerated grunt, one that generated no sympathy from the sheriff or from me, when he bent to help Gardner lift the young woman's body onto the stretcher. They lifted her easily. She could not have weighed much more than one-hundred pounds soaking wet. Rumsey was about fifty-five years old, but stronger than he looked, probably from all those years of hefting dead weight and caskets.

They covered her face again with the sheet that had become her shroud. I took one last look at the nameless woman. She had been so bright and alive just yesterday. Now, she was nothing more than a business proposition for the undertaker, extra work for the sheriff and the coroner, a cause for fear in the community and a damn good story for me. Adele took my hand in hers and gave it a squeeze.

We left. I had enough to get started on my article for the next day's edition. I most certainly had had enough of death for one day.

Sheriff Hoyt Peterson had parting words for Adele. "Miss Atkinson, it would be my sincere pleasure to arrest this man," meaning me, "if he don't show up for your wedding. You just give me the call, little lady."

Adele kissed him on the cheek.

"Thank you, sheriff, I surely will. Hear that, Walter?"

I heard.

CHAPTER 3

Wednesday, July 4, 1933
The Telegraph-Register, Special Edition

WOMAN IN YELLOW DRESS SLAIN, BODY ABANDONED AT CITY DUMP
'A real mystery,' sheriff says

By Walter G. Pratt

A young woman, apparently a stranger in Lincoln County, was found dead yesterday morning, the casualty of a small-caliber pistol shot to the head.

The body was discovered by two boys who were playing at the Paradise City Dump on Missiqua Road.

No arrests have been made and no suspects are currently being investigated. Lincoln County Sheriff Hoyt Peterson said the murder may have happened during a robbery because the victim's personal items were not found with the body.

"There's not much to go on. If the killer was another stranger, he could have hopped on the midnight freight train and be hundreds of miles from here by now. What we got here is a real mystery," Peterson said.

There was no identification on the body. The sheriff urged anyone who might have information about the murder victim or the killer or killers to come forward immediately.

The woman was 20 to 25 years old, five-feet-three-inches tall, slim at about 110 pounds, with green eyes and bobbed, platinum blonde hair. She was wearing a full-skirted, bright yellow dress.

Jeffrey Packard Jr. and Dwight Huff, both 10, found the body about 8 a.m. Packard is the son of Velma and Jeffrey Packard Sr. of 632 East Main Street. Huff is the son of Lavinia and Elliot Huff, of 412 North Columbus Street. Both boys will enter the fifth grade at East Ward Grammar School in September.

The boys said they often ride their bicycles to the dump, where they search to "find stuff."

"We found a silver dollar once and two pocket knives, but nothing like this," Huff said.

"At first, we reckoned it was just some old store dummy that got junked. Then we saw all the blood," Packard said.

After the boys realized they had found a human body, they rode to town to tell their parents. The sheriff and city police were called immediately.

Lincoln County Coroner Dr. Wilson P. Joplin said the woman, who probably had met foul play late Monday, had been in good health and was well-nourished. There were no other obvious wounds or violations prior to death.

Several Paradise citizens reported seeing the mystery woman Monday afternoon.

What little is known about her movements begins about 3:15 p.m., when she got off the westbound New York Central train at the depot. She cashed in the remainder of her unused train ticket.

Everyone who met the woman said she was polite, had a friendly smile and spoke with a slight accent. The accent was variously described as southern, Italian or Canadian.

After leaving the depot, she was spotted walking along Walnut Street toward the center of Paradise. She ate an early supper at the Daisy Diner consisting of beef and noodles, mashed potatoes, green beans, bread and butter, and a slice of cherry pie.

She asked Herbert Daishell, proprietor of the city eatery, whether he knew of any employment opportunities in Paradise and if he could recommend a clean, economical place to stay. Daishell gave her directions to Ida Watson's rooming house at 527 West Walnut Street. She never arrived, said Mrs. Watson.

"She was a real nice young lady. Maybe she was a little sad or had something on her mind. She didn't say much, wasn't what you could call real talkative," Daishell said.

She carried a large, apparently heavy, well-used suitcase reinforced with twine wrapped around it several times and knotted. The suitcase, which has not been found, was brown with tan stripes.

The dump was searched thoroughly yesterday afternoon by sheriff's deputies, city police and numerous civilian volunteers, including Boy Scout Troop 12 led by Arnold Devane. Nothing related to the mystery woman was discovered.

The sheriff said he was going to bring in the bloodhounds owned by Rolland (Rollie) Parker of Rural Route 5. Two years ago, Parker's hounds famously discovered 11-year-old Eleanor Davis alive after she had gotten lost in the Sassafras Swamp.

The body is being held at Rumsey Funeral Parlor and Mortuary pending further investigation and notification of next of kin.

This was the first homicide in Paradise since the stabbing death of George DePuy in September 1929 during a family dispute over an inheritance. DePuy's cousin, Kenneth DePuy, was convicted of the murder in 1930 and sentenced to 22 years in the Michigan City State Penitentiary.

CHAPTER 4

That story was about thirty inches of absolutely nothing except filler and old news. I dropped the newspaper on my unmade bed. I wanted to ball it up and toss it into the nearest fire. I was not happy. The story was beyond sketchy; it was flat and colorless. I could have speculated about the woman and what had happened to her from now until the first dawn after the Second Coming, but I had no facts. And it was facts, I knew, that would make a great story and, not incidentally, reveal her killer.

It was five o'clock on the afternoon of the nation's birthday, and I had nothing to do until six-thirty, when I was due at the Atkinsons for supper with Adele's folks. Afterward, we would watch the traditional torchlight Fourth of July parade from the steps of the newspaper building. Adele and I had our picnic in the newsroom of The Telegraph-Register while I wrote my story, and she put my commas in the right places. She would have made a fine editor. Jeff Heston praised her, too.

I could not rid my mind of the face of the woman in the yellow dress. I was consumed by questions about her. Who was she? Why did she come to Paradise? What had motivated someone to take her life? Why had the killer failed to dispose of her where she could not be so easily found? There were much better hiding places. Why not choose the woods, the swamp, a well on an abandoned farm, an unmarked grave anywhere? Was the murderer, as Sheriff Peterson desperately wanted to believe, another stranger?

There were far too many questions. And far too few facts.

She had been wrapped tightly in a sheet, like a mummy. The boys who found her swore they had not touched her, but the sheet had already been partially pulled off when they stumbled across her. What the sheriff had not said, but seemed obvious to me, was that her makeshift shroud had been moved by a second pair of human hands after the murderer left her there. But whose hands? And why?

The afternoon freight whistle blew. I could just see the roof of the train depot and the railroad tracks from my third-floor hotel window. I pulled aside the dingy curtain. Five men sprawled atop a livestock car slowly rolling through town. I pitied them. The smell must have been dreadful, especially in this heat. How could they stand it? The answer was simple: there was nothing else they could do. They were just five out of the two million or so rootless men in the United States who wandered the country looking for work, dignity, a decent life. Any one of these tramps could been the convenient stranger the sheriff had pegged as the killer. Many of my fellow Paradisans called them bums and turned their backs. Bums? No. Just guys like us, not as lucky maybe, but just like us.

A movement across the tracks caught my eye. It was Doc Joplin carrying his doctor's bag in one hand and a paper sack in the other. He unlocked the back door to his office. Doc's place was one block away on Main Street. If I ducked out the hotel's side door, it was an easy stroll. Better yet, he promised good company and something to do for an otherwise-wasted hour. Besides, I was getting antsy.

I decided to take a slight detour. I cut up Main Street past the Courthouse to Meridian Street, the main north-south drag of Paradise. Cars and horse-drawn buggies clogged downtown. The sidewalks were packed, especially in front of Myer's Drug Emporium, where Jack Myer was making money hand over fist selling ice cream cones. His customers were a mixed lot. The ones clutching pennies lived in the shanties on the north side of town near the Little River, which was little more than a trash-strewn ditch. The ones with dollar bills in their hands occupied the elite's mansions and middle-class bungalows on the south side of town beyond the banks of the Missiqua River, which wound its sluggish, brown way eventually to join the Wabash River and thus, eventually, to empty into the Gulf of Mexico.

Minnie Simpson strolled past me arm-in-arm with her best friend, Constance Brotherton. Mrs. Simpson was a secret drinker who insisted that bootleggers make deliveries to her back door just like other tradesmen of a certain class. Mrs. Brotherton was just as colorful in her own larcenous way. She shoplifted every single time she came to town. All the store owners knew. Her husband went through her clothing and purse every night and returned the stolen trinkets the next day. I could not help but wonder what was in Mrs. Brotherton's pockets at this moment.

"You there! Young Pratt!" Minnie Simpson's whisper could be heard in Pittsburgh.

"How do you do, ladies." I tipped my hat. It was a new straw number, just the perfect, jaunty masculine accessory for a hot summer's day.

"Folderol! When are you people going to do something about that Pearson boy?"

"What do you mean?" I could guess what was coming next.

"Willie Pearson's son, my paperboy. I've called ten dozen times, and you people won't do anything about him. He throws my paper in my rose bushes every single day. Do something, or I'm going to speak with Arletha Heston. Mark my words, young Pratt, *she* will do something, and it won't be pleasant."

"Yes ma'am."

"See that you do, young Pratt." She sidled away, her displeasure leaving an almost-tangible wake.

If you work at a newspaper, the public believes you are answerable for every aspect from the spelling on Page One to errant deliveries to the price of eggs in the grocery advertisements. Go figure.

"Hey, Mr. Pratt.!"

Johnnie Porter clattered to a stop on his rusty bicycle. Dummy. Bastard. Village idiot. Those were some of the nicer names people called him. He had come into the world without a known father. His mother had become pregnant without benefit of clergy. The boy was about thirteen or fourteen, now, and he was far from a drooling simpleton, just very slow. He passed his days cycling around Paradise collecting junk he sold or traded to buy kid stuff – movie tickets, ice cream, shiny toys, little luxuries. He and his mother Julia, lived in a flood-prone, two-room shack on stilts in a mostly hidden low-rent district on the south side next to the Missiqua River. Passersby stepped out of his path and glanced disapprovingly in his direction when they thought he was not looking. There but for the grace of God.

"Hiya, Johnnie. Want an ice-cream cone? My treat."

"Sure. Can I have chocolate? That's the best." His soft brown eyes lit up. His moon-shaped face was not handsome, but his ever-ready smile made it pleasant. I liked him. There was not a nasty, unkind bone in his body. I flipped him a quarter.

"I've got a secret," Johnnie said.

"What's that?"

"Can't tell. Wouldn't be a secret no more. Gotcha!" He giggled and rode off before I could ask him what he had seen and done at the dump before all the adults arrived.

"Johnnie, wait up!" Julia Porter yelled at her son's back to no avail. The boy kept pedaling. He likely could not hear her over the buzz of the crowd.

Julia Porter had dull auburn hair streaked with premature gray that she smoothed back with a work-roughened hand. She had been in Jeff Heston's class at school but was expelled when the powers that be discovered she was with child. She wore a shapeless, hand-me-down dress at least two sizes too big. It had been washed so many times it had faded to the color of Indiana clay.

"You see where Johnnie was going, Mr. Pratt? It's near time for supper."

"Please call me Walter. My best guess is he's headed to Myer's for ice cream."

"He'll spoil his supper. Oh, well, boys will be boys. Can't complain on the Fourth of July. Wouldn't do any good, no how." She laughed, then, and I had a brief glimpse of her lost youth and vivacity.

"I got a raise last week," I lied. "Here's dollar. Why don't you find Johnnie and get an ice cream cone for yourself, too?"

"I shouldn't. Wouldn't be right."

"Sure you can. It's a holiday, so celebrate a little. Besides, you clean the newspaper office, and I can't thank you enough for leaving my desk alone. I know Hattie Webster gives you grief for not dusting it, but if somebody actually straightened my desk, I wouldn't be able to find a darn thing on it. Think of this dollar as a little bonus from me for all your hard work."

She eyed the dollar bill as if it were the Rosetta Stone, the lost chord and the Holy Grail rolled into one.

"Please," I said.

She took the bill, smiled and almost skipped toward the drug store. She waved gaily over her shoulder. I was reminded of the preacher's text last Sunday. It was one of my favorite Proverbs: A merry heart doeth good like a medicine.

I was distracted watching Julia, and Ted Thompson was not paying attention to where he was going. We bumped into one another as he came out of Bartlett's Hardware. He barely managed to avoid dropping a small sack of nails. At last, someone I actually wanted to talk to.

"Ted, got a minute?"

"I guess."

Thompson was stooped, thin and looked a decade older than his thirty years. His ragged overalls were clean, but threadbare and patched. It was difficult to imagine now that he had been a star on the Paradise High School basketball team in his youth, while Jeff Heston, who had more enthusiasm than talent, warmed the bench. Or that he once had an easy-going personality and a sense of humor. Personal tragedy and the Depression had hit him with a one-two punch. All the joy and optimism had been beaten out of him. The hackneyed phrase *a shell of a man* fit him to a T.

"How're you doing?"

"Getting by." He held up the sack of nails, no more than three ounces. "Got to work on the roof. That last storm took a part of it. It's raining in the kitchen." He allowed himself a small rueful smile.

I motioned him into the little walk space, you could not really call it an alley, between the hardware store and Milady's Apparel Shoppe. We were out of the holiday sidewalk traffic and would not be overheard.

"I know this is difficult," I said, "but I need to ask you some questions about what happened after your baby passed away a few months ago. When you sold your farm."

"Mind your own business, Walter."

"Actually, this is more about Francis Rumsey."

"That bastard!" Anger sparked a little life into Thompson's face. It quickly evaporated.

"Bastard how? Did he threaten you? Force you to sell?"

"Like I said, none of your business. 'Sides, I can't talk about it."

"I know it's painful. You suffered a great loss – the baby, the land."

"Can't talk about it," he repeated, his demeanor becoming more agitated by the second.

I probed again, knowing I had maybe one last opportunity before Thompson either ran off or punched me in the face. "Why not, Ted? It's no big secret. Lots of people have lost everything in this Depression. You're not alone. At least you're still living on your homeplace. You're better off than some."

"Better off? That's how you see it? Damn you, Pratt, damn you to Hell. Ain't the same. I'm renting land my great-grandfather settled in 1837. *Renting!* That land would've gone to Ted Jr. if he hadn't got the fever. That was Thompson land, some of the best farmland in the whole county. I can grow just about anything there. Stick a seed in the ground, pray for rain and sun, and there's a crop. Yessir, just about anything – tomatoes, corn, wheat, even sorghum one year. Ain't the same, now. That big city company owns it. They may have a piece of paper, but they can't smell the dirt and tell if it's sour and needs some lime, or if I should let the south field stay in pasture grass another year. That's in my bones. That's who I am."

He drew a deep breath and composed himself.

"I got to be going. My best to Miss Atkinson. And I wish you well on your wedding. Marrying my Sally was the best thing I ever done."

He turned to leave, but I caught his arm. "Look, Ted, I'm pretty sure Rumsey's done this to others folks, too. You can help me here. Just talk to me. Maybe we can figure out a way to prevent Rumsey and those Chicago people from doing this to others, too."

"I'm sorry about other folks, but that's none of my business. I can't talk. Promised. Lawyer stuff." He jerked away from me. "Leave me alone."

I let him go on his way. But before I could get to Doc Joplin's office to pick his brains about the murder, I was stopped by half the populace of Paradise.

Winnie Arbuckle was next. We were in the same class in high school. Every town had a Winnie. She liked a good time with any able-bodied man who would take her dancing and who had a dollar bill or two to tuck in her pocket after a cuddle in the back seat of his Ford.

"Walt, wait up!" Winnie clutched my coat sleeve. The fabric was summer seersucker, and one more wrinkle wouldn't show. "Is it true? Did you really see the body?"

I nodded in the affirmative.

"Somebody told me she'd been cut in half and her heart was missing."

"Cut in half? Where'd you hear such nonsense?"

She shrugged. "Everybody's talking about it. This is the biggest thing to happen in Paradise since – since, gosh, I can't think of anything bigger."

"Winnie, don't believe everything you hear. They're just rumors."

"Aw, that's no fun. By the way, Mr. Almost-Married Man, if you ever get tired of Adele, you know where to find me," she said, then hurried off, giggling all the way.

I tried and failed to avoid the next person.

Patrick Mathews scowled as he limped past. Matthews marched in the regiment of the lost, those veterans of the Great War who seemed forever cast adrift from society. Even tiny Paradise, population 7,213, counted a few of these in their number. Those former proud soldiers had won the war, but marched home vanquished in some deeply spiritual manner that no amount of aspirin and good wishes could heal. Doc Joplin, a little drunk one night, confessed he had performed an abortion on Mathew's fourteen-year-old daughter. Doc suspected Marthews had impregnated the girl. His family had abandoned him shortly after and taken a powder for parts unknown.

"Don't you be looking at me, Pratt," Mathews growled.

"Sorry, Mr. Mathews, I was just passing by. If I stared, I didn't mean to."

"Keep my name out of it. I wasn't there. I didn't do nothing."

"Pardon?"

"Ask your pal, Hoyt Peterson." He stamped off, his right foot dragging.

Helen Little turned from gazing at the display window of McGrory's Five and Dime and caught my eye. She had been tried for murder in 1922 for adding rat poison to her husband's coffee, along with the cream and sugar. She got off by claiming it was an accident, an accident repeated many times over the course of months. But everybody knew Harry Little was a brute who beat his wife and children bloody every time he came home drunk, which was every day. The jury chose to ignore the evidence, do the right thing and acquit.

"Mr. Pratt." Mrs. Little was perhaps fifty years old, but her voice quavered like a woman in her eighties. She had never gotten over having spent half her life in constant dread. "You've got to get the newspaper to do something about those Gypsies."

"Yes, ma'am. Gypsies?"

"Those men. You know the ones I mean. They're camped out by the fairgrounds near the Little River. I can see them from my back porch. They're probably the ones who killed that poor girl. You need to look into that. We won't be safe in our beds while we have Gypsies in our town. They drink and sing songs and make fires. Fires!"

I tried to explain to her that those men most likely were tramps, just passing through. That spot was a well-known campsite for the homeless men who rode the rails. She would not have any of it.

"They're evil men," she insisted. "Mark my words. They worship idols, you know."

Mrs. Little had found religion shortly after her brief foray into justifiable homicide. She was a devotée of Orvis Brunson's New Jerusalem Tabernacle. The Rev. Mr. Brunson was a charismatic Bible thumper without peer. His summer tent revivals were legendary for their fire and brimstone, number of souls saved and overflowing collection plates.

This was my town. Full of secrets. Full of stories. Also full of preposterous theories about the murdered woman, all of which pointed accusations of guilt away from themselves, their friends, relatives and neighbors. Chalk it up to human nature.

CHAPTER 5

"Don't tell me you're here because you gave syphilis to that nice Adele Atkinson." Wilson P. Joplin, M.D., never was one to tiptoe into a conversation.

"How are you? Nice to see you? Isn't this a beautiful day?"

"Horse shit."

"You're in a good mood."

Doc glared over his half-rimmed spectacles.

"Good? What's good about it? I had a dead stranger this morning, a broken leg earlier, and a dead baby this afternoon. That's what I just got back from." He yanked a cigar out of his pocket. "Someday, science will prove these things are bad for you, but until then," he puffed the stogy to life and waved me to a chair, "these are a small pleasure I refuse to deny myself."

"Dead baby?" I prompted.

"Tom and Alberta Stratton. A blessing, really. They already have four little mouths to feed. They're pretty broken up about it. Nothing I could do. Stillborn. Probably the mother's diet. Alberta almost looked relieved. Damn! I hate this Depression! Roosevelt better fix things goddamn quick, or I don't know what's going to happen to this country. If the New Deal turns into the Raw Deal, we're in a shitload of trouble."

I nodded. There was nothing I could add to that.

Doc paced the private office at the rear of his shotgun building next to the railroad tracks. It was small, but efficient. The waiting room faced West North Street. From there, a claustrophobic hallway led straight to Doc's office, with two examination rooms and the nurse's desk in an alcove to the right. The sharp, earthy medicinal odor from Doc's dispensary saturated his office and crept into my nostrils. Doc was famous in a small way for his concoctions – pills, powders, salves, potions – that he fashioned in a closet-sized room to the side of the office proper. Many of these came from plants he collected on his long tramps through the woods. Others came from the memories of aged frontier women, some from Pottawatomie and Miami Indian lore.

"Want some eggs?' Doc asked, breaking the silence. "The Strattons didn't have cash. They paid me with the last of their eggs, which should have fed their children. I couldn't say no. Didn't want to destroy what was left of their pride."

"I'll pass on the eggs."

He changed the subject. "Maybe this'll be the material for that damn novel you're always whining – pardon me, asserting – that you want to write someday."

"That's a little ghoulish, even for you, Doc." I hesitated. "Well, okay. I admit it's crossed my mind. But we don't know how it turns out, yet."

"Don't look a gift horse – *et cetera*. Drink?"

"I will gladly take a drink."

"You're a Methodist. You're not supposed to drink, dance or play cards. You do all three. If I give you a drink, I'll be sending you straight to Methodist Hell."

"Thanks for reminding me. I'll worry about that later. I'm not perfect, but I have faith."

"Glad somebody still does."

I watched Doc pour. His hands fascinated me. They were as big as dinner plates, but his touch was artist delicate. Just like the other contrasts that defined the man. He had just turned thirty-eight, but he had an old man's cynicism. He was an intellectual who read the Latin and Greek classics in the original languages. He swore like a stevedore. He loudly declared that church was for people who could not cope with reality. *The Origin of Species* by Charles Darwin was placed at eye level in the bookcase in the waiting room, cheek by jowl with the two-year-old magazines and the pamphlets on baby care, a spot where no one could avoid seeing it. Right up there with Jeff Heston, who was his antithesis in every way possible, Doc was my best friend in Paradise.

"You're not here to enjoy my charm and scintillating conversation. It's the girl."

"Yeah, you have any thoughts about her?" The whiskey burned my throat.

"She wasn't from around here."

I made a face. "C'mon, Doc."

He swiveled the office chair stationed at his desk to face me. "I haven't had time to perform a proper autopsy. I hope Rumsey kept her

37

on ice. Otherwise --" He let that thought trail off. "I had just gotten started when I was called away to the Strattons. Let me see. Some surface observations from a cursory view of the body. Our mystery lady had a hand-print bruise on her upper right arm. I'm guessing our killer grabbed her to force her with him to somewhere as yet unknown. She also had recent and expensive dental work. A big city dentist, I'm sure. A small-town dentist likely wouldn't have the know-how or the materials."

I took notes.

"What else? She'd been shot at close range above the right ear. Even you could see that. Powder burns. A small-caliber pistol."

"Any clues about the gun?"

"Not really. Maybe a lady's purse gun. Grampa's old derringer. Who knows? Even so, there wasn't much left of the back of her head. Surprisingly, there wasn't that much blood on the sheet she was found in. So, somebody needs to be looking for rags, towels, an old shirt – something that soaked up the blood and brain tissue."

"Jesus! This guy's a nutcase. That took a cool head to pull off. And a fair amount of time. Some strength – or at least determination. And privacy. Unless --"

"Don't tell me."

"Unless he had help."

Doc pondered that. "No, I don't think so. My best guess is we're looking at one man. There were extensive post mortem bruises around her waist and ribs, also her heels. We couldn't see that with her clothes on. No bruises on her ankles or knees, where an accomplice would have picked her up to move her. She'd been grabbed or pulled, then our homicidal maniac dragged her – ka-thump, ka-thump, ker-plop."

"Across rough ground, like at the dump?"

"Possibly. Or down a flight of stairs. Or across a road or parking lot. Or somebody's field or lawn. Remember the dirt we saw on the bottom of her feet?"

"Crap! That describes almost anyone and almost any location."

"Your vocabulary is deteriorating, and you claim you're a writer."

"Yeah, yeah. Anything else?"

"She was a natural redhead, if you know what I mean."

"A redhead?"

"Indisputably. But that's not for publication, per orders from Hoyt Peterson."

I did not like that, but I could see the sheriff's point. "Okay. What about time of death?"

"Same answer as before. Can't say with any certainty. The body being moved. The heat." He thought for a moment. "Best guess is late last night – midnight, a little before. Can't place it any closer than that."

Paradise was sound asleep at midnight. Who would have been up that late?

Doc poured himself another medicinal dose of his special stock of t-genuine Canadian whiskey. We could buy near-beer in bottles only – 3.2 beer at two for twenty-five cents – since last April. The state legislature would not permit draught beer because it might lead to a revival of the evils of the saloon, despite the fact that Hoosiers had voted two-to-one to repeal Prohibition. Governor Paul V. McNutt said he was willing to bend on the issue. Beer was reviving the Hoosier economy. The Owens-Illinois glass plant in Muncie was operating at full capacity making beer bottles. The Centlivre and Berghoff breweries in Fort Wayne ran three shifts, twenty-four hours a day, six days a week trying to slake fourteen years of pent-up thirst. Just a couple of days ago, I read in The Journal-Gazette, Fort Wayne's morning newspaper, that Berghoff bragged that it produced eight-hundred barrels of beer every day. Legal whiskey was just a few months away. The gangsters would have to look for a new line of work. Too damn bad.

Doc angled the bottle toward me.

I shook my head no to the offer and reached for a hard peppermint candy from the jar on Doc's desk. One whiff of liquor on my breath and Adele's mother, a staunch patroness of the Paradise chapter of the Women's Christian Temperance Union, would have a fainting fit.

"Give me something I can check on," I said. "Tattoos. Scars. Laundry marks. Pocket lint. Something. I'm flat out of ideas."

"To answer in order: no, no, no, no, I don't know and aren't you always." He swirled more whiskey around his gums. He claimed it was anti-septic and would keep him out of Gerald Linder's dentist chair. Doc, the model for the original man's man, was afraid of dentists.

"Wait! Sorry, tired." Doc waved his free hand in the air, as if to wipe away his previous comments. "Yes, marks – rather, three marks. You saw that faint bruise on the left side of her face. Could have been from a slap, maybe a fall. Hard to tell. She also had a small strawberry birthmark shaped rather like the state of Florida behind the left ear. Her hair concealed it. More interestingly, there was a band of raw flesh – a strangulation impression – on the throat. It was thin, concealed in the fold of the neck. I didn't see it at first when I looked at her at the dump."

"She was strangled and then shot? That's – pardon the expression – overkill, isn't it?"

"Strangled? Not exactly, not in the sense that it caused her death. It was – and I'm speculating here, so bear with me – caused during a struggle before she was shot. The impression wasn't wide enough or deep enough to have been made by a rope or a belt or anything of that nature. A string or a thin chain, maybe a necklace." He thought for a moment. "That makes sense. Stand up."

I stood, wobbling a little from the effects of the medicine vapors and the whiskey. Doc spun me around, seized the back of my collar with his left hand and yanked hard. I yelped in surprise and arched my back and neck, trying to twist away from him. Doc jammed the lip of the whiskey bottle into my scalp above my right ear. None too gently.

"Bang!" Doc whooped. "Yes, sir. That's it. That's how he did it."

"Run that by me, again."

Doc performed his murder ballet again, this time in slow motion.

"He grabbed her like this." He pulled on my shirt collar. "Only it wasn't her clothing. Imagine your tie is a necklace. The murderer yanked on the necklace and pulled her backward toward him. What did you do? You tried to get away. I think she did, too."

"That's obvious."

"Don't interrupt. Then he shot her while she struggled. It all fits. He had to act fast because the chain on that necklace would break sooner rather than later."

"Okay, I'll buy that. Maybe. But what about our murderer? I'm thinking a big man, young, the strong, athletic type. He had to pick her up and move her from wherever she was killed to the dump."

"Not necessarily. You're what – six-two, six-three?

"So?"

Doc dragged me over to a mirror so I could see what he was doing. "I'm five-eleven. Bend your knees. Stoop down. Make yourself shorter. Pretend you're a girl, a rather short girl." My throat hurt where the collar had bitten into it. Sparkles jiggled in my eyes.

"Thanks, Sherlock."

"Don't faint on me. I don't want another emergency on my hands." Doc pulled up my eyelids and stared at whatever doctors stare at. "You'll live. Not that it matters to me. I could get along just fine without your sorry ass in my way. But Adele would never speak to me if I let you expire in my back room. That would pierce me deeply. I admire that girl almost as much as you do."

"Thanks, again." I tried standing. The room did not whirl quite as madly as before.

"'Sarcasm I now see to be, in general, the language of the Devil.' Carlyle. It doesn't become you, my friend."

Doc was chastising *me* for being sarcastic?

"Damn it, Walter. I came back to this quaint backwater in nowhere Indiana to escape all that. Bloodshed, random violence, race hate, gang wars. Hell, I saw enough of that when I did my residency in New York to last me a lifetime. Not to mention the legally sanctioned murder and mayhem during the war. Give me a case of the croup, lice, a broken arm, a baby to deliver, even Mrs. Christie's never-ending nervous complaints, and I'm a happy man. I can help those folks. I can't do much for scarlet fever or tuberculosis or influenza, but I can at least try. I can't help that poor murdered woman. Damn, here it is again, dumped right in my lap." He poured himself another drink. "Get out of here. Rowena's expecting me home for dinner."

The sign on Doc's back door rattled. *Noli Intrare. Noli Perturbare.* Keep out. Do Not Disturb. It was a good thing I had taken Latin in high school. Doc did not bother with translations.

I weighed Doc's analysis of the mystery woman and how she came to die. In some ways, I knew less now than I had before. We now had at least four missing items – the shoe, the purse and the suitcase, plus the necklace. And the murderer's description fit at least half the men of Lincoln County. The sheriff's declaration that the murderer was a stranger was convenient, but unlikely. I was convinced that only a local would know the dump well enough to feel safe while depositing the body there in the dead of night.

Tall men and southpaws had been eliminated. That much was certain.

Adele awaited.

And, as Doc might say, *Id imperfectum manet dum confectum erit.* It ain't over 'til it's over.

CHAPTER 6

I slept badly Tuesday night. I tried to fit the pieces of the puzzle together in my dreams. Always, I came back to the image of the mystery woman's lovely face covered with flies. She turned toward me and tried to speak, but the flies filled her mouth and no words would come out. Buzzards, all sporting masks of Francis Rumsey, surrounded her like mourners at a casket. Her murderer skulked in the shadows, but I could not find him, although I searched and searched.

Nothing much happened to make news the rest of the week. Kids stole laundry off the line at a sourthside house on Wednesday. A car-buggy accident on Water Street left the Auburn with a big dent; the horse died. Mrs. Chick Grimley's annual summer tea for the Paradise chapter of the Daughters of the American Revolution drew a big crowd. Late Thursday, Orleva Warren, a friend of my late grandmother, died in Prattsburg at the ripe old age of ninety-three. The funeral would be at Rumsey's establishment.

Rollie Parker's dogs found a couple of useless clues in the murder of the mystery woman. The hounds sniffed out a blood-stained pillowcase stuffed under a rotting mattress at the dump. It contained her hat, purse and gloves. The purse contained a hanky, a lipstick, some miscellaneous scraps of paper and a dozen movie ticket stubs. Sheriff Hoyt Peterson burned up the taxpayers' money on long-distance telephone calls and telegrams to track down the theaters. No name, no address, no nothing.

Jeff Heston kept his promise, and I got my day off. Adele and I hopped the 8:10 on Friday morning, intending to spend a relaxing long weekend in Chicago. It was a comparatively balmy eighty-nine degrees in the shade.

Adele was a knock-out. She looked cool and serene in a trim navy ensemble that is called, so I am informed, a traveling suit. A tiny navy straw hat set off her wavy, honey-brown hair. And gloves, of course. Low-heeled shoes. High heels showed off her wonderful long legs, but she had comfort and shopping on her mind. She planned to bring home her trousseau. I planned to catch a Cubs-Phillies game and visit Dugan's Social Club with Barney O'Malley, a Chicago newsman *par excellence* and an old buddy.

The Great Heat Wave of 1933 had begun the second week of June. There was no end in sight. The thermometer outside The Telegraph-Register building had documented the temperature at higher than one-hundred degrees for five days in a row and never less than ninety-three degrees ever since. People moved about only on the most-important errands. Paradise slept on its porches to try to catch the ghost of a breeze at night. There wasn't an electric fan to be found in any store. Cattle died. Children and old folks got sick. Even most of the wild boys stayed home, too wrung out to make trouble.

Herb Daishell, who had his Crosley tuned to Cincinnati's WLW from April to October to catch the Reds games, observed the traffic at Rumsey's establishment next door across the alley, and observed, "Imagine all those folks dying in summer. Humph! Must not be baseball fans."

Adele and I could scarcely hear the Methodist preacher on Sunday mornings over all the noise made by the paper fans in every worshipper's hands. The fans had a picture of a rosy-cheeked, Aryan Jesus on one side and an advertisement for Miller's Funeral Parlor on the reverse. Rumsey used to have all the Methodists locked up in the annual summer fan war, along with the Presbyterians and some of the Lutherans. Miller always stocked the Catholics, the Brethren, the Baptists and some of the smaller, dunk-and-shout country churches. Rumsey claimed his printer went belly up, and he did not have enough old fans to go around, so Miller captured the Methodists and quite a few other pews. This was fuel for gossip over many a Sunday dinner.

Tonight, Adele and I planned to see the picture show at the Biograph Theater, which promised the welcome relief of air-conditioning.

We settled in. The railroad car was nearly full. We recognized two people from Paradise, the remainder had come from elsewhere down the line. Train tickets to Chicago and hotel rooms in the city were at a premium with the World's Fair in full stride. More than a quarter of a million people visited the fair on the July Fourth holiday. On most days, a mere one-hundred-twenty-five thousand attended. We were lucky to have seats.

The whistle shrieked and the train lurched forward, knocking Adele's purse onto the floor. Just as I picked it up, the door banged open. Francis Rumsey, red faced and out of breath, struggled with two large valises. Rumsey fell into the last seat directly across the aisle from us. He tipped his panama to Adele and ignored me.

"Morning, Mr. Rumsey," said Lewis Adams, one of the Paradisans.

"Morning," Rumsey grunted.

Mose Truby, the conductor, took our tickets.

"Another trip to Chicago, Mr. Rumsey?" Mose asked, just making conversation. "You've been such a regular on this train the last few months, you could almost do my job. Ain't that right?"

"Shut up, boy!" Rumsey said. "This is a free country, and I can ride anyplace, any time I want. Leave me alone."

"Yessir, Mr. Rumsey. Whatever you say. No need to get upset, now." Mose backed away from Rumsey, shrugged at me and left the car.

Rumsey, sweating from the heat and the exertion, wiped his face and neck with a large handkerchief. Rumsey had aged in the past year. Where there had been wrinkles, crevices had appeared. The boozer's bags under his eyes were steamer trunks. He had lost weight. and his suit coat flapped from his shoulders like sheets on a clothesline. He looked closer to sixty-five than fifty. What was the matter with Francis Rumsey? That was the question.

"What're you staring at, Pratt?" Rumsey asked.

"Nothing, Frankie. And I do mean *nothing,*" I said.

Adele poked me in the ribs in that way she has of telling me to be a good boy and not make a fuss. She comes by that trick honestly after teaching ninth-grade English for three years at Paradise Senior High School.

Rumsey mumbled something under his breath.

"What was that?"

"You son of a bitch!" He shouted loudly enough to be heard in the next car. "I know about your poking around. I saw you with Ted Thompson the other day. Digging around in the courthouse. Talking to people about me. You're trying to ruin me. I know you are, you little shit."

"I'm a newsman. I go where the story takes me."

"Newsman? You write little stories about little people that nobody cares about. You're just a jumped-up nobody from Prattsburg. Where's your mama? Running around in some God-forsaken foreign country with the Communists, that's where. You want stories? I could tell you *stories* about your mother. She thought she was better than everybody, just like all you Pratts." He paused and shot me a look that would singe asbestos. "Think you're going to outsmart Francis Rumsey, do you? Think again. Go to Hell."

Rumsey was sweating again. But now he had a triumphant, far-away look in his eyes. It was as though he were peering into a secret future that was revealed only to him.

"Mind your mouth, Rumsey. How dare you speak like that in front of my fiancée?"

I jerked off my jacket and stood. Adele grabbed my belt. "That's enough. Sit down, Walt," she said. "He's not worth it." She used her schoolmarm voice, the one that froze fourteen-year-olds in their tracks.

I was not fourteen. I had at least twenty-five years and eight inches on Rumsey. I am not a brawler by nature, but it would not be much of a fight. I would make sure of that.

I had taken one step toward him, when Mose Truby hustled back into the car. Lew Adams trailed after him.

"Mr. Rumsey, Mr. Rumsey. Let's not get too excited, here. There's ladies present. I'll find you a nice seat in the smoker. Come with me." Mose picked up Rumsey's hat and put a guiding hand on his elbow.

Rumsey gurgled in frustration and ripped his panama out of Mose's hand. "Get your filthy hands off me, nigger."

Adele gasped. Our kind of people did not think, much less talk, that way, even in private.

Mose stood like a statue. Coping with Rumsey and his ilk was never pleasant, but Mose obviously had heard it all before. He took it like the calm, dignified man whom we all admired.

"This way, Mr. Rumsey," Mose said, firmly but politely.

Mose ushered Rumsey, who was still swearing under his breath, into the next car.

I collapsed into my seat. "Sorry," I said to no one in particular.

"You should be sorry, Walt," Adele said. "That was disgraceful. You know better."

"Jesus, Addie, I'm not ten years old. I'm a man."

"Then act like one." She turned away and stared out the window.

That put the kibosh on all conversation until we pulled into Gary.

"Why?" she asked at last.

"Why what?"

"Why do you and Francis Rumsey hate each other?"

"I don't hate him."

Silence.

"I despise him."

Silence.

"Look, Adele, that man's a phony, a bigot. You heard what he called Mose Truby, who's one of the nicest people in the universe. Ten, fifteen years ago, when the Kluxers ran Indiana, Francis Rumsey was the grand poohbah of the Lincoln County Klan. Then, everything fell apart for him. The Klan was chased out of the governor's office. Rumsey lost all his influence. His first wife died. He changed. Yeah, he goes to church. He says the right things. Belongs to all the right lodges. But he's bent, seriously bent. Something's not right. Don't tell anybody, but Jeff Heston and I are working on a story about him. We suspect he's working a fiddle to get money out of poor people to pay for funerals. And there are these little trips to Chicago."

Adele arched an eyebrow. *So what?*

I sighed. I really did not want to tell her. "You want the whole story? Okay, here it is – gangsters, drugs, women."

"Francis Rumsey? I can't believe it."

"Believe it. When I was a cub reporter in Chicago, I was working on a story about, uh, sporting houses."

"For Heaven's sake, Walter, this is 1933. I'm no dainty flower who's going to swoon and have the vapors. You can say the word prostitute."

"Yes, well, Hull House was trying to get poor, terrified young prostitutes out of a life of crime and desperation. Some of them were only thirteen, fourteen years old. That's the age of Doc's daughter, Calpurnia. Anyway, I visited a couple of those houses." She gasped. "Don't look so shocked. I was just following a story. I didn't, uh, how shall I put it – uh, participate."

"I certainly hope not. And?"

"I saw Rumsey. He was hopped up or drunk, the life of the party. He was pawing at a pair of red-heads. I felt sorry for them. They tried really hard to hide their disgust."

Adele took my hand. "Those poor women. What a terrible life."

"Yes, it is." I was silent a moment. "I tried to duck out, but Rumsey caught sight of me. I thought he was going to have an apoplectic fit. He begged me – I mean, he got down on his knees and begged me – not to tell anyone in Paradise. There were actual tears in his eyes. I felt sorry for him, don't ask me why. But I left his name out of the story I wrote. I thought he'd be – not beholden, I wouldn't expect or want that, but maybe thankful. Instead, he hated me even more. I know his dirty little secret. That's why he hates me."

Adele thought about that for a minute.

"I see," she said, finally. "That's why he hates *you,* but why do you hate *him?*"

Count on my sweetheart to cut to the heart of the issue. I had fifty years of this ahead of me. I did not want to tell Adele, or anyone, this part of the story.

"Come on, Walter, 'fess up."

I sighed. I could not keep anything from her, even my worst secrets.

"He hit my mother."

Adele stared, shocked into silence.

"And I hit him."

She squeezed my hand hard. "What happened?"

"It was the summer of 1923. I was sixteen. After Rumsey's first wife died, he courted – or tried to court – my mother. You know my father died in the nineteen-eighteen influenza epidemic?"

She nodded. "My grandfather, too."

"Yes. Well. We were at the big ice cream social the last night of the county fair."

"You squired Bonnie Simmons around most of that summer."

"You knew that?"

I got the arched eyebrow again.

"Go on," Adele prompted.

"Rumsey asked my mother to marry him. She said no, thank God. Worse than that, she laughed. It wasn't that she wanted to make fun of him or embarrass him, she just couldn't help herself. He lost control. You saw how he gets. He called her a bunch of bad names and hit her with his fist. I ran up and popped him. He didn't fall, but I staggered him. I went after him again, tried to hurt him, but mother pulled me off." I sighed. "That's why I hate him."

Adele leaned close and kissed my cheek. "I love you, Walter. I love that you stand up for what you think is right."

I ignored the stares from our fellow passengers and kissed her square on the mouth.

At the station in Chicago, I left Adele to guard our baggage and hustled so I was in time to overhear Rumsey give the hack an address I knew was in a part of the city dominated by warehouses and small factories. Adele and I proceeded to our hotel. We had separate rooms. We were a modern couple with modern ideas, but not *that* modern. We came from Paradise, after all.

Adele headed for Marshall Field, and I headed after Rumsey.

CHAPTER 7

"You nuts? There's nothing there," the cabby said through a thick accent.

I threw a few salty words in German at him, and he put his foot on the accelerator.

As forecast, there was a whole lot of nothing in that neighborhood – just empty lots and industrial buildings, most vacant. The occasional truck with hard-faced men behind the wheel whizzed by.

The address Rumsey had given turned out to be a three-story brick building in the middle of a block of small repair shops, a diner devoid of customers, a boarded-up factory. A sign next to Rumsey's destination read: Cook County College of Mortuary Science – Burials at Low Prices for the Thrifty. Much like a beauty school, the mortuary college apparently provided hands-on experience for budding practitioners and cheap funerals for customers who did not mind that their loved ones did not look as though they were sleeping. Families would have to be truly desperate to bring Uncle Morty or cousin Flora here, I thought. The school was more fortress than homey parlor. Iron bars covered blackened windows. A side door was boarded shut. A hearse sat in a wire-fenced, padlocked enclosure next door. Two coatless young men lounged on the front steps smoking cigarettes. Their eyes followed us as Hans the cabby braked to a stop. Neither Rumsey nor his taxi were in sight.

"You want I wait? Don't mind. I bring lunch." Hans pulled a lunch bucket stinking of sausage and garlic from the floorboards. "Take your time, *mein freund.*"

The toughs on the steps refused to move a muscle as I stepped awkwardly over their outstretched legs. A bald man wearing red suspenders over a collarless shirt looked up as I approached the front desk. The interior of the building was as decrepit as the exterior. The floor had not seen a mop since the Harding administration. A moist, faintly medicinal smell suffused the air. It reminded me of an unfriendly version of Doc Joplin's office. I palmed one of the dusty leaflets stacked on the counter just to have something to do with my hands. My greeter kept his right hand out of sight under the counter.

"No classes until October," the man said. "You can sign up then."

"I'm not a student. I'm here about – uh, my Aunt Gertrude."

He stared.

"She died," I added lamely.

"No funerals until October when classes start."

"But I thought – "

"You thought wrong."

"I was told to come here."

He exhibited a little more interest and rested his now-visible right hand on the counter.

"By who?"

I thought fast. "A friend. A friend from Indiana."

The desk man reached over and pushed a buzzer. A bell rang somewhere in the back. A few seconds later, a man buttoning his suit jacket emerged through a side door. The new man had slicked-down black hair, olive skin, a thin moustache and a nose that had been broken long ago and never set properly. He was a boss of some sort, judging by the cut of his suit. He did not button his jacket fast enough for me to avoid seeing a handgun in a shoulder holster. That might have been intentional.

"I thought maybe you'd wanna talk to this guy, Mr. Green." The desk man pointed to me.

"Can we help you?" Green sized up my bank balance in one glance and talked salesman slick, as if he were hawking lawn mowers at Sears & Roebuck. He cracked the knuckles of one hand and then the other. *Pop, pop,* pause, *pop.* An unconscious nervous tic, I thought.

"I have a friend from Indiana."

"Good for you. I have lots of friends across the state line." He let the words settle. "What do you want?"

I took a shot. "Booze. A couple of cases for a party tonight."

The desk man sniggered. "What happened to Aunt Gertrude."

The boss cut him off with a look.

"I think you've come to the wrong place, sonny. This is a school, not a bootlegger's den." He checked his pocket watch, then pointed at the door. "Get lost and stay lost."

The not-so-subtle implication was that if I did not leave of my own accord, he had the means to make me leave. For punctuation, he put a hand on my chest and gave me a firm shove.

I thought about those muscular men on the stoop. I left.

Hans was still chewing on his sausage sandwich when I got in the cab. Smart man. He had left the engine running. I gave him an address loudly enough that the toughs sprawled on the steps could hear. Hans raised his eyebrows but put the car in gear.

"Where we going?" Hans asked after we were a block down the street. "That place don't exist, except maybe in the middle of the lake."

"Are you willing to stay with me for a while?"

"Sure. You got money?"

I handed him two fivespots out of my walking around money. He kept his hand out. I added a tenner.

"*Gut*. What now?"

I told him.

There was something very, very wrong about the Cook County College of Mortuary Science. I had already seen at least one man with a gun. The firepower was not there to keep the corpses in their caskets. I believed the boss, Mr. Green. There might have been a bottle or two on the premises for personal consumption, but the school was not hiding a distillery. The smell would have been unmistakable. Something else was going on.

Hans and I drove six blocks straight ahead. Nobody followed us, so we circled back. We idled in the trash-strewn alley across from the college. From our vantage point in the shadows, we could see the entrance on our right, as well as the parking area straight ahead. The hoodlums had abandoned the front steps.

I gave us twenty minutes to see what we could see, then I would give up and do something sensible, something that would not provoke Adele's ire. I got Hans's life history in the first ten minutes. He liked to talk. I handed him a buck and told him to shut up. My wallet was almost empty. Hans – native of Dusseldorf, émigré in 1907, husband of Inga, father of Rolf, Katrina, Josef and Konrad – grumbled to himself, but pulled his cap down and settled in. Silently.

Hahahahahaha.

I was instantly alert.

The two men from the steps, guns stuck in their waistbands, appeared from a rear door. Behind them, Mr. Green and Francis Rumsey strolled across the parking area, talking and gesturing animatedly. Rumsey acted out of character, behaving deferentially, almost obediently to Green. The henchmen removed the padlock and opened the gates.

"We stay?" Hans asked.

"You bet."

He pointed. "*Ja,* I know that man."

"Which?"

"The ugly old one carrying the small traveling bag. I drive him a couple of times. Hotels, banks, the train station. Always with the red face. Always with the bad temper. Never with the tip. Mean. I not forget that man."

That was Francis Rumsey in a nutshell.

There was a rumble to our left. A few seconds later, a convoy of five big moving vans turned into the lot and backed up to the docks. A dozen men piled out. Two men in tuxedos went inside. The rest, in rough workman's clothes, began unloading their cargo. The first truck disgorged swanky furnishings – velvet sofas, gilt chairs, mirrors, carpets, chandeliers. The second and third held more of the same. I ran the possibilities over in my mind. Maybe the rear of the college was a rather strange warehouse, possibly a holding place for stolen goods. The first three trucks left after the guards checked the street. When the workers began to unload the fourth and fifth vans, the purpose – or at least one of the purposes of the so-called college – became obvious. Roulette wheels. Blackjack tables, Poker tables. A bar. Wood crates and cardboard boxes probably contained smaller gambling supplies. It apparently was going to be a good-time Friday for the high-rollers. The back of the building concealed a mobile gambling casino, a high-class one from the looks of it.

The whole operation took seventeen minutes by my watch. Words such as organized, professional, business-like, and well-practiced caromed in my head. Also words such as criminal, gangster, and felonious. I started to tell Hans to follow the last truck, when another vehicle pulled into the lot. This one was an official Chicago police bus, a meat wagon used to transport large groups of prisoners after a riot or the victims of a natural disaster. This strongly suggested conspicuous police protection and influence at the highest reaches of City Hall. The bus disgorged three dozen people dressed to the nines in tuxes and evening dresses. These likely were the casino staff – dealers, bouncers, waiters, bartenders, coat-check girls, entertainers.

Remarkably, all the women had blonde hair, not all of it bequeathed by Mother Nature. Perhaps that was the casino's signature.

During all this activity, Rumsey and the boss lounged against the fender of the hearse. They showed little interest. I had the distinct impression they had seen it all before, and the boss was there just to keep an eye on things. Rumsey only looked up when the women marched into the building. He might have been looking for someone in particular, but it was difficult to tell for certain.

"*Mein Gott,*" Hans muttered to himself.

I agreed, but shushed him, anyway.

Once the lot had cleared, the police bus whisked away the moving crew. Rumsey and his pal shook hands. Green leaned in close and said a few words to Rumsey. The undertaker nodded vigorously, as if he were agreeing or making promises. The boss signaled to the two guards. One started the hearse and backed it up to the now-vacated loading dock.

"*Mein Gott!*" Hans exclaimed.

I did not shush him this time. I was too stunned.

The men rolled a cheap, wooden casket onto the dock and maneuvered it into the hearse.

"We get out of here, now, yes?" Hans reached for the gear shift.

"Wait. Let's see what happens," I said.

What in blue blazes? Rumsey climbed into the passenger seat of the hearse and propped the valise on his lap. One of the men drove; the other locked the wire gate behind them, then hopped into the rear compartment.

"Follow that hearse."

"I come to America on a stinking ship for this?" Hans looked at me as if I had lost my mind.

Maybe I had. I handed Hans my next-to-last bill, a twenty. Hans sighed, put the hack in gear and backed out of the alley. We followed the hearse at a discreet distance for miles. The industrial district gave way to slums, then cheery suburbs, finally open spaces dotted with small farms. We were somewhere southwest of Chicago proper.

"I know where they go," Hans said, after grumbling to himself for twenty miles in a German dialect, of which I understood very little.

The few words I picked up were not particularly complimentary toward me.

"Where?"

Instead of answering, Hans turned into a farm lane and executed a three-point turn so the nose of the cab faced the road. "We wait a minute," Hans said.

I was in Hans's world, and I was stranded in the middle of a corn field, so I didn't object. I waited, but not long, perhaps four or five minutes. Hans eased the taxi forward until he could see the road in both directions. It was clear.

"We go."

Just ahead on the right was a vast open space, maybe three-hundred acres. It was dotted with a few trees and many tombstones. Three other vehicles were there – the school's hearse at the rear of the cemetery farthest from the road and two cars side by side in the middle. Good, maybe we would not be noticed among the mourners. Hans drove to the middle of the cemetery, not far from the family group tidying a grave. He cautiously bumped onto the grass and steered the cab between a stand of pine trees and a tall, ornate mausoleum containing the mortal remains of Josiah and Nora Bartlett, both dead in 1927. This was the best hiding place available. Hans stopped the engine. There was no point in calling attention to ourselves.

"Stay here," I said. "I'll be right back."

"You bet."

The wind blew hard in advance of dark thunder clouds massed on the western horizon. Sticks and leaves skittered past my hiding place behind a large oak. Evidently, the noise had masked our entrance into the graveyard because the two guards were hard at work, digging in a far corner. They glanced up occasionally, but only to check the progress of the advancing storm.

It took me a minute to locate Rumsey. He stood, head bowed, over a grave about fifty yards to my left. I had a choice. I could leave now while the gun-toting gravediggers were preoccupied and return later to find out what was going on. That was the safer choice, but I doubted whether I could find this place again unless I could also find Hans and had enough cash on me to persuade him to bring me here again. Time was a factor. I had a date with Adele tonight and other pressing business in Chicago tomorrow. It was now or never.

I had another choice. I could sneak up on the men from the mortuary college on my right or try to see what interested Rumsey. Easy. I angled left, ducked as low as possible, and darted from tombstone to tombstone. Luckily for me, most of the inhabitants of this section had been prosperous and their graves were marked with large slabs. I ran out of cover about thirty feet from Rumsey. A sunburnt, raggedy lawn and a dirt lane separated us. Judging by the dates on the headstones I had just passed, this was the newest part of the cemetery and still largely empty. I glanced down. I had nearly stepped into a six-foot-deep hole in the ground. I tried and failed to suppress a little shudder. The earth lay open, probably dug yesterday or earlier today for a Monday burial. The mound of newly turned earth that I hunched beside was fragrant, rich prairie soil, a farmer's dream.

I would not have believed that Francis Rumsey was able to surprise me, but he did. Rumsey was engaged in a one-man, animated conversation – complete with pauses, nods and gestures – whether with himself or with the grave's occupant, was impossible to know for certain at this distance. The wind corkscrewed bits of flowers and grass in all directions. I prayed a twister did not show up for the party, but it was that kind of day, that kind of weather. But the sky had not turned that strange, moldy green that foretold a tornado. We would be spared that, at least.

When I peeked around the tombstone, the wind blew disconnected phrases from Rumsey to me. *Bitch* was prominent among them. Also *sweetie. Why? The other. Money. Sorry. Tricks.*

Rumsey had always been vicious and ugly. Now, I had convincing proof he was crazy as a June bug. But what did it mean?

A car horn tooted. I nearly jumped out of my skin. Please, God, do not let that be Hans signaling that he was leaving. There were shouts in the distance. The men from the mortuary college waved their arms.

"Get the fuck over here. We're done," one said, clearly.

Rumsey scowled, but waved back. He patted the top of the headstone the way you would pet Fido and picked up his valise. He had taken three steps when the wind caught his hat and tumbled it along the ground straight toward me. Even Frederick (1861-1918) and Miriam (1870-19--) Osterbeck's ample headstone would not screen me very long if Rumsey came much closer. The only concealment within reach was right next to me. The diggers had piled the dirt from the open grave at least two feet high. If I could just roll over the top and hunker down, I could wait for Rumsey to pass in relative safety.

I held onto my own hat, made myself as small as possible and scuttled over the mound. Everything went black for a second or two. Once I got my breath back, I realized I had miscalculated the distance and tumbled into the open grave. How much noise had I made? I hoped the wind and thunder had covered my fall. The storm was near. The narrow slice of sky I could see from Miriam's final resting place was black with roiling clouds. My temporary shelter grew darker still. I tried not to groan when I rolled over. I knew what bruised ribs felt like. My fingers scrabbled at the walls trying to get a handhold. I yelped. I could not help myself. My fingers were curled around the handle of Frederick's casket.

"What was that?"

Damn. It was Rumsey.

"Hurry up, Frank. The rain's coming. We gotta get outa here." It was one of the toughs.

"I heard something," Rumsey insisted.

"Sure, Frank. Sure you did." He did not try very hard to hide the sneer in his voice. "Pick up your damn hat, and let's go."

There was a rustling above me and a grunt as Rumsey bent over to retrieve his hat, which must have come to rest against the other side of the Osterbeck's stone. *Donotlookdonotlookdonotlook*, I pleaded internally. Silence. After what seemed like an eternity, I heard a sigh, then heavy footsteps faded into the distance.

When I stood on tiptoe, the lip of the grave was at chin level, too high for me to vault out. With my long legs, I could easily straddle the opening. I planted my right foot a few inches up the wall and put my weight on it. The dirt held firm. By leaning from side to side and raising one foot at a time, I fly-walked more than half way toward daylight. I was congratulating myself on my progress when my left foot slipped on something hard, and I slid back to the bottom. The storm chose that moment to let go. In a minute or less, I was standing in an inch of water.

"Great, just great."

A clod of dirt hit the back of my neck, followed by hail.

"What? You got problem?"

Hans. I had forgotten all about him. He grasped my hand, braced himself and heaved. With his strength pulling and my feet pushing against the wall, I managed finally to crawl over the top.

"You stay there very long, you catch your death." Hans laughed at his own joke. Not funny.

I checked for injuries. Nothing major, just bumps and bruises. My suit was a goner, though, caked with mud and ripped in a couple of places. My hat floated at the bottom of the hole. Forget it, I thought, I am not going back for it. The Osterbecks would never notice.

"We leave, now?"

"Please."

All the way back to the city, I rehearsed how I would explain this to Adele.

"What happened to you?" she asked, wiping smears of dirt from my trouser cuffs.

"I fell under a streetcar."

She did not believe me for a minute.

"Sometimes I think you love gangsters more than you love me." Adele was not happy. She threw hotel towels at me. "Take a shower. You stink. I'll speak to you someday, but not right now. And certainly not while you have enough dirt on you to grow potatoes."

I slunk into the bathroom. Pebbles and clods of dirt rained onto the tiles when I shook off my clothes.

"Hand out your suit. Maybe the hotel staff can do something with it."

"I thought you weren't speaking to me."

"Don't push it."

Adele was seated at the little desk by the window, staring into the dark when I got out of the shower. I no longer smelled like a grave. Clean skin felt good. Adele looked pensive, not angry. That was a relief.

"I laid out a change of clothes for you. The hotel has your suit. They didn't make any promises. Besides, you need a new suit, anyway."

"What's the matter, sweetheart? It's not just my little adventure in the graveyard, is it."

"Look at this." She handed me the leaflet from the mortuary school. I had forgotten all about it. "I found this in your pocket. Look at the back page."

I turned it over.

"Well, well, well. This is interesting isn't it."

Francis T. Rumsey's name was right there in ten-point, serif type, bold-faced. He was listed on the board of directors and as a member of the faculty.

"Mr. Rumsey had a legitimate reason for being there," Adele said. "You chased him for nothing."

"Maybe," I admitted.

But I doubted it. The casino, the men with guns, the cheap casket buried clandestinely all argued against legitimacy for Rumsey's actions.

Adele's mind was practical and analytical, but her heart believed there was good in everyone. I loved her for that. In this case, though, she was wrong – dead wrong.

Before Hans shoved me into his taxi, I inspected the gravesite that had agitated Rumsey. Two fresh red carnations lay in front of a small, plain granite marker that read:

DIXIE LEE RYPANSKI
1912-1933

The site where the men from the mortuary college had been working was filled in. No gravestone. Whoever was down there was nameless and beyond my help.

CHAPTER 8

Saturday, July 8, 1933

I felt as though I had spent the night performing aerobatics in a cement mixer. I awakened at noon Saturday stiff, sore and hungry. Time, a couple of aspirin and a hot bath would fix the first two. Six bits and thirty minutes in a cafe would take of the last item. I would pass. I had been in worse shape after high school baseball games when runners with spikes up slid into me at second. My suit was back. It was not pretty, but it was wearable.

Adele did not answer when I knocked on her door. A note left at the hotel desk informed me she was shopping and would meet me at the State Street Grille for supper at six. Don't be late and don't get dirty. We have reservations. I know you're broke, she wrote. Two ten-dollar bills were tucked inside the envelope.

God, I loved that woman. She certainly knew me. That was enough money to have a little fun, but not enough to get into serious trouble.

I decided to skip the Cubs game. I did not miss much. They lost to Philadelphia 8-3. Maybe the glory season of 1908 would come again someday, but not this year.

Barney O'Malley was easy to find. Most evenings after five, and damn near every weekend, he held court in the back booth of Dugan's Social Club. The hangout, formerly Dugan's Tavern, was two blocks from The Tribune. The so-called social club, the name was a convenient euphemism, was one of those members-only establishments that sprang up on nearly every street corner after Prohibition. The membership requirement was an excuse for the stout locks on the front and back doors, and the so-called members had to be eyeballed through a peephole to gain entrance. Dugan was long dead, but the name lived on. So did the original ambiance, which was of the dark, smoky, low-ceilinged variety right out of the era of Robber Barons and buggy whips. Current owner Shamus Aherne did not worry much about décor or cop trouble. Dugan's patrons were the very people who spelled the cops' names correctly in the city's dailies.

Shamus himself opened the door and hugged me like a long-lost brother. "Holy Mother of God, if it isn't Walter Pratt. Where have you been hiding, my friend? You sick of corn fields? You coming back to the city? Ah, lad, doesn't that girl of yours feed you? You're still as skinny as a telephone pole. Can't even get a decent beer in Indiana, I betcha. Don't worry. I got one right here with your name on it."

When I could get a word in edgewise, I thanked Shamus, took a deep drink of my beer and headed toward the back, where Barney was deep in conversation with two men I did not know. Barney caught my eye, held up one finger to indicate *hold on a second or two*. I leaned against a column and lit a cigar. Barney shook hands with both men, who filed out the back with their faces carefully averted. They obviously did not want to be recognized.

"You old son of a bitch, how're you doing?" Barney pumped my hand and pounded me on the back. "Change your mind about the wedding? If you have, I'm going after that fine woman myself, even if she is a Prot."

"Not a chance pal, not a chance."

We grinned and sank into the booth. My seat was still warm from the previous occupant.

I nodded toward the back door. "What's up with those two? Friends?"

"Not exactly," Barney said. "Informants from the criminal echelons of the city. The mean one's Pete Pierpont. The meaner one is Harry Shouse. Heard of 'em?"

I shook my head no.

"You will. They're trying to give the Italians a run for their money." He paused. "Of course, you have no gangsters in the Hoosier state. More's the pity."

"We have a few. All the politicians, John Dillinger, the Anderson gang. Heard of them?"

"Yeah, but you're writing stories about old ladies and their lost puppies, am I right? By the way, I loved that story you sent me about the frozen rooster."

"Hen," I correct him, "not rooster. There's a difference."

Barney roared. They probably heard him in Milwaukee.

The knock about old ladies hit a little too close to home. "I also sent the county surveyor to the state pen last year. He took bribes to move property lines a few feet this way or that. Tuesday, some kids found the body of a murdered woman in the city dump. Nobody knows who she was. I'm still working on that one." I hesitated a moment. "Barney, you know I've seen lots of bad things – gang killings, floaters, a tornado, streetcar wrecks. Remember that factory explosion? Body parts blown a block away. But I tell you, she was the worst. She was so lonely, so – I'm a writer, and I can't find the word."

"Vulnerable?"

"Exactly."

Barney retreated into his own inner place. He also had seen a host of bad things. We smoked a while. "Tell me something good."

"I sold a short story to The Saturday Evening Post last April."

"That's wonderful, Walter. I mean it." Barney saluted me with his beer mug. "You've got talent, nobody can deny that. You were trying to write stories at night when you were a cub reporter here in Chicago. But too many distractions in the big city, eh? And no Adele."

We drank to Adele.

"I have to confess, though, I do miss the chase after the big story. I miss knowing I nailed the bastards on a daily basis. And I miss the city itself, even the stink from the river."

"Ah, me lad." Barney could turn his Irishness on and off at will. "I can't believe you'd miss that smell. But?"

"But here, I always felt like an outsider. I had a little success. I made great friends. But – home is home. Going back to Paradise was the right decision. I'm happy. Paradise may be small and predictable, but it's where I belong."

Shamus appeared with another round. "And who'll be paying, I'm wondering?"

I reached for my wallet, but Barney waved me off. "Consider this an early wedding present," he said.

I did not protest too hard.

Barney drained half his glass in one gulp. "Speaking of Hoosier gangsters."

"Were we?"

"What do you know about the Underground Railroad?"

"Paradise was right in the middle of it. The whole east side of Indiana was dotted with Quaker settlements. The Quakers and other abolitionists hid runaway slaves and guided them north to freedom in Canada."

"Thanks for the history lesson, but, no, I mean the *modern* Underground Railroad. Hideouts in small burgs or farms an easy car ride apart. Safe places for gangsters on the lam. This operation has tentacles in all the surrounding states. They're loosely connected through some controlling party here in Chicago. Who, I haven't figured out, yet. I've traced seven locations in Indiana as far east as someplace called Muncie. Know it?"

"Sure. It's a big town, small city, county seat about thirty miles from Paradise. It's got a state teachers college, two or three glass factories, a meat-packing plant, good-sized railroad hub. Nothing out of the ordinary."

He scribbled something in a notebook and tore off the page. "This is the Muncie address I was given. Check it out if you get time. Let me know if you hear anything else. I'm this far," Barney pinched half an inch of air before thumb and forefinger, "from putting the whole story together."

"Will do. I also need a favor."

"Name it."

I told him about Jed Bailey, Ted Thompson and the others who had sold property to pay large amounts of money to Francis Rumsey to cover the cost of their loved ones' funerals. Barney raised his eyebrows when I told him about the Chicago real estate company that was the recorded purchaser. I told him about Jeff's and my suspicions that the Chicago firm was a front for Rumsey. I told him the whole story, even the part about my mother.

"So what do you need me to do?"

"Check on that Chicago company, any records you can find."

"Not a problem." Barney took notes in his own peculiar shorthand.

"Names of any other people involved. Look for connections to Rumsey, anybody else in Paradise. Transactions. Is the land being held or sold? You know the drill. I was going to do it yesterday, but I got distracted."

Barney chuckled. "You and Adele alone in a hotel room?"

"Nothing that exciting. I chased a hearse and fell in a grave."

That got his attention. I related the whole yarn. Maybe I embellished it a bit, but not by much. When I described my bruising tumble into Miriam Osterbeck's grave, I thought he was going to have a coronary, he was laughing so hard.

"Only you, Walt," Barney said, when he got his breath back.

"Actually, there might be a story in it for you."

Barney turned to an empty page and licked the nib of his pen. "Spill. I'm working on a couple of things, but nothing that's going to break soon. I could use a good story."

"Well, maybe I should keep this one for myself." I could not resist playing him.

"I'm Irish and you're German --"

"Half German. What does that have to do with anything?"

"Okay, half, but we non-Anglo-Saxons gotta stick together. It's the first rule of the immigrant child."

"Blarney! I've seen Polish immigrants your fellow Papists, beaten up in Irish speaks just because they came from Warsaw rather than Cork. Don't even get me going on how Jews or colored people are treated if they stray out of their own neighborhoods."

"So, arrest me, Officer Pratt. I made that up, but I still want the story."

I gave him the rundown on what I had witnessed at the Cook County College of Mortuary Science.

"All the women had blonde hair?"

"Yep."

"The name of the boss was Green? Broken nose. Little moustache? Real slick."

"Yep."

"So it might be true," Barney said after a pause.

"There's a gang running a floating casino. I've heard rumors about it since last winter. Very high class. Very tight security. Very posh, with social-register types by invitation only. Way I hear it, the participants are driven to the gambling joint in a bus with the windows covered. That's part of the thrill. The players don't know where they've been. Even I can't get in, and I know almost everybody who's worth knowing."

That squared with what I saw.

"This casino's part of a trend," Barney said. "With the end of Prohibition just around the corner, the gangsters have to make a choice – walk the straight path, which is damned unlikely, or find new ways to stay in business. They're expanding – prostitution, numbers, a few pushing dope, hijacking. They're getting organized. Pretty soon, you won't be able to tell the difference between Gangland Incorporated and General Electric or Standard Oil."

I laughed. "My socialist mother claims they're all gangsters. The industrialists rob the proletariat with a little less violence. It's all blood money."

"Yeah, she might be right. They've all got lawyers and accountants. Next thing you know, they'll have time experts with stop watches standing at the door during bank robberies trying to figure out how to make them more efficient. There are a few wild ones still on the loose – John Dillinger and that type – but most of those guys are in prison. They're a dying breed – literally. The smart ones are branching out, taking over legit businesses. That's probably what's happened at that school. They all saw what happened to Al Capone in '31. They're trying to avoid an income tax squeal."

"Sounds like this one will be hard to crack."

"The feds are working on it. They had the location – a warehouse – where I don't know. Agents were ready to swoop down on it in June, but a rival gang beat the cops to it. There was a big holdup at the casino. Shots fired, couple of people injured, lots of chaos. People in the know say a lot of money – I've heard various figures between thirty and sixty thousand – went missing. But the rival gangsters didn't get it. Somebody took advantage of the confusion to make off with part of the night's take. Every hood from Chicago to Atlantic City to San Francisco is looking for that money. It's like the wild west: Wanted Dead or Alive. There's a price on his head."

I steered Barney back to the boss, Benny Green.

"His real name is Benito Verdi, better known as Benny 'The Nose' Green."

"I figured Green for the manager, maybe the owner of the mortuary school. But you're saying he's a boss in the Italian gangs?"

"Middling. But he's ambitious. He might be the ultimate owner, but he's probably using a front. That's easy enough to check."

"While you're checking out the school, look for Rumsey's name, too. He's on the board of directors and a teacher there, according to their literature."

"Consider it done." Barney scribbled more notes. "This Rumsey character seems to have his fingers in a lot of nasty pies, doesn't he? Anything else?"

I hesitated. "Does the name Dixie Lee Rypanski mean anything to you?"

"Dixie Lee, no. What kind of name is that? Sounds like one of those made-up Hollywood names. Now, give me a Kathleen or a Brigit or a Mary – a good, solid Irish name. But Rypanski – that rings a few bells."

Barney signaled for another round and consulted the mental filing cabinet in his cerebrum. I checked my watch. I still had a couple of hours before meeting Adele for dinner.

"Got it!" Barney pounded his beer mug on the table. "I knew I'd heard that name. Met him a couple of years ago at a prize fight. This was just after you left the city. I'd bump into him here and there. Minor hood, on the edges. Big Jim, that's what they call him. He's your height but weighs twice as much. Jim Rypanski. Good looking. Lots of blond hair. Muscles. Makes the ladies swoon."

"Dangerous?"

"Nah, not really. Polish from behind the yards. Maybe a fifth-grade education, but not stupid by any means. Friendly. You'd like him. Heavy fists, and I'd guess he knows how to use 'em. But, sweet Jesus, all he'd have to do is lean over you, and he'd scare you half to death. He's that big. Too bad. If he'd caught half a break when he was a kid, he'd be Mr. Average Nice Guy today. Never had a chance, not where he came from. He was strictly brawn for hire – driver, enforcer, messenger boy – that type."

"Was?"

"Yeah, he's out of commission right now. Last I heard, he was a guest of the taxpayers in the Cook County Jail on a minor beef. What's his connection to all this?"

"Not the first clue. Rumsey was unnaturally interested in a grave with that woman's name on it."

We drank our beers while Barney caught me up to date on mutual friends and bragged a bit about the stories he had broken. He stopped talking in midstream.

"Don't look up. Maybe he won't see us," Barney whispered.

I concentrated on my beer. It did not work.

A pair of highly polished brogues appeared under our table. The shoes were attached to a clean-cut man of about thirty-five wearing a pressed grey suit and a fedora. Everything about him was stiff – from the starch in his collar to his military posture to the creases in his trousers.

"Well, if it isn't the reporter," he said to Barney. "And how are you planning to interfere with my work today, Mr. O'Malley?"

"And a gracious good day to you, George. Meet my friend. This Walter Pratt from Paradise, Indiana. He's getting married in a week or so. We're having a little pre-nuptial celebration."

Our visitor looked me up and down as if I were a bug pinned to a specimen tray.

"Walter, let me introduce Special Agent George McMaster of the Federal Bureau of Investigation. He knows *almost* as much about the criminal milieu as I do. Don't you, George?"

McMaster ignored the dig.

I tried to make nice. "You're one of J. Edgar Hoover's new men, I suppose. I've read about you. College degrees. Scientific sleuthing. None of that hit-'em-with-a-sap to make then talk stuff. Incorruptible. Quite impressive. Very modern."

"Sarcasm is cheap, Mr. Pratt."

I held up my hands in surrender. That was the second time this week I had been accused of unintended sarcasm. "Not my intention, sir."

He rapped his knuckles on the table. "Listen to me, O'Malley. I know you're poking around the floating casino. Stay out. We're close to making an arrest, and I don't want you accidentally tipping off the gangsters and driving them farther underground. Got that?"

"Can I quote you on that, Agent McMaster? Barney asked. "Arrest imminent – *et cetera.*"

McMaster's hands reflexively clenched into fists.

"I guess not," Barney said. "Tell you what – I'll do my job, and you do yours. I'm close to breaking that story. If I get to the criminals before you do – well, that's life in the big city. Isn't that right, Walter?"

I agreed.

"Stay out it," McMaster warned again. "I'll make sure you get your story, but on my terms. Understood?"

"Loud and clear. But, pardon me for just a moment while I look up the First Amendment. I think that applies here," Barney said. "You remember the Constitution? It's a little piece of paper. I think you swore to uphold and protect it."

McMaster glared at us, then retreated to buy himself a drink and keep an eye on us in the mirror over the bar.

"What was that all about?" I asked.

"The usual. The government thinks they own the news and can parcel it out like gift baskets to the poor at Christmas. My sources are as good as his, and I refuse to grovel like a grateful beggar. Let's get out of here." Barney look at his watch. "Got some time to spare?"

"Sure."

"Let's do a little hunting. I've got an idea."

We walked a block to a cigar store, where Barney was greeted as a member of the family. He made three phone calls. "Got it!"

His Chevy with the souped up engine was parked behind the store.

"Where are we going?" I asked.

"Big Jim Rypanski, remember him?"

"We're going to the Cook County Jail?"

"Nah, his apartment."

Barney drove to a down-at-its-heels neighborhood near Northwestern University that I had never visited. He checked the address and pulled to a stop in front of a dilapidated, three-story Victorian that had not seen a coat of paint since William Howard Taft pulled on his pants in the White House. The house, once a mansion, dominated a large corner lot. In design, it was a hybrid of wedding cake and Bavarian castle – all towers and turrets, with tiny upper porches and oval windows tucked into odd corners of the facade. A *porte cochere* that once allowed guests to step out of their horse-drawn carriages without getting wet was made impassable now by a parked tricycle and a row of ash cans. A few well-tended rose bushes beside the porch hinted at the home's former dignity. Eight rusting mail boxes and a row of buzzers flanked the front door.

"Rypanski's place? Looks too proper for a gangster," I said.

"We'll see."

Barney ran his forefinger down the hand-written names next to the door bells. He punched the third from the top. We waited three or four minutes. The shade under the porch roof was welcome relief from the heat, but sweat bees and flies were eating us alive.

"It was worth a try," I said. "C'mon, let's go."

Barney punched the buzzer again. "Give it --"

"Hold your horses, sonny, I'm coming." An elderly, but firm voice came from within.

When the door opened just a crack, we discovered the voice belonged to a small woman of at least seventy, with a cane in her right hand. Thick glasses dangled from a string of what appeared to be thumb-nail sized, genuine Japanese pearls around her neck. Those pearls could be worth thousands, but she wore them as casually as if they were cheap fakes from Woolworth's.

"Miss Fisher? Miss Catherine Fisher?" Barney asked, hat in hand.

The lady nodded, put on her spectacles and looked us over.

"You're policemen," she said matter of factly. "In my day, if your type came to one's home, you used the servants' entrance. But that was a long time ago. What do you want, now?"

This former *grande dame* displayed an imperious fortitude little dimmed by time and circumstance.

Barney and I glanced at one another. Policemen?

"It's about that nice Rypanski couple, isn't it? I don't know where she is, haven't seen her for weeks. The rent's paid until the end of the month. You already know where he is." She sighed and opened the door all the way. "You may as well come in."

The spacious entrance hall was old oak, aged to a dark glow even under the dust. Gas lighting fixtures had been converted to electricity, but half of the bulbs were missing. One of Miss Fisher's economy measures, I deduced.

"What can you tell us about them, ma'am?" Barney asked.

"They were Polish, at least he was. We had a Polish cook once. Mother let her go for fooling around with the chauffeur. Her? Southern, I think. Nice manners. Didn't get home until the wee hours of the morning, either one of them. She was a singer, I think. Entertainer of some sort. Always heard her humming when she skipped down the stairs. Very lively. Nice girl, even if she did wear too much makeup for my taste. Looked like a tart but acted like a lady."

"Did they have many visitors?" I let Barney take the lead. He seemed to have established a rapport with her.

"Not many. I discourage that sort of thing. Children are bad enough with all their dirt and noise. You never know about visitors. They might steal something. The Rypanskis, though?" She thought for a moment. "Some men came once – not you police – but rough-looking men just the same. There were loud voices, and I think some drinking. I don't allow that, either."

She pointed to a sign posted in a square frame next to the door: Rules of the House. No Drinking on Premises was Rule No. 2.

"Mr. Rypanski apologized, said he'd make sure it wouldn't happen again. It didn't. But you police took him away soon after that."

I chimed in. "Did they mention any family? We're trying to get in touch with their relations."

"I think Mr. Rypanski was an orphan. She said something about a sister, maybe it was sisters. I don't remember things as well as I used to."

"Could we take a look at their apartment? We won't disturb anything, we promise," Barney said.

"You won't find much. Your friends were here before. Go ahead and look. It's the first apartment on the right on the third floor. Used to be a maid's room. I'd show you up, but stairs and I don't get along so well since I had that fall three years ago. It's unlocked. Help yourself." She let a small but bitter laugh escape. "I would have the butler show you out, but he died in 1913."

The stairs challenged even my twenty-six-year-old legs, especially above the second floor, where they became steep, twisty and narrow. Barney huffed beside me. Miss Fisher's long-gone servants must have been in great physical shape after navigating these steps several times a day.

The door on the left opened wide enough to expose a three-year-old boy with huge eyes under a mop of blond curls. I guessed the tricycle outside belonged to him. "Get back inside, Roger." A young woman in a faded housedress and apron peeked out. "More gangsters. This was a respectable place. It was bad enough when *they* were here." She pointed across the hall. "Go away."

First, we were taken for policemen, now gangsters. What next – meter readers, deliverymen, encyclopedia salesmen, visiting clergy?

I started to reply, but got no further than "No, ma'am," when she slammed the door shut and turned the lock.

"Don't bother, Walter," Barney said. "Let's get in and out before real cops show up."

As promised, the door was unlocked. Someone certainly had been there before. The tiny, one-room apartment was a mess. The bathroom must have been down the hall and shared by everyone on this floor. The room contained a bed, a tiny table and two chairs, a hot plate, a closet, a dresser, a radio, a padlocked door that likely led to another room on the other side just like this one. Men's and women's clothes were strewn everywhere, drawers pulled out. The mattress on the double bed had been slashed and bit of stuffing floated in the air. A thin layer of dust covered every surface. The room gave every impression of not having been occupied for some time.

"What do you think?" Barney asked.

"The Rypanskis weren't real popular with somebody. A friend didn't do this."

"You might say that. Let's give it five minutes, see what we can see, then beat it out of here."

"I feel like a burglar."

"Get over it," Barney said. "We can't do any harm."

"Fine by me."

Barney took the left side of the room and the closet. I took the right side with the bed and the dresser. All the drawers were pulled out, some broken. The woman had been petite and favored bright colors, that much I could make out from the clothing. The man was big and liked white shirts with soft collars and blue ties. A pile of broken glass next to the dresser might have been a perfume bottle. The glass shards were covered with face powder.

"Anything on your side?" I asked.

"Bunch of hangers. Ripped clothes. No suitcases. A couple of old newspapers from early June. What's left of a green satin evening grown – pretty ritzy for Mrs. Rypanski, wouldn't you say? Ugh Rotten food in a paper sack. Might have been a sandwich. Hard to tell. You?"

"Not much. Wait a minute, what's this?"

I tugged a large book from under a pile of women's silky underthings. The cover had been torn off, but the pages were intact. It was a large-format scrapbook filled with newspaper clippings and photographs. I started to flip through the pages when I heard a scuffling noise in the hallways. I did not know why, exactly, but I stuffed the scrapbook into the back of my waistband and smoothed my suit jacket over it.

"Find anything useful, gentlemen?"

Agent George McMaster lounged against the door jamb.

"Christ on a crutch! You damn near gave me a heart attack," said Barney. He melodramatically clutched his chest while one of Jim Rypanski's undershorts dangled from his fingers.

I fervently prayed McMaster did not possess X-ray eyes that could penetrate my body and see what I had hidden. The scrapbook burned against my back. But that sensation mostly likely was guilt. Or fear. I hoped the G-man assumed my normal posture was this erect.

"I thought I told you to stay out of this," McMaster said. He looked about the room. "Never figured you for the breaking-and-entering type, O'Malley."

"We had permission from the landlady. Ask her."

"I did. Only problem is, you told her you were policemen. That's slightly illegal everywhere, except in your circles."

"She assumed what she wanted to assume," Barney retorted.

McMaster gave us the silent treatment. "Maybe," he conceded. He fished one of Mrs. Rypanski's filmy nightgowns off the floor. "What're you boys doing here? I've been following you since you left Dugan's. I had a hunch you were up to no good."

"And I suppose you'll be shopping?" Barney could sneer with the best of them. "I don't think that's your size."

"Yeah, shopping – shopping for information." McMaster let the nightie drop.

"We don't have any." Barney gestured to take in the tiny room, which had shrunk considerably with the intrusion of the federal agent. "Looks like somebody beat us to it. If there was anything here to begin with."

"What do you want with Rypanski. He's still in jail. I checked."

Barney tried his best Irish grin. "You know me, George, I try to stay in touch with all the gangsters. I figured for sure he'd be out by now. I thought I'd bring my friend from Indiana here to meet a genuine Chicago hoodlum. A little something off the usual tourist track. More exotic than the World's Fair. Maybe we'd do a little night-clubbing later. But – no Rypanski."

Maybe we could pull this off. Barney had never introduced me to McMaster as a fellow newsman.

"Uh-huh." McMaster was not buying Barney's story, at least not all of it.

"Why are *you* interested in Rypanski?" When in a tight place, the best defense is a good offense. That was Barney's theory.

"Benito Verdi? Benny Green? I'm sure you've heard of him," McMaster said. "Rypanski was occasional hired help. Benny's missing some money, so I hear. Big Jim might know where it is. So, if you find that missing forty grand, don't spend it all in one place. That money belongs to the government as the fruit of criminal activity. I mean to have it. Don't get in my way. Consider yourself warned. If you cross my path again, you will find yourself facing a federal charge of obstruction of justice. I'll make sure it sticks, and you go to prison."

"Yessir, your lordship." Barney tugged his forelock in a mockery of obsequiousness.

McMaster was right, of course, within his limited way of viewing the world. Prudence would have dictated that Barney keep his mouth shut, but prudence was not Barney's style.

"Tell you what," Barney said. "When I get the story, all of it, I'll be sure to grab the first paper off the press and bring it to your office, autographed. That good enough?"

McMaster swept some of the Rypanski trash out of the way with his foot. "They did this to Rypanski and his wife. You get too damn close, O'Malley, they could do this to you, too – or worse. It's not just me who's after their money and the casino. It's every hood in town. If I could find you here, so could they. Your life would be yesterday's news." He snapped his fingers. "That fast. Like I said: stay out of it."

"C'mon, Walter, let's go. It's a little too stuffy in here for my delicate constitution," Barney said.

McMaster stood on the porch of Miss Fisher's crumbling mansion and watched us pull away from the curb. I waited until we were two blocks away, then retrieved the scrapbook, which had banged painfully against my bruised ribs all the way down those long stairs. I had prayed every step of the way that it would not fall out at McMaster's feet.

"What's that?" Barney tried to steer and look at the book open on my lap at the same time.

"The Rypanski family album. I don't know why I took it. McMaster came in. There wasn't anywhere to hide it, so I just stuffed it in my pants for safekeeping."

"Always said you had good instincts. Maybe it can tell us something."

Boy, did it.

The proof was on the third page. It was the Rypanski couple's formal wedding portrait taken September 12, 1931. It was one of those traditional photos in sepia tones that could be found on a brick-a-brack shelf in almost any parlor in the country. He was seated, hair slicked back, staring straight ahead, looking stiff and uncomfortable in a new suit and a tightly knotted tie. She stood slightly behind him, her right hand on his left shoulder, wearing a slim wedding gown made of some shiny fabric with a wide, round collar. Adele would know how to describe the style. The bride had a tranquil smile and pale eyes that had been green in life.

Dixie Lee Rypanski was my woman in the yellow dress.

There was no doubt in my mind that the happy woman in the photograph and the woman with the back of her skull missing were one and the same.

At least now she had a name. I took some small satisfaction in that. But why did she have two graves – the one with the headstone in Illinois that Francis Rumsey had visited and an unmarked one in Paradise? How could there be *two* Dixie Lee Rypanskis? And how did Rumsey connect to her?

And – this thought really disturbed me – why had Rumsey told Sheriff Peterson that he did not know her? That he could give her a name, could send her back to her family where she belonged? Francis Rumsey was a boil on the backside of humanity, but I had a hard time imagining him a cold-blooded killer.

"What's the matter with you?" Barney asked. "You just turned all green and stiff as a board. Thinking about the wedding?"

"No, murder."

CHAPTER 9

Sunday, July 9, 1933

"Where are we going?" Adele asked as we sped through light city traffic early Sunday morning.

"You'll see. I have a treat for you."

Our taxi, thankfully not driven by Hans, dropped us off at a three-story apartment building in Over the Rhine. Our bags were packed, and we were set to return to Paradise on the afternoon train.

I knocked on the door of the front, right apartment. The windows had been painted recently, and there were pots of petunias on the front stoop.

"*Ja, ja.* Keep your shirt on." The voice was a German-accented grumble.

Two locks clicked.

"Walter!"

We were greeted by the world's biggest smile. It burst out of a forest of whiskers on the old man's face.

"Uncle Adolphus," I said.

He leaned his crutches against the door and crushed me in a bear hug.

Adolphus Mueller may have been seventy-nine years old but was as mentally alert as a man a third his age. Actually, he was my great uncle, my grandfather's younger brother. As boys, they had come to America in 1866 and taken vastly different directions in life. Although Adolphus had lived in this country for nearly seventy years, his speech, with harsh consonants and flat vowels, still contained remnants of his birthplace. My grandfather Gustav – that was where I got the G in my byline – became an anarchist and labor organizer. He barely escaped lynching after the Haymarket Riot. Adolphus, a quiet, gentle progressive, became a prosperous brewer. Prohibition forced him into retirement, but he owned the roof over his head and was relatively secure.

"This must be the lovely Adele." He kissed her on the cheek. "Ah, the wedding is not so far away. You are nervous?"

Adele blushed. "A little."

"You should be nervous marrying this one." He laughed. "I kid you. He's a good one."

"Usually good. He has his moments," Adele said.

"You know him well, I see." He tucked the crutches under his arms. "Come in, come in."

The interior of the two-bedroom shotgun apartment was clean and tidy, as always. It was stuffed with heavy furniture and hundreds of books. The perfume of pipe smoke, sauerkraut, sausage and beer instantly brought back the two years I had occupied Uncle Adolphus's spare room. It was the closest thing to a home I had known since childhood.

"Sit. How long are you staying this time?"

"Just an hour or two. We have to get back to Paradise," I said.

"You seem to be getting around pretty well. How's the leg?"

"The same. Today's a good day. It's always better in the summer. Don't worry. I'll be there for your wedding. Greta, too. She should be here soon."

"Mr. Mueller, I am so happy to finally meet you," Adele said. "Walter talks about you all the time." She pointed to the crutches. "Did you have a fall."

"Uncle Adolphus was – "

"Shush. This is my story, and you will not tell it."

I shut up.

"I had a little brewery. If I may boast just a little, we made the best lager in Chicago. It was a cooperative. The workers shared in the fruits of their labors. I am no Robber Baron becoming rich by stealing from the poor. Then came the Prohibition." He scowled. "I had a little money saved, I would be okay. I would live the quiet life with my Greta, smoke a pipe, go to political meetings, read my books. But after the Prohibition, came the gangsters."

I had heard the story before, spiked with German expletives. The gangsters tried to force Uncle Adolphus to make beer for them. He refused. They broke his left leg in five places before they finally gave up. He had been beaten by federal agents during the Palmer Raids after the World War, when the government hounded communists and socialists. Most of those the federal agents rounded up were immigrants. Foreigners were considered suspect and subversive during the Red-baiting mania that followed the Russian Revolution.

"They're both criminals – the government and the gangsters," Uncle Adolphus continued. "If I had to choose, I'd say the criminals are worse, but not by much."

Adele reached over a patted his knee. "You've suffered so much, but you have zest for life. What's your secret? Most people in your shoes would be bitter, would have given up."

"Thank you, my dear, but that was long ago, and life goes on," he said. "One copes. One adjusts. Ah, would you say our Walter is a little, shall we say, stubborn?"

Adele laughed. "More than a little."

"That's the Mueller side of him. It's in the blood. I'm too damn stubborn to give up. Rust and rot and wait for the undertaker? Never. Not as long as I have breath. Not as long as I have a beautiful woman lying beside me every night. And I have hope. Maybe, if I live long enough, I'll see the bastards in their graves. An old man's revenge is to outlive his enemies."

"That's terrible, Uncle Adolphus," I said. "You live for revenge? Getting even keeps you alive? What about justice. Or love. Or duty. Don't those mean anything?"

"Walter, you're a prig," Adele interrupted. "That's beneath you. Not to mention dishonest. What about Francis Rumsey? Don't even *try* to tell me you don't want revenge. That's the real reason behind your crusade against that man. Rumsey might be bad, is bad, but what you're doing is personal. It has very little to do with justice or duty. You can't see what your face looks like when you talk about him. I can. You hate that man."

"Damn it, Adele, I'm a newsman. Rumsey is a story, whatever our personal history."

"Partly," she said. "You're a sensitive, thoughtful, caring man. I've read your fiction, remember? But there's this whole other part of you that wants blood. Which is the real Walter Gustav Pratt?"

Adolphus laughed so hard his eyes watered, and he had to reach for a handkerchief. "I have no fears for your marriage. You'll do just fine."

"Thanks, I think," I said.

"Ah, Walter, you combine the best of both your grandmothers. You're part the dutiful Mrs. Pratt and part the free-spirited Mrs. Mueller. They were both idealists, but so very different. Yes, I met Frau Pratt from Prattsburg. We had many conversations, many letters after her son married my niece. I would even call her a remarkable woman. A little stiff in her beliefs and standards for my taste, but many fine qualities."

"Stiff? That woman was as hard and unforgiving as a rock," I said.

"So was your Mueller grandmother. Unbending, even fierce. She and my brother were wild ones when they were young."

"If you say so." I was not quite ready to concede my uncle's point. He had never experienced Leonora Pratt's whip hand when I broke one of her thousand rules of proper behavior.

"Take a look at yourself, Walter. I am serious. You have a soft heart and a hard head. You love poetry and facts equally. You were raised among the higher classes but blend in among the lowlifes and the under classes. And when it comes to faith, the dissenter and the believer in you live side by side. That's you. That's the heritage of both sides of your family."

Adele smiled at me. "That's you, indeed."

"Some combination, wouldn't you agree, Miss Atkinson? At least, my dear, you'll never be bored. My Walter will always be a little of this, a little of that."

Adele laughed. "Bored? I have no fear of that."

He grew quiet, almost somber. "Someday, Walter, you may have to choose between the two sides of you. A portion of you will want to do the correct thing according to society, the Mrs. Pratt in you. Part of you will want to do what is right morally, whatever the cost, and that is the Klara Mueller part of you. I pity you. If it comes to that, you will be forever changed. Reality, that's your job, Miss Atkinson. You will be the place where the two Walters can find a home and be one. You are a lucky man, Walter, so very lucky. Forgive me. I am an old man, and I talk too much."

"That's an understatement, dear. You never stop talking." A straight-backed elderly woman entered, removed her hat and kissed me on the cheek. "Good to see you, Walter. You don't visit us often enough."

Greta Hauptmann had been a great beauty in her day. I had seen photographs. She was still pretty and plump, with a thick braid of silver hair wound atop her head like a crown. Her spicy tongue and take-no-prisoners manner had kept her in the forefront of the suffragette movement most of her adult life. She had been my uncle's companion for thirty years, since he had been widowed. Legally, she was his common-law wife. Greta refused to surrender to any convention, including marriage, but she lived here and was his wife in every way. I used to hear the bed springs sing at night while I scribbled in the room next door.

We sipped tea and ate sandwiches. Uncle Adolphus showed photos of the Mueller side of my family to Adele. Greta fussed and argued. She and Adele hit it off instantly – two women with strong opinions who believed in female equality in all matters. I listened with half an ear. My mind was occupied with Dixie Lee Rypanski, and how I could write the story about her identity without tipping off Rumsey that I suspected he was involved in her killing. Was I obliged, morally and legally, to tell the sheriff? That question rattled around in my brain, too. I had no proof, after all.

Adele elbowed me back to attention. Her eyes held questions. So, this is what you wanted me to see? Is this what we will be thirty years from now?

I hoped so.

CHAPTER 10

Late Sunday, July 9, 1933

The wedding dress was a state secret. It was wrapped securely in tissue paper and tucked into one of the six Marshall Field boxes we brought back to Paradise. When prodded, Adele admitted it cost an eye-popping $98.75 and was guaranteed to make all the other girls jealous. She giggled when she told me this – and Adele was a woman not given to wanton giggling – and would not even let me carry this precious box onto the train. I pretended to be a pack mule and carried the remaining five.

Our train had been shunted onto a siding in South Bend to let another train pass. The conductor said it was President Franklin D. Roosevelt's personal train, which, of course, took priority. The President's car passed scarcely five feet from our window. We could tell from the bunting and flags draped on it who rode there. All the windows but one were covered by drawn curtains. I would have sworn I saw that familiar profile – tilted chin, cigarette holder, perhaps the hint of a grin – in that window. But my imagination -- or was it wishful thinking? -- was a powerful thing.

"Father would be having a conniption fit about now," Adele said. "He'd say that Republicans wouldn't make us wait like this."

"Your father! Can't say I'm surprised." I liked the man well enough, but his idea of a great president was Warren G. Harding.

"You and father might as well stop voting. You're only going to cancel out each other's votes," Adele noted.

We got into Paradise about nine o'clock. The depot was dark and long closed when we stepped off the train. My beautiful maroon 1931 Buick 8 sedan, for which I had paid $645 out of my short-story money three months ago, and which I loved almost as much as Adele, was parked under one of the elms next to the station. It was well past dusk, but not yet full dark.

"Drop your purse," I said under my breath.

"What?"

"Shh. Just do it."

She dropped her purse onto the platform and let out an exaggerated sigh. I bent over to pick it up and checked the car from a lower angle. I was right. I had seen someone standing near it. Most of him was in shadow next to the building, but his feet caught a bit of the station's new electric lights. He must have sensed me looking in his direction because he flattened himself against the wall.

"Stay here," I said to Adele.

"No, Walter. I don't know what you're playing at, but I'm tired and I'm going home with you or without you. *Right. Now.*"

I put my arms around her and pulled her tight to my chest. No one in Paradise would think it out of the ordinary for two almost-marrieds to have a cuddle, even in public.

"Listen," I said quietly. "There's a man hiding beside the car." She started to turn her head. "No! Don't look! There's been too many strange things, dangerous things going on in Paradise lately for me – us – to take any chances."

"Oh, Walter, really. You're imagining things."

"I'm going to say this once. Look at me!" I caught her chin with a finger and turned her head to face me. "I'm going to say something about looking for our luggage, then I'll walk around the building and come up behind him from the other side. You sit over there on that bench where there's light, and you'll be safe. It might be nothing, but I want to make sure. Here are the car keys, just in case you have to make a run for it."

"Walter?"

"Just do it. Please."

"For God's sake, Walter, this is Paradise not Chicago. You won't find a gangster behind every tree."

"Just stay here." I patted her on the fanny. She did not like that, either. I raised my voice. "Oh, sweetheart, where'd they leave our other bag? Do you see it?"

"Hurry up, Walter," she whispered. "This is ridiculous."

"I'm looking." I made an elaborate show of searching. "Just a minute. Maybe it's over here."

I slid off the platform and tried to stay off the gravel of the parking area to avoid making noise. There was a narrow lawn on the street side of the depot, and I made good time crossing it. I sidled up to the far corner and peeked around it. The man was still there, about seven or eight feet away. He wore a suit and a hat, that much I could make out. Not a tramp, then, the clothing was wrong for that. Not a kid sneaking a smoke away from his parents' eyes. I took one cautious step, then another. He must have heard something because he turned toward me. The next thing I knew, he was on me. He threw a wild punch that landed on my right temple. I tried to hit back, but he was too close and my reach was not an advantage. He was shorter than me and wiry, but strong. He connected again with a couple of quick rabbit punches to my already sore ribs. This nearly took my breath away.

"Stay out of it," he said. With that, he kicked my feet out from under me and started to run. I managed to grab an ankle and pull him to his knees. He was on his belly, so I crawled on top of him and tried to turn him so I could see his face. I smelled something on him. Not cologne, not that strong – hair pomade, maybe soap. He broke free of my grasp. I crouched, intending to tackle him football-style, but he landed another punch. I fell again.

"Stay out of it," he whispered again, and hit me in the kidneys.

"Out of what? What are you talking about? *What?* "

There was a solid *thunk*. The man groaned, staggered and clutched his arm. He sprinted for downtown, lurching a little off balance from cradling his injured arm. He dodged the streetlamps, so all I could make out was a dark shape in dark clothing running in the night.

When I looked up. Adele held my baseball bat in her hands. "Walter, are you all right?" She helped me up.

"Keys?"

"Right here."

"Get in the car."

"What happened?"

"Later. Where'd you get that bat?"

"In the back seat. I saw it when I threw the packages in there."

I fired up the Buick, put the car in gear and headed east along Walnut Street toward the main drag. I was moving before Adele had her door closed.

"Thanks. I'm going to call you Babe Ruth from now on. Maybe just Babe." I stepped on the gas.

"Where are we going? Home's the other direction."

"After him."

The man looked over his shoulder, his face a featureless white blur, then ducked into the alley between Mercer's Cigar Emporium and Winston's Haberdashery. He had two blocks on us.

"Did you get a good look at him?"

"Male. Not young, not old. That's about all." She pointed. "Watch out!"

An old Model A clattered down Main Street toward us at a stately fifteen miles per house and started to turn onto Maple, which paralleled Meridian Street one block over. I honked the horn. The Model A ignored us completely and kept turning, right into my path. I stood on the brakes. Nothing. No response. I pumped the brakes. Nothing. The only choices were hit the car ahead or hit something else. I swerved to the right and banged into a light pole. I had lost my man, and I lost the right front fender of my car. Also, most likely, the brakes.

No injuries from the car wreck, thank God. I suffered Adele's indignation and the humiliation of having to call Mr. Atkinson to get a ride for Adele. The nearest phone was in Mercer's, which always stayed open late to accommodate the poker game in the back room.

At least Adele now believed me about the danger that I – make that *we* – were in. I tried to convince her to go to Fort Wayne and stay with her older sister, Marie, for a few days. No dice.

"Are you completely mad?" she said none too quietly. "Our wedding is a little over a week away. I have a bridal shower. Flowers, presents, thank-you notes – a million and one things to do. You have to move to the new house. So do I. The house needs cleaning and decorating – curtains, paint, wallpaper. Go to Fort Wayne? Not on your life, Walter Gustav Pratt. I'm staying right here."

She softened a bit and placed her palm against my cheek.

"Besides, Walter, remember the Bible verse. It's from Ruth – 'Intreat me not to leave thee, or to return from following after thee: for whither thou goeth, I will go; and where thou lodgest, I will lodge.' I won a ribbon for reciting that in a Sunday school convocation when I was eight and never forgot it. We are a *we*, now. We are a team. Your joys are my joys. Your dangers are my dangers. I'm with you one-hundred percent every day for the rest of our lives. Your choices may not always be my choices, but I promise to respect them, even if I reserve the right to disagree. Loudly at times."

The fortunate appearance of Mr. Atkinson in his sedate black Packard saved me from a paroxysm of guilty apologies or from bursting into tears. I kissed Adele on the cheek, whispered *be careful* and declined her father's grudging offer of a lift. Adele had forgotten or deliberately neglected to remember the rest of that verse from Ruth: "Where thou diest, will I die and there will I be buried." I tried not to think about the implications.

The attackers repeated words – *stay out of it* – vibrated in my ears. I had heard that voice before, I was sure of it, but couldn't place it. Not Rumsey, wrong voice, wrong size, wrong age. The man who attacked me was too young, too fleet of foot, too agile to be deep into upper middle age, out of shape and out of breath. Was it someone from out of town brought in to do a little dirty work? One of Benny Green's business colleagues, perhaps? I could not make sense of it. Every possibility I considered was too far-fetched for my rattled brain to contemplate and come to a rational conclusion.

I limped back to the Travelers Hotel. My knee was bleeding, and my trouser leg was shredded. During the fracas, I had fallen onto one of the white-washed rocks that circled the depot's flagpole. The trousers belonged to the same unlucky suit I had worn when I fell into Miriam Osterbeck's grave. The suit was destined for the dump.

There was not one proper bandage to be found among all my possessions, so I wrapped a clean sock around my knee and held it in place with a rubber band. It hurt like Hell. I counted my wounds – ribs bruised twice in the past three days, a big lump on my head, a black eye, a knee gushing blood, assorted cuts and scrapes. I browbeat the deskman to bring me six aspirin and a pint of whiskey. I slept, but not well. The Sandman was not my friend this night.

CHAPTER 11

The Telegraph-Register
Monday, July 10, 1933

MYSTERY WOMAN'S IDENTIFY REVEALED!

WIFE OF CHICAGO MAN WAS ENTERTAINER; SHERIFF STUMPED, KILLER STILL AT LARGE

Dixie Lee Rypanski half of 'nice couple,' landlady says in exclusive interview

By Walter G. Pratt

I had finished the story, managing to leave out the floating casino, Jim Rypanski's gangland connections, the missing $40,000 and Rumsey's involvement. That was not easy. I had told Jeff Heston the whole tale, and we agreed we could always put those nuggets of information in another story once we had more tangible proof. A late lunch was the next item on today's agenda.

I limped to the Daisy Diner with one of the first papers off the press tucked under my arm. Doc Joplin had cleaned my wounds, clucked about my habit of getting violence committed upon my person, taped my ribs and put a clean, proper dressing on the knee. My ruined sock went into Doc's wastebasket. The tape around my aching ribs itched almost as much as the knee hurt. Doc took one look at my black eye and pronounced that there was not one damn thing he could do. It would have to heal on its own. The bump on the back of my head was a worry, Doc said, but only if I got hit there again.

My Buick was in Vance White's garage undergoing repairs. I took it to White's rather than Pilcherd's because Cole Pilcherd was the police chief's brother in law. Vance knew how to keep his mouth shut. I had bought a couple of bottles of hooch from him in Prohibition days. Vance promised the Buick would be back in running order in a day or two. As I had suspected, the brakes had been tampered with.

"Somebody sure don't like you, Walter," Vance said. "You ought to tell the police about this, you know."

I should, but I chose not to. What had happened was between me and the faceless attacker.

The diner was packed. Herb Daishell spoke to a man I had never seen in Paradise before who was seated at the window table. Herb motioned me over. "Sorry, Walt. Busy Monday. Mind sharing a table? He's new in town. Be nice."

"No problem. How're the Reds doing? I haven't been paying attention to the box scores."

"Losing. Need a decent pitcher." Herb slapped a menu on the table. "We're out of the ham steak special, but we've still got plenty of the chicken and noodles."

"Just a Daisy burger, scalloped potatoes and iced tea. Make sure the hamburger's well done. I don't want it to moo when I bite into it." I stuck my hand out to the stranger across from me. "Walter Pratt."

The stranger showed a row of perfect white teeth. He was about my age, middle height, trim, with chestnut hair that might look blondish or reddish depending on the light. I was sure the girls would call him handsome, even though he lacked any trace of the Hollywood pretty boy about him. He wore a tan, summer-weight suit, but he had draped the jacket over the chair next to him. He had rolled up the sleeves of his shirt to the elbows, sensible in this heat, revealing a tattoo on his left forearm. Not many tattoos in Paradise.

"Homer Vaughn," he said, and shook my hand.

I took the seat opposite Vaughn, an uncomfortable spot for me. I always sat facing the door. Always. Old habit. Good practice. Gives me a chance to see what's coming at me.

I looked him over. Something wriggled in the back forty of my memory. I could not pin it down, though. "You look vaguely familiar," I said.

He laughed with a knowing sparkle in his eyes. "I get that a lot."

"New in town?" I asked.

"Passing through."

"Let me guess – salesman."

He grinned. "No, not exactly. You ask a lot of questions, don't you?"

"Occupational hazard." In for a penny, in for a pound. "You staying at the Travelers?

"The hotel, you mean?" He frowned. "Nah, I guess you could say I'm staying with a friend of a friend. Save a buck or two."

I heard the slap of the diner's screen door behind me. My tablemate looked up, and I think he tried to suppress a shudder, but I would swear in a court of law that I saw a black look cross his face, one comprised of part disgust and part sheer hatred. I looked over my shoulder and spotted Francis Rumsey's wife, Louise, advancing toward us. All two-hundred-fifty-plus, well-corseted pounds of her thumped across the floor. She planted her feet and stared at my lunch companion until he flinched. Her eyes, a watery blue, almost disappeared in her boiled cabbage of a face.

She ignored me completely, for which I was grateful.

"Mr. Vaughn." She actually hissed. Her attempt at a whisper could have been heard in Dubuque, Iowa. "My husband wanted me to give this to you." She flicked a folded note onto the table as if it contained the plague. "Somebody telephoned from Chicago. Long distance, can you imagine that? What could be so important it couldn't wait a day or two for the mail to arrive? Never mind. What difference does it make? You big-city people wouldn't know good manners or respectable conduct if it fell on you from Heaven. That's a place I doubt you've ever heard of." She started to turn away, thought better of it and added, "When you call back, reverse the charges. I'm not paying for your frivolity. Long distance? Really!"

As she stamped out the door, I could still hear her muttering *long distance* to herself.

Vaughn, of the spendthrift long-distance telephone call, muttered, "Maybe somebody'll call me and tell me she's dead." He shook himself and flashed an apologetic smile. "Sorry. That woman is a --"

"Pain?"

"I had a few other words in mind, but that'll do."

We ate in silence for a few minutes. Vaughn finished his ham steak and ordered a slice of Reba Witherspoon's rhubarb pie. "I'm all for the city life, but I gotta admit I can't get pie like this in Chicago speaks. Here now, I never asked. What do you do for a living?"

"Newspaper reporter. The Telegraph-Register here in town."

"No kidding? Is that where you got that black eye?"

I grunted in the negative. "No, I tripped and hit a table on the way down."

"I bet," Vaughn said and laughed in a man-to-man kind of way. "You might want to work on that explanation, though." He put down his fork and stared at me with sleepy blue eyes. "Say, you saved me a trip. I was going to find the newspaper office later today. Might have a story for you."

That got my attention.

"I'm a scout. Kind of an advance agent," he said.

"Baseball? What team?"

He laughed again. "No, but I used to play a little. I'm in the motion picture business." He patted his pockets. "Sorry. I'm all out of business cards. But I'm with Warner Brothers, the Chicago office. The studio's thinking about filming a picture off the studio lot. Looking for – what's the word? – authenticity, that's it. Someone suggested Paradise might be a good location."

"Ah, c'mon."

"Nope. Strictly on the up and up."

"A movie in Paradise?" I was thunderstruck. Imagine seeing a picture show starring Paradise, Indiana, at the Primrose Theater not three blocks from where I sat.

"Sure, why not? I walked around a little bit. Pretty little courthouse. Very scenic. Could tap the locals for extras, maybe a speaking part or two. Put a little money in people's pockets. Bed and board. Wages. Incidentals. A lot of businesses would make money.

Maybe I could talk Harry – that's Harry Warner – to having the premiere right here in town."

"You *are* a salesman. This could be a big boost for Paradise. Not just the money, although that wouldn't hurt. How long are you going to be in town?"

"A day or two." He made a sour face. "I tried the coffee shop at the hotel for breakfast. The food's terrible. Somebody said to come here. And look – I run into the one man who knows this burg better than anybody, I bet. What do you say?"

"The movie? Fantastic idea. I can almost promise you that every man, woman, child and dog in Paradise will help you out."

"Got some time this afternoon? How about we take a tour of your little town and some of the countryside? I bet you dollars to doughnuts you could tell me all kinds of colorful stories about the places around here." He reached into his back pants pocket and pulled out a fat wallet. "There's a finder's fee. I could advance you a little."

I waved away the offer. He shrugged and put his money away.

"That it? The paper, I mean," he said.

"Sure. Hot off the presses. Take a look."

He scanned the front page, chuckling when he came to this headline:

MAN BUILDS HIS OWN COFFIN, INVITES MOURNERS TO 'SERVICE'

Vaughn lingered over the Dixie Lee Rypanski story. He started to ask something.

"Don't worry, we don't get many murders here," I said, feeling as though I needed to put a bright gloss on Paradise for the benefit of this stranger.

"That's good. Looks like the sheriff's having some trouble finding the guy who did it. How're the police? Can we count on them? We'll need security. You know – fans out of control, petty thefts, vandalism, that sort of thing."

"Shouldn't be a problem. Like any town, we've got a couple of Keystone Kops who put in their time and collect their pay, but I can vouch for the sheriff. Good man. By the way, what's the picture about?"

"Gangster stuff. Pretty much the usual, except some famous writer's doing the dialogue. I forget his name. Wrote a bunch of books, highbrow stuff. Anyhow – a gang of crooks on the lam hit a small town in the Middle West. They need money, hold up the bank. It goes bad. Guns. Bang, bang. A couple of people get killed. Gangsters end up on – and here's the kicker – a little Amish farm, hold the family hostage. Can't you just see the costumes. Guns versus pitchforks."

"The Amish are peaceable people. I can't imagine them attacking anybody with a pitchfork or any other weapon," I said.

Vaughn thought about that. "I'll tell the producer. Anyhow, the gang leader falls in love with the farmer's crippled daughter. The cops come and surround the farm. There's a shootout and the hero gets shot and dies in the girl's arms. It's very poetic." He sketched the words in the air: "THE END."

"Who's going to play the gangster?"

"I'm not supposed to tell," he said.

"But --"

He lowered his voice. "Okay, but swear you won't tell anybody. My buddy at the studio says George Raft and Jimmy Cagney are fighting over who gets to play the lead. They actually had a fist fight over it, that's what I heard. Raft put Cagney on the floor with one good jab. Glass jaw, I guess."

"Wow! Cagney or Raft." Reality brought me up short. "Uh, I'd be happy to show you around, but my car's out of commission."

"We'll use mine. You point, and I'll drive."

My fingers itched to get to the typewriter keys, but this story would have to wait for the next day's edition. Plus, I needed a photographer, and Phil Stiles was taking pictures at one of Mrs. Arletha Heston's society events. He would not be available for an hour or so, but Vaughn and I could start out in the country and catch up with him later. At least the prospect of a movie was good news. Jeff Heston would jump all over this one.

And, it was something to replace the tale of Dixie Lee Rypanski, the dead woman in the yellow dress – a story that was rapidly going nowhere. Barney O'Malley had not had time to dig around and get back to me. Without the real estate records, the story about Rumsey's funny business with the funerals was also on hold.

Ditto the casino in the mortuary school. Ditto the Gangland Underground Railroad.

I uncapped my pen. "How do you spell your name?"

CHAPTER 12

I picked up Adele at seven o'clock. We had a date at one of my least-favorite places – Rumsey's Funeral Parlor.

This was the last night of visitation for Mrs. Orleva Warren from Prattsburg. I had a store of fond memories of the woman. I had never understood the friendship between Mrs. Warren and my grandmother. They shared a passion for flowers, elaborate embroidery creations and Prattsburg's Grace Evangelical Methodist Church. But where grandmother Pratt was cold and demanding, Mrs. Warren radiated warmth and acceptance. Her home was a lonely child's Garden of Eden. I was allowed to run inside the house. She always had fresh bread and homemade quince butter or blackberry jam on hand for a hungry kid, and I was always hungry, especially at her table.

And, better still, she had books, hundreds upon hundreds of books – history, fiction, biography, travel, philosophy, science. She lent them to me and discussed them with me in a serious fashion, as if I were an adult, an equal. Mrs. Warren's house was a place of refuge. When I was eleven, mother and I moved to Paradise after father and my sister, Nellie, died two weeks apart of the Spanish Influenza that had raged through the village. I missed Mrs. Warren terribly, then and now. With her death, I lost another piece of my childhood. I dreaded this visit, but it was an innocent excuse to be inside Rumsey's lair.

Ralph Gardner greeted us at the door, wearing his uniform of starched white shirt, dark suit and tie. He held himself more stiffly than usual. He twitched when he saw Adele, but quickly recovered. Adele sometimes had that effect on men. His flat stare took in my black eye. He suppressed a smirk. I offered to shake hands, but he turned away.

"The Warren viewing? Come this way, please," was all he said.

"Walter, take a look," Adele whispered.

"At what?"

"It's bare," she said.

The foyer was empty. "So?"

"There used to be a small antique chest of drawers over there. I'd bet my last dollar that chest was Philadelphia Federal period. Very valuable. And two chairs. And a lamp. A bench along that wall. They're all gone. I was here just last month for one of daddy's distant Atkinson cousins. That furniture was here then."

"Redecorating?"

"You're a professional observer, and you're blind. Look at the carpet."

I looked. It was a carpet. "So? It has holes in it. More like dents, really."

"But what does that *mean?*" she asked in that challenging Adele Atkinson teacher's voice. "You're the Rumsey conspiracy expert, you figure it out."

The Rumsey Funeral Parlor and Mortuary was grand by Lincoln County standards. It had two viewing rooms. A smaller one on the left opened off the entrance hall through an arch made of elaborately carved oak with cupids, or maybe they were supposed to be angels, flitting among bunches of grapes and unidentifiable greenery. Farther along the hall, also on the left, was Rumsey's office. A discreetly closed door at the end of the hall presumably led to the embalming room, living quarters and other working parts of the establishment. Gardner hovered at the slid-back pocket doors of the second, larger viewing parlor up ahead on the right, waiting for us to catch up. He motioned us inside. This room was much more sedate and decorated in somber walnut paneling.

Adele signed the guest book first. As I put pen to paper, I suddenly realized that the next time we came here, we would take up only one line in the book as Mr. and Mrs. Walter G. Pratt. That was sobering.

The room was packed and noisy. There must have been at least fifty people there, many of whom I recognized from Prattsburg. The open casket was in a curtained alcove at the rear of the room. Mrs. Warren's two children were there. The daughter, who lived on a farm outside Prattsburg in Lafayette Township, and her son, who used to work at an auto plant in South Bend, were both well into their sixties. A gaggle of middle-aged grandchildren and great-grandchildren of a variety of ages surrounded them, trying earnestly to avoid looking at what was once Mrs. Warren. There were nieces and nephews and cousins of every degree. The hubbub was perfect cover for the exploration I planned later.

"Excuse me, Walter, may I speak to you privately. If you'll pardon me, Miss Atkinson." It was Rowland Shuster, the lawyer, dressed, as always, in a pin-striped suit of an old-fashioned cut.

"Of course," Adele said. "I'll make our condolences to the family. Take your time."

Shuster led me outside. A little breeze had kicked up. Perhaps we would get a storm. The crops certainly could use the rain.

"Mind if I smoke?" he asked.

"I'll join you."

"I don't indulge very often, but Mrs. Warren's death has hit me pretty hard. My father before me did all the legal work for Mrs. Warren's husband after they found oil and gas on his land, and they started making real money. Mr. Warren wasn't Rockefeller rich by any means, but he was able to buy more land, make conservative investments. They were more than comfortable. After her husband died in 1913, Mrs. Warren stayed with the firm. After my father passed over, I took care of her legal necessities. What a wonderful lady, as I am sure you would agree."

"I do. I do, indeed."

"Yes. Well." He took a breath. "I wanted to talk with you because there's something you need to know. Mrs. Warren left a bequest to you in her will."

"Me? I can't imagine."

"Yes, you, and I think you'll be pleased."

"May I ask what? I don't want to sound mercenary. I'm just curious. I never expected this."

"Certainly. I'll file the probate papers in a day or two. Shouldn't be any problem from the family. They've all been well provided for, and they're aware of your bequest. You'll need to come to my office to sign some documents. You don't have a will, as I recall. You need one, after all you're getting married soon."

"Trolling for business, Rowland? Shame on you." I laughed, but the lawyer looked so hurt and offended that I would suggest such an inappropriate thing that I immediately apologized. "The wedding's a week from Saturday. And, yes, I don't have a will. I suppose I need one, but, God, what a thing to think about when you're just starting out in life. Maybe I should talk to Adele about that."

"Good plan, Always involve the wife. I could tell you stories, sad stories, terrible stories about husbands who left the little woman in the dark about financial and legal matters. Then, after he dies, the poor woman can't cope with the simplest decisions. Doesn't know how to pay a bill or read a bank statement. Sad. Needless heartbreak. Don't get me going on that topic. It's one of my pet peeves. But I digress. Anyway, as I was saying, you are to receive a nice present from Mrs. Warren."

"What, Rowland? I don't mean to be rude, but Adele's waiting for me."

He cleared his throat.

"You are to receive eighty acres in Missiqua Township. It's decent farm land. Gilbert Owens has rented it for years, so you'll have a regular income from that. Plus, there are two oil wells. The wells aren't producing like they used to, only a few barrels a week, but, again, it's a little money in your pocket. And it's pretty country with a creek running through it. You'd have a nice site for a house there someday, if you want. You could pond the creek, make a swimming hole for your children, when they come along. It's right in the middle of the old Missiqua Indian Reservation in that little range of hills northeast of Prattsburg. The Sassafras Swamp's on the border of the property, but you've got the high ground, so that shouldn't be a problem, even in a flood."

"Land? Oil wells? My God," I squeaked out. "I know the place. I used to play there all the time when I was a kid. Found arrowheads."

"And something else." he added. "This doesn't have any monetary value and you might want to pass on it, but Mrs. Warren left you her entire library -- six-hundred-thirty-two books to be exact. If you don't want the books, Mrs. Warren's instructions are that they are to be left to the town of Prattsburg to form the foundation for a free lending library."

"Can I pick and choose? I mean, there are some I know I want. But, let's leave the rest to the town."

"Not a problem. You may take whatever you like. I'll start drawing up the papers." He patted me on the back as we stepped inside the funeral parlor. "Nice wedding present, wouldn't you say?"

I was too stunned to reply. I was a man of property. Two properties, actually. Adele's father had purchased the little house where

Adele and I would live. He had wanted to give it to us free and clear, but Adele and I insisted that we buy it from him. We would pay him in installments at low interest. But, eighty acres of prime farm land. I thought of Ted Thompson. He had lost his land through no fault of his own. I suddenly owned land through no effort of my own. It was a crazy world.

The cause of Ted Thompson's loss stood in Ralph Gardner's former spot outside the door to the parlor. Francis Rumsey glared at me, then caught sight of Rowland Shuster and composed a more appropriate expression on his face.

"Ah, Francis, just the man I want to see," Shuster said. "Do you have a minute? Lawrence Farrell showed me some contracts between you and a client of mine. The client asked me to chat with you about some of the details."

Rumsey showed Shuster into the unused second viewing parlor. Before they disappeared out of earshot, I heard Shuster complain mildly, "Where have you been the past week? I've been trying to get hold of you." I nearly laughed aloud; I knew where Rumsey had been.

I glanced toward the chapel where the Warren viewing was still going strong. Noise spilled into the hallway. Rumsey's office door was open. I have never been what one could call an impulsive man, but I figured it was now or never if I wanted to get a look at Rumsey's records, assuming I could find them quickly. I had no idea where Ralph Gardner was, but I would deal with that if and when.

Rumsey's office occupied a room at the rear of the entrance hall. I had been there before. I was just a child at the time, but mother had dragged me with her when she had made the arrangements for Dad and little Nellie. "You'll need to do this someday, Walter, so you may as well start learning now," Mother said in that matter-of-fact way she had of dealing with any emotionally fraught episode.

I had dreaded funeral homes, even then. The dead were set on a throne and laid out in a big, fancy, satin-lined box like an inert birthday present. Adults wept. Children were lost in the sea of grief engulfing them. They wandered about in their best clothes trying to get into trouble to be noticed or trying to stay out of trouble to avoid being noticed. One funeral was etched indelibly on my memory. I was about ten at the time, and the old-fashioned viewing was conducted in the front parlor of the dead woman's home in Prattsburg. A little girl of about four was lifted by her father. "Kiss Granny goodbye," he ordered as he tilted her over the open casket. She kicked and fought. He pinned her arms and lowered her toward the dead woman's face. "Kiss her, or I'll never love you again," the father said. That was when I fled the room, the little girl's screams still ringing in my ears.

Okay, Pratt, I told myself, you are a man, not a child. The scariest thing in Rumsey's office would be Rumsey, and he was elsewhere. Do it.

The restrooms were at the rear of the hall on the right with Rumsey's office directly opposite. I sauntered in that direction, trying to look casual. I checked behind me. No one. I darted into the office. It was tasteful, professional, the size of an average bedroom, say ten feet by twelve feet. It held a large oak desk and a matching office chair. Two comfortable chairs for the bereaved sat in front of the desk. A four-drawer wood filing cabinet stood behind the desk. There was what appeared to be the door to a coat closet on another wall. No window. Instead, a bland painting of a calm outdoor scene occupied the side wall, with curtains on either side to complete the illusion of a window. There were unoccupied spaces along the walls, formerly containing pieces of furniture judging by the telltale dents in the carpet. Why was Rumsey getting rid of furniture? And by the truckload, apparently.

The desk lamp was lit. It gave off enough light for my purposes. Where to start?

The filing cabinet was a no-go. It had a sliding steel rod that threaded through the handles and was padlocked top and bottom to connecting rings. That left the desk. The top was clear of anything interesting. Pens, ink, letter opener, blotter, calling cards, a thick casket catalog. The center drawer held more of the same. The two side drawers held stationery, envelopes, blank billing forms. I heard movement in the hallway, and I peeked out the door. No one there. I quickly scanned the rest of the room. No obvious safe. There might have been one in the wall, but I did not have the time, tools or know-how to open it, even if I found one.

The upper left drawer contained bookkeeping journals – one each for the past five or six years. I flipped through the pages. Nothing interesting or damning. Names, dates, type of services rendered, charges, when billed, dates paid. I compared 1928 to the current 1933 ledger. In the past, Rumsey had let customers pay when they could, a down payment followed by installments. A few were written off –

Charity Case scrawled in the PAID column in a different color ink. There were charity burials in the first few months of 1930, but none in any of the later books. Something had happened during the spring of 1930, that was evident. Maybe it was a coincidence, but that was about the time when I had run into him in that whorehouse in Chicago.

I froze. Voices outside. A door closed. The men's room. I shook my hands and arms to release some of the pent-up tension. A sane man would have known this was the time to leave. I grabbed the letter opener and set to work on the locked bottom drawer.

I tried to work carefully, but the wood was dry and it split. There was no longer any point in trying to hide my inexpert sleuthing. The lock finally popped. Another set of bookkeeping ledgers sat there. Rumsey was meticulous, with all of his income and outgo listed in compulsively neat columns. Salary from the Cook County College of Mortuary Science with amounts and dates paid. But the same amounts of money immediately were paid to one Mr. Benjamin Green. This money appeared to have been due on a promissory note tucked into the back pages and duly autographed by lawyers and bearing a notary public's seal. Business loan, it said. Another ledger contained records of the Lincoln county real-estate deals through Copper Beeches Property Development of Chicago. Names, dates, deed numbers.

I wanted those records. I certainly was not a cop. I was not even a rough-tough private eye in the movies. I was a small-town newspaper reporter with the biggest story of my life staring me in the face.

What would happen if I did not take them with me? The answer: Rumsey could make them disappear as fast as he could light a match. Arguing against that scenario was Rumsey's obvious love of keeping detailed records. But the shattered drawer made it evident that someone was onto him. Rumsey had numerous people to fear. I was least among them. Benny Green could make him dead; I could only put him in the state penitentiary.

I was breaking a couple of Bible commandments and a few more state and local laws, but I took the books. I rationalized it as safekeeping, but the truth was I simply wanted to nail the bastard any way I could. Now, I had the power to do so in my hands. *Hahahahahaha* to you, Frankie.

Hahahahahaha. Rumsey's real laugh sounded in the hall. Close by.

I looked at my watch. I had been gone more than ten minutes. Adele would be calling in Rollie Parker's dogs to find me if I did not show up soon. I heard Rowland Shuster's voice.

"Francis, just come to my office tomorrow," Shuster said.

"No, you're here. Let's get it over with. You'll bill me, anyway," Rumsey said.

I used my Chicago trick and tried to slide the ledgers down the back of my pants. Not enough room. I filched a manila envelope off Rumsey's desk and stuffed the ledgers inside. I managed to close the closet door behind me just in time.

"Rowland, I fudged a little. This isn't really about the land contract."

"Then why'd you haul me in here? I haven't properly paid my respects to the Warren family, and my wife was expecting me home a long time ago," Shuster said.

"This room is soundproofed, and I don't want anybody else to hear," Rumsey said.

"If this is a criminal matter --"

"No, no, nothing like that. I'm thinking about selling the business."

"Why don't you call Lawrence Farrell? Doesn't he take care of your legal affairs?"

Rumsey snorted derisively. "Farrell's good enough for most things, but he can't keep his mouth shut. I don't want this news all over the county by noon tomorrow."

Shuster maintained a noncommittal stance. "Why now? Unlike some folks, you have a steady income here."

"Been thinking about it for a while," Rumsey said. "Take the wife and go someplace where I don't have to shovel snow and smell the dead."

"Sounds like a wonderful dream, Francis, but how are you going to afford this new life? I know you've been converting a lot of your assets into cash. In fact, this has me a little worried. I'd like to be assured that is all above board. People around town are talking, you know. I'm afraid you haven't been very subtle with your customers. Your tactics haven't been, well, very nice."

"I don't give a whore's fart about *nice*. Besides, that's all done with. I've got my little nest egg. I just have a couple of small details to work out, then this business is somebody else's problem. Don't you worry about Francis Rumsey, no sir."

I could picture the smirk that accompanied the self-satisfied tone of Rumsey's voice.

"I must say, anybody who has managed to keep a nest egg intact through this Depression is one very lucky or very careful man," Shuster said.

Yeah, I thought, my best guess was that Rumsey had kept that nest egg intact courtesy of Dixie Lee Rypanski and that missing $40,000.

"What do you want me to do," the lawyer continued.

"Draw up a bill of sale for the funeral parlor. Leave blanks for the buyer's name, date, amount of purchase, witnesses – that sort of thing."

"Easy enough," Shuster said. "When do you need it?"

"Soon. This week."

"That's fast. And here I always pegged you for the slow, methodical type."

"Situations change. People change," Rumsey said. "Have to go with the times. Streamlining. Efficiency. Speed. Those are the watchwords of the modern businessman, wouldn't you agree, Rowland?"

"Yes, indeed, Francis."

I could almost hear the adding machine keys clacking in the lawyer's skull. His bill would be ready before Rumsey's paperwork was finished.

"I'll need the property records," Shuster said. "Deeds, any liens, *et cetera.*"

"Got it right here."

The office chair creaked. Rumsey's heavy steps stopped next to the closet door. I prayed fervently that those records were not in the closet. I tried to remember if there was anything else along this side of the office. A mirror, some doo-dads, plaques, hand-shake photos of Rumsey at civic events. A shadow obliterated the thin sliver of light that outlined the closet door. Rumsey grunted. I was becoming all too familiar with that grunt. A hinge squeaked. A metallic spinning sound was followed by a soft *chink* and a well-oiled whisper of machinery.

"Well, well, Francis, that's clever – a wall safe," said Shuster admiringly.

"That was my father's idea. You'd be surprised how many people pay in cash. At least that damn Democrat in the White House got the banks straightened out last spring. I'll give him that much."

"We lost only one bank in Paradise and another in Kirkville. I guess we should consider ourselves lucky," Shuster said.

"You make your luck," Rumsey stated flatly.

There was a rustle of papers.

"That should do it," the lawyer said after a moment's pause. "Anything else?" There was another pause and a muffled reply. "Thanks. It is a pleasure doing business with you, Francis."

The air in the closet was growing hotter and stuffier by the second. I felt a sneeze start to work its way up my nasal passages. The office door opened and closed. I reached for the knob of the closet door, then jerked back my hand. What if only Shuster had left the room? I counted backward from one-hundred by threes. Not a sound. If Rumsey were still in the office, I would have heard something by now – papers crackling, the rustle of clothing, a sigh, something. My blood raced loudly in my temples, but there was not one sound in the office.

Nothing ventured, nothing gained. I cracked open the door a scarce half inch. The mirror was at a forty-five-degree angle to the wall and blocked most of the room from my view. I could see the desk chair. Empty. I opened the door the rest of the way. No Rumsey, but I had to get out of here now. I chanced a quick peek in the safe. Papers, empty cubbyholes, a small metal box similar to the one we used for petty cash at the newspaper. No stacks of greenbacks.

Before I closed the closet door, the light caught a shape at the back partially concealed by a hanging winter coat. A brown suitcase with tan stripes. There was no way I could casually stroll out the front door with it. It would have to remain where it was for the time being. It might not be there later, but that was a chance I would have to take.

Voices in the hall brought me out of my woolgathering. I was prepared to dart back into the closet, when I recognized one of them as Adele's. I dashed to the office door, sidled though it as inconspicuously as possible and came up behind Adele and a young pregnant woman, most likely one of Orleva Warren's great-grandchildren.

"Sorry, dear." I pointed to the men's room door. "Must have been something I ate. I'm still a little queasy. Mind if we leave?" I turned to the young woman. "Please give my apologies to your family."

I steered Adele toward the front door.

"Walter, what's the matter with you," Adele whispered.

"I opened my suit jacket and showed her the manila envelope. She raised an eyebrow. I cradled it against my ribs with my left arm like a quarterback running for the end zone. That forced me to walk half bent over – a good strategy that complemented my pretend stomach ailment. Adele and I almost made it outside before we ran into Gardner, who emerged from the second parlor carrying a broom and a dust pan.

"One of the children knocked over a vase of flowers," Adele said to him. "I'm afraid the carpet's wet, too." To me, she said, "Let's get you home, Walter. You're looking worse by the minute."

I let out a groan worthy of an Academy Award. I hoped it sounded authentic in Gardner's ears.

"I'm taking you to Doctor Joplin's first thing tomorrow. No arguments," she said briskly.

I clutched my stomach tighter and heard the envelope crackle.

"Good night, Mr. Gardner," Adele said over the noise and pushed me out the door.

"This better be good," she said once we reached the car.

"It's good – very, very good," I said.

CHAPTER 13

The Telegraph-Register
Tuesday, July 11, 1933

SILVER SCREEN COMES TO PARADISE, WARNER BROS. MOVIE TO BE SHOT HERE
'We're all excited,' says Mayor Browne

By Walter G. Pratt

Homer Vaughn came to Paradise this week with a list. He needed a bank, a police station, a farmhouse, a filling station, a cafe, open roads, busy streets – and lots of help.

He found all that and more.

Vaughn, 28, a native of Fort Wayne, is a production scout for Hollywood's Warner Bros. Studio, working out of Chicago. The studio plans to shoot a gangster picture on location in a small town in the Midwest, and Vaughn said Paradise is at the top of a short list of communities under consideration.

The proposed three-week shooting schedule could bring thousands of dollars into the local economy, said Vaughn.

"This will be the biggest thing to happen to Paradise since the tornado hit in 1924," said Mayor Robert L. "Brownie" Browne. "We'll help these folks any way we can. We're all excited."

Mr. Stephen R. White, president of Lincoln County National Bank and Trust, welcomed Vaughn and gave him a tour of the bank.

The bank building, an ornate limestone edifice built in 1894, dominates half a block of Meridian Street in downtown Paradise.

"It's a beauty, very photogenic. I can see lots of possibilities for camera angles," said Vaughn.

White showed Vaughn the tellers's cages, the lobby, executive offices, the alarm system and the large, walk-in vault. Vaughn took copious notes and made drawings, which he said will be forwarded to Hollywood.

"We have the most up-to-date alarm system in this part of the state," said White. "There hasn't been a bank robbery in Paradise since the one in 1897."

The plot of the film, which is expected to be shot next spring, involves a bank robbery in a small town. The robbers escape only to be tracked down and killed during a shootout at an isolated farm where they have held the farm family hostage.

Vaughn said the names of the stars, which he stated will be top caliber, cannot be released at this time.

Mrs. Dorothy Rogers Pugh, chairwoman of the Paradise Dramatic Society, met Vaughn. Mrs. Pugh, last seen on stage in March in a well-received production of "Thy Neighbor's Wife," promised the full cooperation of her organization in providing players for small roles and extras for the filming.

"We have 36 members and a dozen more who show up once in a while. All of them will help with the movie. I'm sure of that," said Mrs. Pugh.

Vaughn visited several other possible locations yesterday. These included the Daisy Diner, the Travelers Hotel, the railroad depot, the Lincoln County Courthouse and White's Service Station. He scouted two farms in Washington Township north of town on U.S. Highway 1 owned by Mr. DeWayne Parker and Mr. Curt Gates.

Officer Marcus Slack, of the Paradise Police Department, showed the Hollywood representative around the city's police station in the rear of City Hall on East Main Street. Chief Thurl Gaskins was out of town. Officer Slack said providing protection for the film crew would not be difficult. Every member of the city's three-man police force would be made available.

Drawing attention to the station's holding cell, Slack said, "It ain't big, but it's strong."

Vaughn agreed, posing behind the bars for The Telegraph-Register's photographer. (Turn to Page 3 for additional photographs.)

A decision on which town will be chosen will be announced by the end of August, said Vaughn.

CHAPTER 14

Later Tuesday, July 11, 1933

"Where the Hell have you been?" Jeff Heston leaned against my desk and did not look terribly happy. He automatically tossed a dime onto Hattie Webster's desk. "It's almost ten o'clock."

"I went to Doc's to get the dressing on my knee changed, then I went back to the dump. I thought I'd look around again, see if I could find anything else connected to Dixie, the girl in the yellow dress. Remember her?"

I was more-than-a-little irritated. Jeff was in unaccustomed, full-on editor mode.

"While you were out chasing a fantasy, the city cops arrested the woman's murderer. Get over to the county jail and get the story."

My irritation disappeared to be replaced by chagrin. I felt as though Jack Johnson had just punched me in the solar plexus. "Who did they arrest?"

"You're not going to like this – Johnnie Porter."

"Christ!"

I dug out my own dime and handed it to Hattie.

In my haste to get to the jail, I forgot to tell Jeff about the Rumsey ledgers. They were currently residing in Doc Joplin's locked dispensary. Rumsey would not think to look there. I hoped.

Hoyt Peterson hunched over his desk, wrestling with a stack of paperwork. He put down his pencil. He looked relieved to see me, if for no other reason than to provide a distraction from his fiscal duties. Peterson was not a numbers man, even if he could compute batting averages in his head.

"Wondered when you'd get here," he said.

"Johnnie Porter – you must be kidding."

"'Fraid not. Thurl Gaskins brought him in last night."

"He's only fourteen."

"Fifteen."

"But – "

"I know, I know. Ain't easy to believe. But Thurl found evidence."

"Thurl Gaskins couldn't find his own kitchen without a road map. I find it hard to believe a child could commit such a cold-blooded murder. Especially Johnnie. He rides all over town on that bicycle of his. He can't drive a car. How the heck could he get the body out to the dump?"

"Coulda put the body in a little red wagon, maybe a wheelbarrow and pulled it behind his bike."

"That's a stretch, sheriff."

"Maybe." He shrugged.

I tried another argument. "He's not, well, smart enough."

"Not right in the head? Village idiot? Them's the words you're looking for?" the sheriff said.

I gave the sheriff's slurs a pass. I tried another tack. "Besides, everybody knows him. He wouldn't hurt a soul."

"But *she* didn't know him, did she? We don't know what goes on in Johnnie's head. Maybe it's easier to hurt somebody you don't know," the sheriff suggested.

That brought up an interesting point. Maybe *she* did not know her killer, but her killer knew *her*.

Only one person in Paradise had a connection to a not-very-successful singer, a natural redhead-turned-blonde, from Chicago. That singer was married to a borderline gangster who occasionally worked for Benny "The Nose" Green. The mob boss ran a mortuary school that employed our local undertaker. That same undertaker had been observed displaying an extramarital passion for redheads in the past. That same man had visited the dead woman's supposed final resting place in Illinois. That circle of relationships pointed to the one person in Paradise who might have had a reason to make Dixie Lee Rypanski's second death a final one – Francis Tolliver Rumsey.

I had been avoiding this conclusion, but it made sense. It was all coincidence, or as the lawyers would say, circumstantial – but it fit. What I could not put together was Rumsey's motive for killing Dixie, assuming he needed a motive.

Hoyt Peterson leaned across his desk and snapped his fingers. "Hey, boy, where you been? You faded away there for a minute."

"Motive, that's the key." I was not answering the sheriff. I was thinking about Dixie and Rumsey. My pulse raced. Oh, there was a motive, a big motive, a motive worth at least $40,000. Perhaps Rumsey knew or suspected that Dixie had make off with the gambling take, but she had not noticed him.

"Motive's for books and made-up stories. Judge Taylor wants evidence," Peterson said. "You've been to his trials. A real stickler, he is."

"Evidence?"

"Bunch of it." Peterson reached behind him and pulled a brown paper sack out of a file drawer. "Take a look."

He made space on his desk and dumped out the contents.

A woman's wallet. No money. A couple of wrinkled snapshots: Dixie and Jim, Dixie as a young teen-ager posed with half a dozen people who looked just like her. An Illinois driving license bearing her name, birthdate of April 14, 1912, and listing Miss Fisher's address. A gold necklace with a pendant that spelled out TRIXIE dangling from a broken thin chain. A white towel matted with brown stains that could be only dried blood.

"Jesus!"

The sheriff nodded. "Thurl Gaskins found this in a cardboard box under the Porter's house."

"How did Thurl know to look there?"

"Tip, he said. "Citizen called in."

"That's convenient."

Peterson shot me a black look. He did not have much respect for the police chief's abilities, but the city cop was a fellow officer, and that brotherhood stuck together tighter than any secret-handshake fraternal lodge, assassin's cabal or pack of wolves.

"Does this good citizen have a name?" I asked.

"Not so as Thurl mentioned. What you'd call anonymous."

"That citizen could've been the killer trying to throw the suspicion of guilt on somebody else."

"You're making this too complicated, Walter," the sheriff said. "This here evidence is all that counts."

"Look, sheriff, I know Johnnie couldn't have done this."

"Know, or want to believe? There's a difference, son. Can you prove it?"

"No, damn it!" I wanted to tell Sheriff Peterson about Francis Rumsey – Chicago, the gangsters, the money, Dixie's connection, the land scheme, everything – but there was little I could relate that constituted definitive proof or that would not implicate me in my own less-than-strictly-legal activities. Otherwise, all I had were fanciful speculations that could not compete with the concrete items spread out on the sheriff's desk.

"If you can find one stitch of evidence, I'll let Johnnie go in a minute and do it with a glad heart. He's a nice kid, just a little – well, you know."

I knew. "Can I see him?"

"Don't know why not," Peterson said. "You won't get much out of him. He keeps bawling, afeared somebody'll steal that old bicycle of his. Wants his mother. Scared half to death, I reckon. Go by the kitchen and check with Juanita. Maybe the kid'll take a cup of coffee or milk or a sandwich. I don't think he's et since he come in here. Wouldn't touch a bite of breakfast. Maybe he'll eat some if you give it to him. He's in the first cell on the right. Door's open. Ain't nobody else back there. Been a slow week. Johnnie ain't going nowhere, and I didn't want to scare him worse that he was already."

"Has Julia been here?"

"Yeah, I finally had to shoo her out of here. She's worried sick. Told her to talk to lawyer Shuster. He knows her. I think she cleans for the Shusters once in a while. He might help without charging her a pretty penny. Poor woman. She's about all done in. Stop back here before you leave."

I did as I was instructed and carried a tray back to the cells. I nodded to the jail deputy, Milt Chandler, who had his feet propped on his desk and was reading a book on car repair. If Hoyt Peterson lost the next election, Milt might be out of a job. The sheriff could hire and fire at will. Milt already worked part-time at Vance White's garage, just in case.

"Saw your Buick. You were lucky. The brakes were fiddled with, for sure. Vance is about done with it. You could use an oil change. Want me to tell Vance to go ahead?"

"Thanks Milt. Have Vance fix whatever needs to be fixed. Adele and I are driving to Wisconsin for our honeymoon. I was going to bring it in for a once-over in a couple of days, anyway."

"Wisconsin, huh?"

"We rented a little cabin. Thought we'd go fishing."

He chuckled. "I bet."

The honeymoon snickers were rapidly wearing thin. "Here, thought you'd like a cup of coffee."

"Thanks. Johnnie's right through there. He's quieted down some. Sheriff said to go right back."

"Oh, Milt, do me a favor, will you? Don't tell the sheriff about my brakes."

"Already done did."

Great. Wonderful. Just what I did not want.

The jail, built about 1900 when the county was floating in oil-and-gas money, was elegant red brick and limestone on the outside, prosaic concrete and iron on the inside. In a pinch, it could hold thirty prisoners in five double cells and three large group cells on two floors. There was one woman's cell down the hall from the sheriff's living quarters on the third floor. The jail might have been bare and forbidding, but it was scrupulously clean courtesy of Hoyt Peterson's rules and the merciless scrutiny of his wife, Juanita Peterson, the jail matron. The usual run of prisoners included drunks, vagrants, reckless drivers, petty thieves and brawlers. There was the occasional confidence artist and flimflam man. Every August, the jail filled up with transient Mexicans who had been transported by the busload to Lincoln County to pick the tomato crop. The Mexicans tended to settle disagreements with fists and knives. Its most famous prisoner had been James Anderson of the notorious Muncie-based Anderson Gang. There had never been an escape, although a few had tried.

I pushed open the steel-barred door behind Milt Chandler's desk with my foot and eased through, trying to keep the tray balanced. I stopped at the cell door. Johnnie Porter was curled into a tight ball on the concrete floor. His pudgy arms covered his head.

"Hey, Johnnie. It's Walter Pratt. Brought you something."

He tucked his knees tighter into his chest.

"C'mon, Johnnie. We need to talk. That's the only way I can get you out of here."

He muttered something.

"What was that?"

"I want Mommy."

"She'll be by later on. Is it okay if I come in? I have chicken-salad sandwiches and cookies. Molasses cookies. Mrs. Peterson made them just for you."

That got his attention. The boy had a sweet tooth.

"Cookies?" He uncurled and looked at me for the first time. His dirty cheeks were tear streaked. He had wet his pants.

I gingerly folded my legs and tried not to flinch from the bruises. I sat on the floor opposite him and placed the tray between us. "Help yourself."

He crammed cookies into his mouth. Crumbs fell everywhere.

"You have to tell me what happened with the lady in the yellow dress. You know, the one at the city dump. You were there. I saw you."

He nodded. His mouth was too full to talk.

"Did you hurt her?"

He shook his head no.

"Are you sure you didn't hurt her? This is really important. You have to tell me the truth."

No again.

"People are saying you hurt her and took – stole – things that belonged to her. Those things were found under your house. Do you understand that?"

A guilty look passed over his face. He knew something. He reached for the glass of milk. Half of it disappeared down his gullet in one gulp.

"Nice and cold," he said. "Hot in here."

At least he was now communicating in words, even if his words did not answer my questions.

"It was hot out at the dump, too. Remember? That was exactly one week ago today, the Fourth of July."

"I 'member. You give me a quarter for ice cream. You're a nice man."

Good Lord, this was becoming more difficult by the minute. Johnnie grabbed another cookie, put it down and took a sandwich, instead.

"What happened at the dump?"

"Them kids was playing. Wouldn't let me play with them. They throwed tin cans at me. Told me to go git. I hid out and watched. That's 'bout all I do is watch things, people. You know."

"What did you see when you were watching?"

"I wanted to make sure she was okay, you know, but them kids found her, anyway. She was real pretty."

"The pretty lady in the yellow dress?"

Johnnie finished the milk and wiped his mouth with his shirttail.

"Uh-huh. I seen the sheet, see. My mom could use a new sheet, so I was gonna take it. I find good stuff all the time. But the lady was in it. I seen her face."

"You pulled back the sheet and saw the woman wrapped inside it. Is that what happened?"

"Yes, sir. I didn't take nothing. I'm a good boy." He grinned. "Most of the time."

"You certainly are, Johnnie. Your mother's proud of you." That solved the mystery of the second pair of hands at the dump.

His grin evaporated. "They said I was bad. Said I'd go to jail."

He started weeping, huge sobs shaking his body. I passed him my handkerchief. I felt helpless, so I patted him on the knee and waited. A full two minutes passed before he regained control of himself.

"Johnnie, a bunch of stuff was found in a box under your house. What do you know about that?"

"Nononono. No! Somebody found my secrets?"

"What secrets?"

"Oh, I got lots of stuff – marbles, a two-dollar bill, a canteen. I found a knife, but Mom took it away. Too scary. Found a real nice pocket watch. Mr. Gold give me three whole dollars for it. Lots of stuff. I check the river banks and the dump and the alleys. Lots of good stuff in people's trash." He looked up at me. "I can write my name. I can count to seventy-eight without stopping. Wanna hear? Onetwothreefourninethirteen --"

"That's great. You can show me some other time, okay?"

"Okay." He looked crestfallen. He obviously took pride in this skill.

"Did you take any secret stuff from the lady?"

He looked at me as if I were the less-than-smart one in this six-by-eight-foot room. "Wasn't nothing to take. 'Sides, didn't have time. Them kids come."

"Thanks, Johnnie." I gave his shoulder a squeeze. "You be a good boy and do what Sheriff Peterson tells you. "You still hungry?"

He nodded.

"I'll see if Mrs. Peterson can bring you another glass of milk and some more cookies."

With that, Johnnie went limp and flipped over onto his side. He was completely senseless for a few seconds. Then he eyes flickered and his feet twitched rhythmically. I had the odd impression he was trying to run, much like a dog chasing rabbits in a dream. When he came to, he was bright-eyed and refreshed, as if he had just awakened from a short nap.

"Does that happen often?" I asked.

"What happened?"

He was completely unaware of what he had just experienced. A seizure of some sort, I thought. Could Johnnie have had one of these fits – maybe like sleepwalking – and killed Dixie while he was under its spell? Maybe Doc Joplin would know.

Hoyt Peterson was still in his office.

"Johnnie Porter didn't do it, I'm positive. He found the body before the Huff and Packard boys got there and chased him away. Says he didn't hurt her or take anything belonging to her."

"I'd like to believe that, I surely would," the sheriff said. He tapped his pencil on a scratch pad filled with sums. "What're you keeping from me, son? I'll help you if I can. I knew your father pretty well. Did a lot of business at the Prattsburg State Bank when I was in the oil equipment business afore I got into politics. Fine, fine man. Helped me through a couple of rough patches, he did. I owe him to keep an eye on you."

I stood and could not completely suppress a groan. Damn this! Sitting on that concrete floor had not helped.

"Why're you walking funny?"

"Fell. It's nothing."

"Fell, huh? This got anything to do with the brakes on your car? I heard about that."

"You're a sharp one."

"I try." He turned back to his paperwork. "When you want to tell me, you know where to find me. By the way, that's some black eye you got there. Try steak. Always works for me."

CHAPTER 15

Tuesday, July 11, 1933

PORTER BOY ARRESTED IN RYPANSKI DEATH

Woman's trinkets found under house

'I didn't hurt her,' boy says

By Walter G. Pratt

I had two bylines on Page One. The movie story was happy news; the other was not. I looked at the Porter headline again. It was solid, the writing tolerable, but the content made me sick to my stomach. I still had not figured out a way to clear Johnnie Porter. Doc Joplin was in Indianapolis at a medical conference. There was one other person who might be able to help. It was four o'clock. I took a chance she would be home.

Julia Porter opened the door of her house by the river. I smelled coffee. She was wrung out. Her eyes burned from lack of sleep, and her jaws were clenched as if she were fighting back a scream.

"Tell me Johnnie's okay." She twisted the rag in her hands so violently it tore.

"He's fine, Julia. He's scared, but he's doing okay. Mrs. Peterson is keeping an eye on him. She made cookies for him. The sheriff's trying to help, too."

"That's good. That's good. Johnnie's a good boy, he really is. He wouldn't do – do anything – you know, bad."

"I know. I'm trying to help him." I tried my best smile. "Could I come in for a minute? Maybe we could figure out something together."

"Uh, I don't know, Mr. Pratt – I mean, Walter. I have company."

A man appeared next to her in the doorway. My jaw dropped. It was Ralph Gardner wearing no shoes or socks, casual trousers, no belt, a strap-type undershirt. He looked right at home, with a cup of coffee in his hands. He had a livid bruise turning green on the edges of his upper right arm.

"Maybe he can help, baby," Gardner said in that soft, uninflected way of his. "Come this way, please." He let out a small, self-deprecating laugh. "Sorry, professional habit."

The interior of the tiny, one-bedroom home was painstakingly clean. The left side of the front room was a kitchenette with space for doing the washing and ironing she took in. On the right was a sitting area that doubled as Johnnie's bedroom. Julia's bedroom, one apparently shared by Ralph Gardner, and a small bath occupied the rear.

"What happened to your arm?" I nodded to Gardner. I was not comfortable enough to call him by his first name, so I avoided any name at all.

"Your girlfriend should play for the Cubs. They could use a good pinch hitter."

"*You!*" I took a step toward him, but Julia stepped between us. I tried to dodge around her. "*You're* the one who fiddled with my car at the depot?"

"What's he talking about, Ralph? What car?" Julia looked back and forth at us.

"That's one of the reasons I came here, honey. I can't work for that man another minute." To me, he said, "I'm sorry, Mr. Pratt. I didn't want you to get hurt. I can see you're limping. You jumped me pretty good. I played some football in school. I'm not one of those physical culturists but lifting caskets and dead people keeps your muscles in shape. You got in a couple of good pops, then your girlfriend just about knocked me into the next county. If she could have seen where she was hitting, she'd have brained me good. I'm lucky, I guess."

"I think that's the most I've ever heard you say."

"I try to stay in the background," Gardner said. "I keep my mouth shut. I do my job. Try to help Julia and Johnnie."

For a second or two, Julia's eyes filled with a pure, shining love that drove away the pain.

"You owe me nineteen dollars and fifty cents for the repairs," I said. "Pay me, and I'll call us square. The coppers don't know about our little wrestling match at the depot, so you're in the clear."

I should have had him thrown in jail, but I could not bear the thought of being responsible for piling more hurt on this woman, who already had so much pain in her life. Gardner looked shamefaced, then relieved. He pulled a twenty out of his wallet. "Keep the change," he said.

"Done," I said and pocketed the bill. "We'll talk more, Gardner. I need to know what's going on in that funeral parlor. Right now, Johnnie's the bigger problem."

"I'll do anything for that boy. Anything," Julia declared.

"Can we sit? This might take a while to sort out."

"Sure. Come in, please," she said.

We settled at her kitchen table. She fetched cups of coffee all around, then sat with her hands folded on the table like a schoolgirl. The windows were wide open to let in a breath of air. They also let in the stink from the brown rivulet the Missiqua River shrank to in mid-summer. This time of year, the river was little more than an open sewage drain.

I opened my notebook. "Let's start by agreeing that Johnnie did not murder Dixie Lee Rypanski."

Julia and Gardner nodded in the affirmative. "That's obvious," Gardner said.

"Not to the cops. Not to the Lincoln County Circuit Court, once – if – the case gets to that point. They like evidence. The sheriff is on our side, but his hands are tied without something more substantial than a hunch to rule out Johnnie as a suspect."

"What can we do, Walter? I'm desperate," Julia said.

"Let's start with the truth, all the truth. Let's start at the very beginning."

We began.

Johnnie birthdate: June 1, 1918.

Years in school: through the fourth grade at South Ward Elementary. He repeated the second and third grades twice. Then the teachers threw up their hands and said they could not do any more with him.

Mental condition: beautiful, healthy baby, but slow from early infancy. Late to sit up, late to walk, late to speak.

Friends: not really, keeps to himself.

Hobbies, activities: riding his bicycle, collecting things.

Employment: sells objects he finds, helps people with shoveling snow, raking leaves, easy things requiring only a strong back and willing hands.

Achievements: can write name, read a little, count a little.

"The teachers said it was hard teaching him to write, him being left-handed. They tried to make him use his right hand and taped up his left so he couldn't use it. That didn't work. He is what he is," she said.

"He's left-handed? You're sure?"

"Of course, I'm sure. I'm his mother. I ought to know," she said irritably. "Is that important?"

"I don't know. Maybe." I had the vivid picture in my mind of Johnnie grabbing for the molasses cookies with his left hand. And Doc Joplin was convinced the killer was right-handed. This information could not be put forth as hard evidence, but it certainly blew large holes in the cops' theory of the crime. Back to basics.

Firearms: none in the house, never, would not allow it, too dangerous with a child like Johnnie around.

Previous violent behavior: none.

Hurt animals, her, himself: never.

"Julia, who was Johnnie's father?"

I had heard the expression *green about the gills* all my life but had never actually seen it. Now I had. A thin, greenish line circled her mouth, and she shuddered as if taken with a sudden chill.

"Can't." She choked out the word, then dashed to the bathroom. Gardner and I fiddled with our coffee cups while she retched. When Gardner could not stand it any longer, he went to her. "It's okay, baby. It's okay. Maybe it's time to tell. I won't let that bastard hurt you anymore. We'll go where he can't find us."

Water ran. There were splashing sounds. When they re-entered the front room, Gardner placed an arm around her shoulders to steady her. She refused to look me in the eye.

"C'mon, honey," Gardner pleaded. "Tell him *Tell him.* He already knows, 'cept he doesn't know he knows."

That had me stumped. "I --"

Julia spoke, the words coming from a faraway place deep inside herself. "Rumsey. Francis Rumsey is Johnnie's father." Tears coursed down her cheeks. "I was pretty then. I had red hair. I wasn't one of the rich kids, but I was what you'd call popular these days. I had lots of friends. Everybody liked me, I think."

Once she started telling her story, she could not stop. I sat perfectly still, so I would not distract her.

"My father died when I was eighteen months old. My mother worked herself into an early grave. My getting with child didn't help her any. Mr. Rumsey was like a father to me – always with the hugs and the squeezes and little presents now and then. My mother cleaned at the funeral parlor, and I helped out sometimes. Then she got really sick, I spent that summer -- the summer after eighth grade – working there by myself. It was hard work, but I felt so grown up, so proud of myself. I was keeping our family together. His wife -- his first wife, Lavinia, nice lady she was -- was sick, too. Cancer of the bosom, I think. Then Mrs. Rumsey died in the summer of 1917.

"Then he, Mr. Rumsey, he changed after that. Got all bitter and angry and drank a lot. Smashed things. Hollered. He never used to be that way. I was thirteen going on fourteen. One day, when there wasn't no business, nobody around 'cept us, he --" She took a moment to calm herself. "He hugged me and wouldn't let go. He was crying. Calling me her name, his wife's name. She had red hair, too. Then he – he had his way with me. I was scared, but I couldn't tell my mother. I was afraid we'd lose our job. We needed that money. That was all we had in the world. He cried and promised it wouldn't ever happen again. And it didn't. But every now and again, he would just look at me – you know, *that* way – and I'd know what he was thinking.

"Then I found out I was with child. I had to stop out of school half way through freshman year at Paradise High. My belly was out to there. My poor mother was so disappointed. She wanted me to be the first in my family to graduate high school."

"It's okay, baby, go on," Gardner said.

"After Johnnie came, and it was obvious he wasn't, well, quite right, Mr. Rumsey gave us, my mother, this house free and clear so we'd have a roof over our heads. But Mr. Rumsey won't look at Johnnie, doesn't want to be seen next to him. If you look real close, they look a bit alike. A little bit in the eyes, the chin. He kept me on to clean for him. It isn't easy trying to make a living when the whole town sees you as a sinner with a bastard child. He couldn't make me respectable again, but he protected us a little. He helped me find other little jobs here and there. But --"

"But what?" I asked.

She looked directly at me for the first time in this long recitation.

"He changed again. This was maybe three, four years ago. He'd gotten married to that awful Mrs. Rumsey what used to be Mrs. Harry White – married her because she had family money. Louise treats me worse than the dirt I sweep up. I think she suspects about Johnnie. Then he hired Ralph to help out at the funeral parlor. He needed the help because he was gone all the time. Chicago mostly, I think. There were arguments about money. We had the Depression happening, but this was something different. Then the money thing seemed to go away."

"Did he change in other ways?" I asked. "Did he act like he had secrets, was hiding something?"

"Yes, now you mention it, he sure did. Kept his office locked most of the time when he wasn't in there. I think that was to keep Mrs. Rumsey out, more'n anything. He wasn't as nice to the families of people who had passed over. He used to be. Not anymore. Relatives left there crying and not just because somebody died. He got real hard-hearted. Folks still came to Rumsey's place, but they didn't feel good about it. He was scared, too, real jumpy sometimes, especially in the last month or two. It's like he's looking over his shoulder in case somebody's chasing him. Does that make sense?"

More than you know, Julia, more than you know. "That makes a lot of sense," I said aloud. "Thank you. I know it wasn't easy for you to tell me all this. But it's important."

I patted her hand. Gardner got up and located another handkerchief for her. I refilled our coffee cups. I checked my watch. It was almost five. Tonight was Adele's bridal shower. I was not invited, of course. I had made a date to have supper with Homer Vaughn, maybe find a pickup game of baseball, have a little fun. First, there was more to settle here.

"Ralph – may I call you Ralph?"

"Sure, Walter." He smiled in his shy way. He struck me as a man who had been waiting a long time to make a male friend in Paradise.

"Now it's your turn to spill. What's going on with Rumsey?"

He took a pull of coffee and stirred another spoonful of sugar into it.

"He's mad as Hell. All the time and mostly at you. He knew you loved that Buick of yours. That's why he had me fix the brakes. I don't think he wanted you hurt or dead, nothing like that. He just wanted to hurt something you loved, teach you a lesson, that sort of thing. That's my guess. I was just ready to leave when you jumped me." He grinned sheepishly and rubbed the bruise on his arm. "Scared the living daylights out of me, I don't mind saying."

"Okay, I'll buy that story, for now. I'm not sure that's the whole truth, but I can live with it," I said. "What did you mean by *stay out of it?*"

Gardner shrugged. "Those were Mr. Rumsey's words. He said, if you run into him, tell that SOB Pratt to stay out of it. I didn't ask why. I just did it."

"Oh, Ralph! I can't believe you did awful things like that for Mr. Rumsey," Julia said.

Gardner showed a spark of anger and slammed a fist on the table. "It's a *job,* Julia. You want me riding the rails, being a bum, a tramp? It's a *job*. There used to be five funeral parlors in this county. We've got three, now. It's the same all over. Where would I get a job?"

That was an explanation, not a good one, but I let it pass.

"I quit, didn't I? I'll just have to take my chances," he said to her. "Friday's my last day," he told me.

"What else, Ralph? Any other extracurricular *jobs* you performed for him?" I asked.

He looked away, clearly uncomfortable.

"C'mon, Ralph."

"He – okay, *we* – had little ways to make more money. We switched less-expensive caskets for the nice ones. Promised marble headstones, delivered limestone painted to look like marble. Took jewelry off the bodies. Dug gold fillings out of teeth." A wave of remorse, perhaps revulsion, swept across Gardner's face. "I didn't do that. I wouldn't – the teeth, I mean. That was going too far for me. Rumsey sold the gold in Chicago, someplace where they wouldn't ask too many questions, I 'spect. Those were all little things, but they added up. I got a percentage on top of my wages." He hung his head. "I wasn't raised that way. I think that's one reason why I never spoke much to folks. I couldn't look people in the eye. So I just stayed quiet. Out of sight, out of mind, like they say."

"Why'd you quit? You might not have been proud of yourself, but, like you said, it was steady work and good pay."

He rolled his eyes, had a *you-won't-believe-this* expression on his face.

"Monday night, last night, he exploded. Something happened. He lost complete control of himself. Broke a chair. Cursed at the top of his lungs. Actually went into the Warren viewing – you were there, weren't you? – and chased them all out. Called all those folks names. Said they, or somebody, stole something. One of Mrs. Warren's grandsons took a swing at him. I dragged Rumsey out of there and apologized to everybody. He locked himself in his office. I had to take care of Mrs. Warren's burial by myself this morning. Oh, those folks are still hopping mad. They're going to talk. The business is probably ruined. Who'd want to come to Rumsey's, now?" He kissed Julia's cheek and hugged her.

"At least we can get married, now." He paused. "I'd probably be out of a job pretty soon, anyway."

I had a thought.

"See this black eye?"

"Yeah, sorry about that."

"You can pay me back for it."

He laughed. "You want to hit me? Take your shot. I guess I deserve it."

"No, nothing that simple."

He stared, suddenly still.

"You're still working until Friday, right?"

"Yes."

"How about committing a friendly burglary? There's a brown suitcase with tan stripes that's hidden under a coat in the back of the closet in Rumsey's office. I want it. You can get it for me."

Julia and Gardner looked mystified.

"A suitcase?" Julia asked.

"It might be the one belonging to the mystery woman from the dump," I explained.

That sobered the pair.

"Do you think Rumsey could have murdered her?" I asked. Best to get this question out in the open, I decided.

Julia and Gardner look at one another, then came to the same conclusion: no.

Julia laughed. "He's afraid of his own shadow."

"He makes me put out the mouse traps and dispose of the dead mice. Doesn't want to touch them," Gardner added. "He'll touch people after they're dead – I mean, that's been his business for thirty years, but – *kill?* I can't imagine that."

"What about if he was angry, really angry, in a rage? You've both said you've seen him lose control more than once."

Julia shook her head no.

Gardner thought for a moment. "I don't know. Maybe. He hasn't been himself lately. Sorry, maybe's the best answer I've got."

"Would he cover up for somebody else?" I was becoming desperate. I wanted Rumsey to be the murderer so badly that I was willing to clutch at straws.

"That's a little easier. Sure, if he had a good reason," Gardner said.

"What reason?"

"Fear," Julia said.

"Money," Gardner offered.

Those two words summed up Francis Rumsey neatly.

Back to basics.

"How did the box with the dead woman's belongings get under your house?" I asked Julia.

"I've wondered and wondered about that," she said. "Somebody put it there, but I don't know who or when or how. Johnnie keeps what he called his 'secrets' down there, little things he picks up around town and plays with. They're not worth anything, so I never thought much about them."

"Did anyone else know about Johnnie hiding place?"

"Not that I know of," she said. "Does any of this help Johnnie? I have to know."

I hesitated. "I hope so."

Julia and I made trivial conversation while Gardner excused himself to change. It was his night to stay by the telephone at the funeral home in the event of emergencies. I excused myself for a few minutes to check under the house. Nothing there. Lots of little hidey-holes. Johnnie's precious secrets and the empty boxes that had held them were scattered everywhere. Thurl Gaskins had been thorough and needlessly inconsiderate. With the first hard rain, all of them would be washed down the river. I gave up. This was another dead end. Gardner came out of the bedroom dressed in his usual black suit and white shirt. He offered to walk with me to downtown.

"Aren't you afraid Rumsey might see you with me?"

"Do I look like I give a damn? The Hell with him," he said and lit a cigarette.

"I've never seen you smoke."

"Not proper in my job," he said. "But that was yesterday. New day today."

"Let's get back to Rumsey," I said.

"I'm sick of that man." He spat. "What do you want, now?"

"Does he own a gun?"

"Never seen one, doesn't mean there isn't one."

"Okay, remember back to the Monday before the Fourth of July. What happened that day?"

He thought. "Nothing special, I don't think. I worked on the hearse. It wasn't running right. Changed the oil. Washed it."

"Any funerals, visitors, anything out of the ordinary?"

"Let's see. Dardanelle funeral in the morning. Some men came to visit in the afternoon. I saw them go into his office. Mrs. Rumsey had a screaming fit later. Rumsey sent me home early – yeah, now that was unusual."

"Uh, Tuesday morning. Picked me up to help with the dead body at the dump." He hesitated. "Funny. The hearse was dusty when I drove us out there. Maybe he used it later Monday. He does that once in a while, if his wife needs the car."

My knee burned under the bandage. Damn, I would be glad to get my car back tomorrow. Gardner could not add much to his previous account. He promised he would try to get a look at the suitcase and bring it out if he could. Gardner and I shook hands. We were not exactly lodge brothers, but I felt we might become friends. But that would not happen until my black eye faded completely. I had been given strict orders by Adele: no black eye at the wedding. Either that, or I'd have to wear makeup. And that's not going to happen, dear, not going to happen.

I limped back to the newspaper office. I was surprised at how Gardner's revelations made me feel lighter, a little more optimistic, even cool despite the heat waves shimmering off the pavement. Perhaps things were looking up. I was worried about one thing: if I nailed Rumsey for his land deals and the thefts from the corpses, how would I keep Gardner out of it? Should I try to keep Gardner out of it? That was a tougher question.

I was a newsman. All I did was root out the facts and report them as faithfully as possible. After that, any consequences of that reporting were out of my hands. Let the chips fall where they may.

Sometimes – rarely, but it happened – the facts and the truth were not quite the same, and they struggled to occupy the middle zone between those opposites. The *fact* was that Ralph Gardner had played, perhaps was still playing, a significant role in Rumsey's myriad swindles. The *truth* was that Ralph Gardner was basically a decent man just trying to get by in tough times, and a man who loved a wronged, wounded woman and her damaged son.

A news story was a carefully orchestrated recitation of events. If you were good at what you did – and I liked to think I was – you sprinkled them with quotes from the people interviewed. Quotes were the salt that brought out the perfect flavor of what you tried to convey. Of course, your quotes must be accurate. But they were not always an exact transcript of what had been said. The stutters, pauses and repetitions were left out for the sake of clarity.

What I needed right now was clarity. The big picture eluded me. Perhaps the jigsaw puzzle that was Francis Rumsey and Dixie Lee

Rypanski might be larger than the pieces I had on my table. I had big holes and needed more pieces to fill them. Perhaps I had more than one puzzle and did not realize it. That thought gave me a headache.

I took four aspirin.

CHAPTER 16

Wednesday, July 12, 1933

I got my car back first thing Wednesday morning. I paid for it with Ralph Gardner's twenty. I kept the fifty cents change, you bet I did. I earned it. Vance White had done a good job, but I could still see the ding in the fender. No one else would notice, but I would know it was there – a little reminder that Rumsey was dangerous and had named me his personal Enemy No. 1.

"You look terrible," were Jeff Heston's opening words to me.

"Hangover."

"Drinking away your sorrows?"

"No. Spent last night with Homer Vaughn, the movie guy. We looked at some more locations, played a little baseball with the Paradise Robins. They were having a practice. Vaughn's a pretty good shortstop. They stuck me in right field, but I got a hit. Then we found a bottle. The rest you can imagine."

The Robins, a touring semi-pro team, were the pride and joy of Paradise during the summer. The winter sports obsession, of course, was high school basketball. This was Indiana, after all.

"Sounds like a fun night. Back to work. What's on your agenda today?" Jeff put on his editor hat.

"How about a story about how farmers are coping with the heat? The crop outlook."

"Useful, but boring, and it'll take too long to have it ready for today's paper. What else?"

"I could run over to Prattsburg. Orleva Warren left her book collection to the town to start a lending library. Find out where they plan to locate the library. Get local reaction. That sort of thing. I have to take a look at the books, anyway."

"Perfect. We can always use good news, happy news. If anything breaks here, I can send Delores. Go. You're not going to get the story sitting here on your lily-white duff."

I went. I saw. I, if not conquered, at least got a decent story out of it, plus four boxes of books – a complete Dickens, poetry, a life of

George Washington, a history of Lincoln County, *War and Peace, Les Misérables*, some contemporary novels, Ralph Waldo Emerson, Galsworthy. I left the books in my car. I would drop them off at the house later.

Before I left The Telegraph-Register, I called Wayne Cartage, where I stored my grandmother's household goods. That was one more item I could cross off the list of things to do that Adele had given me. My mother sold the house in Prattsburg after my father, sister and grandmother had died. When mother left Paradise in 1929, she told me to keep the furniture; I would need it someday. I had not wanted it then, but that *someday* had arrived. The furniture was not exactly what Adele and I might have chosen for ourselves, but it was free, and newlyweds needed every break. The basics were covered. We would have places to sit, eat, sleep and store books. I was contributing the furniture and a pile of books to our new household. Adele was bringing more books, linens from her Hope Chest and the bridal shower and an upright piano. I told Ocie Wayne the key was in the mail box, to let himself in, and I would be over later. While he was at it, would he stop over at the Atkinsons and pick up the piano. He groaned good-naturedly.

Jeff Heston had seen the paper put to bed precisely at one-fifteen, as it was every afternoon, except Sunday, when we did not publish. He left early to get in a round of golf. I had an appointment with Adele to talk to the pastor about final arrangements for the wedding ceremony. Simple was my only requirement. Pastor Clark Migglin walked us through it. He instructed us that July 22, although a happy day of celebration, was less about a wedding ceremony and more about beginning our marriage, which was a commitment for life. He took our hands in his and offered a prayer. I was suitably subdued.

"With all my worldly goods, I thee endow," I reminded myself after we left the church. I informed her, rather proudly, that Ocie was delivering our furniture at that very moment.

"I'd better get over there," Adele said. "He won't know where to put anything. Knowing Ocie, bless him, the dining room table could end up in the bedroom and the davenport in the kitchen." She looked at the list, where I had drawn a line through item five, *have furniture delivered,* and pointed to item eleven, *buy cleaning supplies,* which was followed by an entire catalogue of essential things -- mop, broom, bucket, rags, polishes, soap and more.

"Good grief, Walter," she said, "nobody's used that furniture for years. It'll be filthy. We'll start cleaning tonight."

She was her father's daughter. That starchiness was her father's managerial style but softened with a bone-deep femininity that was all Adele, with none of her mother's helpless hand-wringing.

I reassured her that the furniture was clean and well cared for, had been covered with cloths all this time. Per my mother's instructions, I had checked on it periodically. Not as faithfully as my mother might have wished, but I had checked.

Adele gave me a look. "It still needs to be cleaned," she said firmly. "Thoroughly."

And that was that. I kissed her and went in search of cleaning supplies. She said she would sort out Ocie and the furniture placement, get something to eat and meet me back at the house at half-past seven. I would shop, grab a bite, pack some of my belongings at the hotel and join her.

My hands were full. I had stopped by Bartlett's Hardware and picked up cardboard boxes. I had relatively little to move from my hotel room. Maybe four dozen books. Three suits. Shorts, socks, undershirts. My typewriter and writing supplies. One comfortable, overstuffed chair from my old childhood room at home. Shaving gear, toothbrush. Not much to show for my twenty-six years on this earth. I struggled up the three flights of stairs at the Travelers Hotel and dropped the boxes in front of my door. It was ten after seven, and I had little time to spare. I thought I would toss extra clothes and books in the boxes. That was five minutes, if I dawdled. Then ten minutes and three trips to get the boxes to my car. That left five minutes to get to the house to meet Adele. That was optimistic. I would be late, I knew it.

Very, very late, as it turned out.

CHAPTER 17

Later Wednesday evening, July 13, 1933

I started to put my key in the lock when I realized the door was open a crack. Mrs. Dottie Alexander, the hotel's elderly char lady, worked two or three days a week or whenever she felt like it. She swept and changed the towels when she got around to it. The permanent residents did not complain; we shifted for ourselves when she was not there. No point in arguing with age and rheumatism. Mrs. Alexander was getting forgetful, too, so the open door was not all that surprising, just mildly annoying. I picked up the boxes and pushed open the door with my rear end. I realized the room was dark. The window shade was pulled down. I always left it up. Someone, a relatively short man with strong arms, grabbed the back of my coat collar and yanked hard enough to choke me. I tried to twist and break free, and I landed an awkwardly aimed elbow in what might have been his ear. He grunted in pain but held on tightly.

"Everybody dies," he said, the voice like gravel. "Take a look."

I looked. Even in the dim light from the hall, it was obvious that Ralph Gardner was dead. He was seated in my soft chair by the reading lamp. He had a bullet hole in the middle of his forehead.

"Good night," the voice said. He began to laugh.

That laugh was the last sound I heard, except for the swishing that something very heavy, very hard made cutting through the air before it made contact with the back of my head.

My skull exploded. Its shattered pieces lay everywhere. White shards of bone covered my shoulders and chest. But if my head was gone, why could I think, have all my senses intact? I smelled blood and perfume and cigar smoke, and I had a taste in my mouth that reminded me of sucking on a dirty nickel. I heard voices. My hand floated in front of me as if it belonged to someone else. I lazed on a warm and cozy cloud. I hope this is what Heaven is like, I thought. I ordered my hand to touch my face. For a moment, I was eight years old when I was hit in the head by a swing on the playground during recess at Prattsburg Elementary School. No. I felt stubble on my cheek. I remember, now. I was twenty-six. I was a man.

Someone batted my hand away and said, "Stop that, or I'll shoot you myself."

I opened my eyes. The light hurt. Bad. I shut them.

"Is he going to be all right, Doctor Joplin?" It was Adele.

"He'll live. He's a Pratt. They're practically indestructible."

"Open your eyes, Walter," Adele said. There was a strange note of pleading in her voice that I had never heard before. Adele did not beg.

"Give him time, Adele. He's coming around," said Doc.

Another voice – no, two voices – cluttered the background of my consciousness. This floating sensation was delicious, and I wanted to stay in that cocoon of warm blackness. I could not truly enjoy this Heaven because the pain kept jabbing at me like a punch-drunk fighter whom no one had bothered to inform that he had already lost the match.

"Damn it, Walt. I told you not to get hit on the head again." That was Doc.

"Goldangit! This makes me mad." Sheriff Hoyt Peterson was one of the other voices. What was he doing here?

I remembered.

"Gardner," I said and sat bolt upright. I instantly wished I had not. My brain felt as though it had been rocked by a bomb explosion. I realized I was lying on my bed in the Travelers Hotel, not on a cloud in Heaven.

"Walter, I was so scared. After I found you --" Adele started to say.

"In a minute," Doc interrupted. "Walt, look at me."

I opened my eyes again and tried to focus on the location of the sound. I was overwhelmed by a sudden nausea and felt as though I were sitting in a very small rowboat in the middle of a very large ocean and had been hit by a thunderous wave. I forced myself to concentrate. Adele was sitting on one side of the bed holding my hand. She was the source of the perfume scent. Doc Joplin on the other side wielding a stethoscope and a small flashlight. I winced as the light probed into my pupils. The light did not hurt quite as badly as before.

"What happened?" I asked.

Doc sighed. "Concussion, Walt. Blow to the back of the head."

I tried sitting up. With help from Doc and Adele, I managed to scoot back and lean against the headboard. I shook my head to clear the fog. Bad idea.

"Can't you give him something?" Adele asked.

"No. Head injuries are tricky. I could give him something for the pain, but that might mask other problems. We'll have to watch and wait." Doc picked up my wrist to check my pulse.

Reality flooded back. I looked past Doc. Ralph Gardner was still seated in my reading chair, still with a bullet hole in his forehead, still dead. He had slumped to the side.

"Ralph?"

"What about Gardner? Did you shoot him?" the sheriff asked.

"God, no!" I said. "He was – when I – sorry, not thinking too good. I mean too well."

"Take it slow, son. We've got lots of time," the sheriff said. "What happened here? It sure looks like you and Gardner had a fight. You shot him, then passed out." Peterson walked to my desk and picked up a revolver. It was small, maybe a woman's purse gun. "This yours?"

"No. Never saw it before."

"Miss Atkinson found it. It was on the floor next to you. She come up here looking for you."

"Still doesn't belong to me. Don't own a gun." I was starting to get some of my snap back. Maybe I could write a best-seller about the healing effects of anger. I stifled a laugh. I knew it would have hurt.

"Okay," the sheriff said, "if it's not yours, how'd it get here?"

"Don't know. Don't know, damn it." I stopped, thought, tried to force the vague constellation of images from the past few hours into some recognizable order. "There was a man."

"What man, Walter?" This was from Adele.

"The one who hit me."

"*Who* hit you?" the sheriff demanded.

"Don't know." That seemed to be my answer for everything.

"By gum, you better be telling me the truth, son."

"Scout's honor."

"Walt, be serious." Adele was in schoolmarm mode. "just start at the beginning and tell us what happened."

"I don't remember a lot."

Doc spoke up before the sheriff could get a word in. "That's typical in head trauma. Memory can be lost permanently or temporarily. He might lose short-term memory from a few minutes to a few days before he was hit. It varies. He might remember more later, he might not."

"Walt, tell us what you *do* remember," the sheriff said.

"I remember it being dark in here. I remember seeing Gardner. Couldn't forget that. Heard a swish. Got hit, I guess. Then I woke up with you folks. That's all."

Chief Thurl Gaskins, who was on night duty apparently, cleared his throat. "Do we arrest him?" Thurl's had been another of the voices I had heard.

"He couldn't have done it, Chief," Doc said with an acidic edge to his voice. "When you're hit that hard, unconsciousness is immediate. He could not have been hit on the head, shot Gardner, then collapsed. Medically impossible. And Walter did not, could not have hit himself on the head, if that's what you're thinking. Gardner was shot, then the shooter hit Walter. I'd say Gardner's been dead since early afternoon. The timing's all wrong. That is my professional opinion as a doctor of medicine and as Lincoln County Coroner."

"Take it easy, Thurl. No arrest. This is a set-up if I ever saw one," the sheriff said.

The fog in my brain had started to clear. I needed to know some important facts. Who, what, when, where why, and how? Reporter's instincts kicked into gear. "How did you find me?"

"I was angry at you, really angry," Adele said, picking up the thread of the story. "You promised you'd meet me at seven-thirty. You never showed up. I finally came looking for you here about eight, maybe ten after, to give you a piece of my mind. I found you lying on the floor, unconscious. I called Doctor Joplin."

"And I called the authorities," Doc added.

"What I want to know is why was Ralph Gardner, of all people, murdered." The sheriff scratched his scalp under his thick thatch of iron-grey hair. "He was a quiet man. Hardly made a peep. Never riled nobody I know of."

Gardner had been doing something for me – a task, an errand, something. I was almost certain of that, even if I was completely in the dark about the events that led him, or his corpse, to my room.

"When was the last time you saw him?" Thurl asked.

"Uh, let me think. Orleva Warren's visitation at the funeral parlor on Monday. I think it was Monday." That was the night I had hidden in Francis Rumsey's closet. That was clear enough.

"What about yesterday – Tuesday?" The sheriff clearly was impatient.

That drew a blank. I must have had a half-witted look on my face, because Adele jumped in. "Do you remember yesterday, Walt?"

"Yesterday was Tuesday?" They all nodded. "Sure it was. I went to work." I looked around the room. "Where's the paper, Tuesday's Telegraph-Register?"

Thurl Gaskins walked a wide circle around Ralph Gardner and pawed through the pile of junk on top of my chest of drawers. Finding the paper was neither quick nor easy. The room was a mess. The closet door was open, its contents on the floor. The dresser drawers had been pulled out, with my unmentionables strewn everywhere. The bottom had been busted out of at least one of the drawers. He ultimately found the paper on the floor next to Gardner's body.

I scanned Page One. Roosevelt was hashing over production and labor issues with industrial leaders. There was a photo of Mrs. Arletha Heston looking richer and more smug than usual at a Daughters of the American Revolution luncheon. Government statisticians reported times were getting better. The reason was revealed in a United States Postal Service report that stated the postal service was delivering to more addresses this year compared to last year. This meant fewer families were doubling up. Two blocks of West Water Street had been closed for repaving.

There it was.

WARREN ESTATE DONATES BOOKS, KERNEL OF FREE PUBLIC LIBRARY FOR CITIZENS OF PRATTSBURG

Generous gift applauded by residents

By Walter G. Pratt

That portion of yesterday flooded back. I went to Prattsburg. I took some books for myself from Mrs. Warren's personal, now public, library. I talked to people. I hope I added *kernel* to the headline. Great word. After that, the day's events were a jumble.

"And after that?" The sheriff echoed my thoughts.

"Not sure. I must have done something."

"Walter, we went to the pastor's office at church in late afternoon," Adele said. "We made the final decisions about the wedding. Don't you remember that?"

"No, sorry."

"You had your mother's and grandmother's furniture moved to the new house."

"I did? Sorry. I meant to do that days ago."

"Them boxes in the hall. Yours, I take it," the sheriff said.

"Don't know."

"Yes," Adele said. "He was on his way to pick up cleaning supplies after we left the church. He said he was going to move some of his belongings tonight."

"What do we do, now?" Chief Gaskins asked the sheriff.

"First, call Miller and have him come get the body. Then we'll talk to Francis Rumsey. He might know what Gardner was up to."

"What about me? I want to go with you when you question Rumsey. I have some questions of my own."

"You'll do nothing of the sort," Doc interjected. "You're coming home with me. You need looking after. Technically, that's called medical supervision. The first twenty-four hours are crucial. I'm pretty sure you won't have any permanent damage, but I want to keep an eye on you. There's always a possibility of vomiting, seizures, other complications."

Adele gasped. Her fingernails dug into my forearm.

"Don't worry," Doc said. "That's a remote possibility. But he will need rest. No stress and strain. He'll have to take it easy for a few days."

"Have to work," I protested.

"Not for a few days. That's final. I'll take a look at you Saturday. Until then, you keep still and stay out of trouble. Doctor's orders."

"Damn!"

Damn Ralph Gardner. Damn Francis Rumsey. Damn.

CHAPTER 18

Thursday, July 13, 1933

Thursday morning bright and early found me at the Joplin's dining room table. Doc Joplin's wife, Rowena, fussed over me and outdid herself with a special breakfast of eggs, pancakes, whole-hog sausage, homemade strawberry jam, real maple syrup – the works. I swallowed as much as I could to be polite, but I had no appetite, a strange and unsettling experience for me. Throughout the meal, Doc's daughter, Calpurnia, observed me closely. She was a fifteen-year-old budding beauty. The girl had inherited her mother's looks and her father's direct approach.

"Who beat you up?" she asked between forking bites of pancake for herself and sneaking sausage to the Joplin's huge Alsatian dog, Caesar. The dog looked like a wolf but had the cuddly personality of a kitten. "You look awful."

"Callie!" Her mother was aghast. "Mind your manners. Mr. Pratt is a guest."

"It's okay, Rowena, really." To the daughter, I said, "I don't know for sure, but I have suspicions, and I will find out who and why."

"Hmm." Calpurnia looked thoughtful. "Maybe Dad was right."

"How's that?"

"That Pratts live on stubbornness, rather than food and water and air, I mean oxygen."

I laughed aloud. That made the pain reverberate as if the clapper of a bell banged against the walls of my skull.

"You are your father's daughter," I said.

"Yep, sure am, gonna be a doctor, too. It'll be the Joplin and Joplin Medical Practice one day."

"Don't say 'yep,' Callie," her mother admonished. "It's uncouth and unladylike. It has no class. Don't say 'gonna,' either."

The girl covered her lower face with her hands, but I still saw the little smirk that played around her mouth. She winked at me.

Annoying her mother obviously was a favorite game. Judging by the warmth displayed by all around this family's table, no one kept score.

I never doubted that Calpurnia would achieve her MD degree. Whether a female doctor could have a successful practice, whether patients would trust her with their ailments, those were other questions. She was smart enough. I had heard that from Adele. And Doc Joplin had taken her with him on house calls since she was a small girl. It was an introduction to real life, he had said, a way to toughen her up. That was his contribution to her life education. He mother taught her how to cook, write a sincere thank-you note and set a fine table. At her tender years, Calpurnia Joplin already had seen babies born and old folks die. She was steady, had sure hands and never lost her composure. She might be serious, but never somber, a smart aleck with a ready laugh. She was fifteen going on thirty.

Doc heard her say that and beamed. He leaned back in his chair at the head of the table and cast a critical eye over me. "How're you feeling this morning, Walt?"

"The head hurts, but that's about all. The dizziness has just about gone away. I'm going to work."

"Not today and not tomorrow, at the very least. I already called Jeff Heston, so don't argue with me," Doc said. "You might be able to go back to work Monday, but only after you've consulted with me. That's final. Don't be alone. Make sure there's somebody nearby who can call for help, if anything, uh, untoward happens. And no physical labor or emotional jolts, especially in this heat. No point in asking for a stroke."

"I have to move."

"Call Ocie Wayne. Let him do the heavy lifting. You can supervise." He turned to his daughter. "Why did I tell him that?"

Calpurnia launched into a detailed analysis of my condition, complete with proper Greek and Latin terms, that earned her father's approval.

I thanked Rowena for her hospitality, and Doc gave me a lift to the hotel. I called Jeff Heston and Ocie Wayne. Jeff told me to take care of myself and not to worry about the newspaper. Ocie did not answer.

Bill Andrews, the desk clerk, scowled at me. "That's a business telephone, not for the personal use of guests," he said. "It'd be nice if you'd pick up your messages. You don't look so good. You room is a mess. Does this mean you're leaving for good?" I thought I heard him mutter *I hope* as he reached under the front counter and brought out an envelope with my name on it. "This here's your final bill. Fifteen dollars for past rent. Plus twenty cents for delivering the aspirin to your room the other night. Plus four dollars for the broken chest of drawers. That's nineteen dollars and twenty cents total."

"I can do arithmetic. Gosh, Bill, thank you for caring about my dreadful ordeal, especially since you're the person in charge of the security in this place."

He growled.

"I'm a little slow today." I rubbed the sore spot on the back of my head. Bad idea. "Uh, what messages?"

He turned to the wall of cubbyholes behind the desk and pulled two envelopes out of the box for Room 305. I did not recognize the handwriting on one. The other was from Adele. I read Adele's. It was filled with sweet concern and orders to meet her this morning. I stuffed the other envelope into my pocket. Adele came first. I had no pressing responsibilities today. A wave of dizziness knocked me sideways when I turned away from the front desk. I had to grasp the back of a chair to steady myself and catch my breath. I decided to take Doc's advice. This time.

I caught up with Adele at Gold's Jewelry Store. She and Bonnie Simpson were chatting about china patterns, and which pieces were important and which would be needed only on special occasions. It was the ultimate female talk. Men talked about weather, crops, automobiles, politics, sports -- manly things like that. Linens, crystal and china as serious conversation gave me another headache on top of the one I had already. I would rather kiss Comrade Stalin than discuss stemware, whatever that was. Well, almost.

Adele informed me that our new front yard looked more like a pasture than a civilized lawn. "Buy a lawnmower or buy a cow, but take care of that lawn," she said. She looked me over critically. "How are you feeling? Your color's better than last night. I was pretty worried about you. Is your memory back?" I could tell from her gush of words that she was barely holding herself together.

"A little. Still fuzzy." She still looked troubled, so I drew her close. "Don't fret, sweetheart. I feel much better, really. Doc ordered me not to work today, so I'm going to take it easy. I plan to clean up the mess in my room and move into the house. How's that?"

"No need. It's already done," she said. "I called Ocie Wayne first thing. Your room is cleared out. Ocie had a terrible time getting that awful old chair you love down the stairs. How'd you ever get it up there?"

That question spun my brain in a different direction. Questions popped up like bubbles in a glass of beer. The first question was: How did Ralph Gardner get up there? Had he walked on his own, intending to meet me or leave something for me? Had he been forced at the point of a gun? Or had he been carried there, already dead? Dixie had been moved, perhaps Ralph had, too. Wait! Doc said Gardner had been killed earlier in the day. I had forgotten to ask Doc about the specifics. I had forgotten a lot of things.

More questions: Had Julia Porter been notified? How was she holding up? Had Ralph told her anything else? What did Rumsey tell the sheriff? Did we know whether the bullet from Gardner matched the one from Dixie? Had Gardner found Rumsey's suitcase? *The suitcase!* Had he gotten the suitcase from Rumsey's closet?

It was all coming back.

"That's it!" I shouted. I threw my arms around Adele, picked her up off the floor and whirled her around. This brought smiles from most customers and twitching frowns from others. "I remember. *I remember!* Wednesday afternoon, it's back – part of it, anyway – Pastor Migglin, Ralph and Julia, the hardware store. *I remember!"*

"That's wonderful, Walt. Really wonderful. I was so worried." She kissed me discreetly on the cheek and whispered, "I love you, even if you are a lunatic."

"I have to go."

"Walt, the rings."

"Tell Mr. Gold I'll be back later."

"Walt, don't do anything stupid, you hear me. You're not healed, yet."

"Me? Stupid? Nah, I'm crazy like a fox. I love you. See you later at the house. No, make it the Daisy Diner for lunch – half past twelve, okay?"

I urgently needed the sheriff's information, but I was equally certain that Julia Porter's need of comfort was of greater importance. The sunlight stung my eyes, but I was grateful that the pain seemed to be receding. I eased myself into the Buick and proceeded to the little shack by the river where I had talked to Julia and Ralph on Tuesday.

Was that only two days ago? It seemed like a lifetime. It certainly was a lifetime ago for Gardner. There had been far too many deaths in my small town in the past few weeks. Good people like Orleva Warren. Decent-if-flawed people like Ralph Gardner. The mysterious Dixie Lee Rypanski. Not to mention whoever was in that grave in Chicago. Too many deaths. I felt a chill despite the heat.

A haggard Julia Porter answered my knock. Her eyes were sunken and dazed, and she had not washed or combed her greying auburn hair, which hung limply to her shoulders. She was a complete blank, a *tabula rasa* as Doc Joplin might have said. She gave me a stony look and started to close the door in my face.

"I just wanted to offer my condolences, Julia. That's all."

Her expression did not alter. "You killed him, Mr. Pratt, good as you pulled the trigger yourself. I don't think I want you in my home right now."

I might have been able to take her accusation better if she had shown some emotion. She had put into words what I had avoided coming to grips with.

"I have to ask you, did Ralph tell you whether he found anything for me at Rumsey's? Anything at all? It's important."

"The last I saw him was Wednesday morning when he left for work. Don't matter now, does it?" She blinked back tears.

"I'm sorry, Julia, truly sorry."

"'Sorry' doesn't bring Ralph back. 'Sorry' doesn't get my Johnnie out of jail." With that, she closed the door. I thought I heard a sob, but it might have been my imagination.

On my way to the jail, I stopped in at Bartlett's Hardware and bought the lawnmower. Jeb Bartlett promised to deliver it today. "You're a homeowner, now," Job reminded me. "Want me to put together some tools for you, too? You're going to need a hammer, a couple of screwdrivers, a wrench, nails, screws, pliers, lubricating oil, stuff like that. I'll bring it over with the lawnmower. Put it on your account, Walt? Tell you what – I'll throw in a nice handyman's tool box as a wedding present, least I could do."

Sure, I said, and wondered why grooms did not have showers the way brides do. We could have a party with masculine gifts like screwdrivers and cigars and hedge trimmers and snow shovels and pocket knives. Marriage was an expensive proposition, I was learning to my chagrin. The precipitous drop in my bank account was proof positive. Wedded bliss was becoming costlier by the minute.

"Out of the way." Ted Thompson, wearing his usual threadbare overalls and a scowl, barreled past me without so much as a hello. He looked like a tornado on two legs. He clutched another small bag of nails.

"What's the hurry, Ted?"

"Gotta get home. Got company." For some strange reason, he refused to look me in the eye. "Sorry, Pratt." He edged past me and bolted out the door.

Jeb Bartlett's teen-aged son had been waiting on Thompson. The son, who worked in the store when he was not in school, had his fists clenched. As I paused at the display of flashlights near the door, I overheard Jeb tell him, "Howard, the man has troubles. Cut him some slack. Besides, he is a customer. You don't have to like them. Just take their money and smile."

Good advice. I yelled at Jeb to add a couple of flashlights to my order while he was at it.

"Wondered when you'd get over here. I figured it'd be the forenoon, and I was right," Sheriff Hoyt Peterson said. He was seated at his desk with his feet propped on an open drawer. "How're you feeling? I must say, you look a lot better today than you did last night. Kinda worried about you, son."

I appreciated his concern, but I was getting tired of answering the same question *ad nauseum.*

"Fine," I said. "Thanks for asking. How's Johnnie Porter doing?"

"Better. Nice boy. I think he's helping Juanita in the kitchen about now. I've pretty much given him the run of the place." The sheriff looked me over closely. "What do you want? Sure as shootin' this ain't a social call."

"It isn't, although it's always a pleasure to see you, sheriff."

Peterson hesitated a moment. I could almost see him weighing whether I was making fun of him or being serious. I decided to jump back into the conversation before he could come to the correct conclusion.

"Did you ask Rumsey directly if he killed Gardner?"

"Yes, I did."

I waited, but the sheriff did not elaborate. "Come on, God damn it, tell me!"

Peterson pointed to the sign next to his door: DO NOT TAKE THE LORD'S NAME IN VAIN ON THESE PREMISES. Prisoners caught swearing more than once were denied Juanita Peterson's desserts for three days. That was enough incentive to bring them around to the sheriff's way of thinking. That was the rumor, anyway. I had never been able to confirm it.

"Sorry, sheriff, and I mean that sincerely. It's just that this, this – you know, what's happened in the last couple of weeks -- has gotten kind of personal. If you don't think so, look at the lump on my head."

The sheriff resettled his feet on the floor, leaned his massive forearms on the desk and stared at me for a second longer than was comfortable. "Guess you got a point there," he said, finally.

"So, Rumsey denied it. He's not in jail, or I would have heard by now."

"That's right. Rumsey said he hadn't seen Gardner since early afternoon. Sent him home early. Mrs. Rumsey – my stars, ain't she a piece of work, wouldn't want her mad at me – anyhow, Mrs. Rumsey said the mister was home all night."

"Rumsey, or somebody, had plenty of time to get up to my room. He could have taken the back stairs from the alley or the fire escape."

"Yes. Still don't budge his alibi, though."

"Did you search Rumsey's place?"

"Nope. No cause to. Besides, he had an alibi."

"But --"

"I know, I know. I can only go so far. What do the lawyers call it – probably caused?"

I let that *faux pas* pass. "But Rumsey is the only person in Paradise who has connections to everyone else involved in this."

"What, exactly, is this?"

I hesitated a fraction of a second too long. The way the sheriff eyed me could have melted the moon. I suddenly realized that I needed to tell somebody the story, the whole story. Barney O'Malley knew the Chicago pieces. Adele knew about the past relationships. Jeff Heston was up to date on what we had learned so far about the real estate deals. But I was the only one who knew everything. And it was all in my head, not on paper. If I met the same fate as Ralph Gardner, God forbid, I doubted whether anyone could or would put the whole shebang together. It would be a dead story in more ways than one. And not just a news story. By now, it was fast becoming a legal story, one that seemed to be spiraling rapidly out of my control.

But I was not quite ready to tell all of it to the sheriff. As sympathetic as he might have been, stealing Rumsey's bookkeeping records was still a felony. I could be sharing a cell with Johnnie Porter. Plus, I had not quite woven together all the threads in this story. I had a strong impression that all those separate elements were connected through Rumsey. The problem was that I could not prove a damn thing. I also had to admit to myself that my conclusions about Rumsey might be colored by wishful thinking and obsession. An action here, an event there – however damning – did not add up to a cohesive whole, a pattern that I could place before the sheriff and a judge or on Page One with absolute certitude.

I decided it was in my own self-interest to tell the sheriff the whole story. Somebody, preferably somebody with the power of arrest, needed to know. And I needed to tell, if for no other reason than to provide a small guarantee of my own safety. Hoyt Peterson listened carefully. I even told him what I heard while I had hidden in Rumsey's closet. I also decided it was in my own self-interest to leave out the part about taking the ledgers.

"That there's some story, young man. I ain't sure what it all adds up to, but it sure gives a man pause, don't it?" He folded his arms over his chest and stared at me in that calm way he had. It was more unnerving than loud words and physical threats.

"Let me tell you something about me," he continued. "I graduated eighth grade out at the township school in Lafayette Township, and that was something in those days, getting that far in school. Not too many did. I was a pretty big fellow even then. Fourteen, but could pass for eighteen, if you didn't look none too close. I ran away from home. Ain't too proud of that now, but I did. Couldn't stand the thought of staying on the farm, being chained to that plow like a mule with two legs. 'Bout broke my mother's heart. Well, can't change the past – what's done is done. So I joined up with Teddy Roosevelt and went to Cuba. You think what we got here is hot, well, you ain't been to Cuba. They invented hot. Didn't know that, did you? That was in eighteen and ninety-eight."

I was fascinated. I had never bothered to wonder about the sheriff's personal history.

"I can see you're wondering where this is going, right?"

I nodded.

"Well, I saw a lot of boys, good boys, die on them mountains in Cuba. Most of 'em from the fever. But a lot of 'em from Spanish bullets and bombs. I saw things that shake my soul, even to this day. Arms, legs, heads, guts – all gone, blown to heck and beyond, a worse sight than butchering hogs in the fall. Ain't no sound like the sound of a man praying for death, begging for water, screaming for his mama, when there ain't no help a-coming."

The sheriff's warm brown eyes turned hard as sunbaked Indiana clay in August.

"I ain't never told nobody this, not even my Juanita, but that's one big reason I run for sheriff. The other was that the previous sheriff had been dipping into the public trough and putting the money in his own back pocket, but that's another story. Made me mad. And – trust me, son -- you don't want Hoyt Peterson mad at you, and that's for darn sure." He paused. "Anyways, I seen enough slaughter in Cuba to last me a lifetime. Ain't gone hunting since, neither. When I was a kid, I put meat on the table regular with my daddy's rifle. Not no more. Back to being a sheriff. I thought maybe if I got the sheriff's job, I could keep more blood from being shed. Folks get all het up. That's the natural order of things, but it don't have to lead to fists and knives and guns. Now, I'll be the first to admit that some folks get a tad upset about me breaking up fights and grabbing feuding neighbors and tossing them in a cell overnight to give 'em time to cool off and think about it. But they can darn well think what they want. I want to head off trouble, not clean up all the mess after trouble happens. That's my job. That's how I seen it from the start."

Peterson scrutinized me over the rims of the half glasses he wore only for close work.

"Been too much violence in Paradise lately, son, and that don't make me happy. That ain't part of my plan for Lincoln County, and I got a plan, believe you me. The problem is you're right in the middle of this mess we got here. Not sure I know exactly why that is or what to make of it. I do know this as certain sure as I know Jesus is my Savior." He reflexively patted the six-pointed star on his left breast and fixed me with a Medusa stare. "Son, you ain't telling me everything. In fact, you're hardly telling me anything. I know it, and you know it. Here's a for instance: why'd somebody search your room, toss everything to heck and gone?"

"Looking for something?"

Thank God, the ledgers were safely under lock and key in the medicine storage room in Doc Joplin's office.

"Uh-huh," the sheriff said. He did not sound convinced. I could not blame him.

"There's a lot I don't know yet, myself," I offered by way of an admittedly weak explanation.

"Uh-huh."

I tucked my tail between my legs like a beaten pup, metaphorically speaking, and scuttled out of Peterson's office. His warning rattled in my ears: *Stay away from Rumsey, son. He ain't worth your time nor the trouble you'd get from me.*

CHAPTER 19

Friday, July 14, 1933

I had to admit it felt strange to sleep on my grandmother's double bed. It was wide and feather soft, unlike the rock-hard slab at the hotel I had slept on for two years. My toes hung over the foot of Grandmama Pratt's bed, but that was the price I had to pay for being tall. Adele had used old sheets scrounged from her mother. It was comfortable enough, but it just did not feel like my – make that, *our* – bed, not yet.

That thought made me sit up straight and head for the shower. I checked my physical condition: the shakiness was almost gone, the lump on my head had shrunk although it was still tender to the touch, and the dizziness had nearly disappeared. I pronounced myself on the mend.

I had met Adele for lunch Thursday, as planned. Then I came home and slept for five hours straight, ate a light supper, and immediately went back to bed again. I had felt as though someone had let the air out of my tires. Head injuries were exhausting, I had discovered. Adele had left a note on the bathroom mirror where I could not possibly miss it. She wrote that she had stopped by but had not had the heart to wake me.

Friday had dawned bright and sunny. Judging from the view from our kitchen window, it was going to be yet another day without a rain cloud in sight. Only a few curly wisps scooted across the sky. The view also confirmed Adele's remarks about the lawn. I would need to get busy with the lawnmower Job Bartlett had stowed in our tiny garage yesterday. It was that or park the car outside and convert the garage into a milking shed.

Ocie Wayne knocked on the back door at seven-thirty sharp. I was still working on my first cup of coffee. Adele had stocked the house with a few basics – bread, milk, eggs, butter, coffee, a coffee pot, towels, a couple of mismatched and dented cooking pots, soap –

enough to get by for a few days. I had contributed shaving supplies, aspirin, my reading chair and an alarm clock.

Ocie was one of those ageless men who could have been forty or sixty. He had moved my mother and me from Prattsburg to Paradise, where he had been a fixture for as long as I could remember. He was short, wide, bald, with long arms and legs and no neck. Strong as the proverbial ox, too. If something needed done, Ocie was the man to call.

Odd jobs, small repairs that did not require a specialist, storage, moving, deliveries, hauling, lifting things so old ladies could dust under them, a wrecker to pick up your smashed automobile, digging garden beds – Ocie did it all.

He was not rich, but managed to scratch together a steady income, his time was his own, and he never had to report to a boss. If he felt like taking a day off to go fishing, he draped the CLOSED sign on his shop door and off he went.

When I was a kid, I had thought he had the best job in the world.

He was a deacon at the tiny, brick African Methodist Episcopal Church on West Water Street. When he filled in for the preacher who traveled a circuit of Negro churches throughout east-central Indiana, his shouts of joy could be heard all the way to the street. Many a Sunday, Mother had handed me off to Ocie to attend services with him in the morning, then to go fishing or explore the Sassafras Swamp in the afternoon. This had raised a few eyebrows about town. I may have returned home muddy with scrapes and scratches, but I always returned happy and safe. To me, he was more an adopted uncle than a hireling.

"Morning, Ocie. Cup of coffee?"

"Thanks, Mr. Pratt. I surely will."

"It's Walter, not Mr. Pratt. For Heaven's sake, Ocie, you've known me since I was eleven years old."

"That I have."

"To what do I owe the pleasure of your visit?" We settled at the kitchen table where I had done geometry and Latin homework for Paradise High School. If I looked hard enough, I might still be able to find the initials I carved into the underside when I was seven. Grandmother Pratt had taken the dreaded carpet beater to my backside for that one.

"Well, now, Miss Atkinson asked me to get started on that ugly yard out there. Whoo-ee, boy, that yard looks pretty bad. It does."

"That it does. But I can take care of it."

"No sir. No, sir, can't do that," Ocie said, shaking his head with firm determination. "I've got my marching orders. Miss Atkinson said I wasn't – what did she say? – yessiree, it was 'under no circumstances are you to allow Mr. Pratt to touch that lawn.' Those were her exact words."

"Yes, dear," I said with an exaggerated, man-to-man sigh. Ocie laughed and slapped his knee and laughed some more.

"You're going to make a good married man, in spite of yourself. Speaking of the wedding, my Lizzie has planned to bake a special cake with butter icing. Her own recipe. Homemade strawberry ice cream, too, the last of this year's crop. Your mouth will water, I promise." Ocie paused, then stared straight through me with those warm brown eyes and made his voice preacher-stern. "Now you listen to me, boy. Miss Adele Atkinson is one of the smartest, kindest, most good-hearted people in this whole town, and I mean everybody, colored or white. If I ever hear that you laid a hand in anger on that fine woman of yours, you will answer to me. Is that understood, boy?"

"I understand, Ocie, I most definitely understand. But no worries there, you have my word on it. I don't mind telling you I love that woman more than life itself. She makes me crazy sometimes, but I love her."

"*She* makes *you* crazy? That's a good one, boy, that's a good one." With that, Ocie politely rinsed his coffee cup in the sink, stretched his arms and headed outside. At the door, he shook his head. "That's a fine mess out there, it surely is. But Ocie'll have it looking pretty in no time."

I never doubted he would.

Ocie's unexpected appearance meant that I had an entire Friday before me with nothing to do – no work, no stories to write for the newspaper, no husbandly home duties, nothing to compel me to stick to a schedule or answer to anyone. The drafts of two or three short stories were somewhere in the small room that Adele and I, rather grandly, called my study. I could polish them, but I had no clue where they were in the pile of boxes. Besides, I was not in the mood, and my brain still groped at times to make all the proper connections. I decided to obey Doc's orders to take it easy and stay around people.

Right now, I preferred to be around people who would bring me food.

I yelled at Ocie, who was already attacking an overgrown lilac bush with sharp snips, to help himself to the coffee and the bathroom. I proudly took one last look at my new home, rinsed my cup, threw on an almost-clean shirt and tie, and headed downtown.

Breakfast at the Daisy Diner was nectar and ambrosia with red-eye gravy on the side. I seemed to have my appetite back, one more milestone on my climb back to normality. Several folks stopped to ask how I was feeling and, more importantly, to probe for details about the murder of Ralph Gardner, which they could then grind even finer through the Lincoln County gossip mill. Not remembering much came in handy in this situation. I could be polite and not lie to my friends, neighbors and readers. Finally, Herb took pity on me and started shooing people away.

I spread open the fat, child's writing tablet on my regular table by the front window. Most of its lined pages contained scribbled snatches of short stories, descriptions of people and places, assorted lists and notes of goings-on about town. So much had happened since the last entry dated Monday, July 3. That was a brief description of the woman in the yellow dress. I now knew the mystery woman's name. She was Dixie Lee Rypanski, late of Chicago, Illinois. I also knew she was a wife and a sister. In my mind's eye, though, she remained the enigmatic stranger about whom I had speculated. That smile, that unmistakable yellow dress. That was how I would always remember her – vibrant and alive, not cold and covered with flies.

I started a list. That process always got the little grey cells moving. Pick up pay envelope at the newspaper office. Chat with Jeff, maybe clear off my desk, find something to work on. No. Scratch that. Stick to Doc's plan. Grab my pay and leave the paper as quickly as possible. Go to First National Bank, make a deposit, check on the balance. Stop by The Travelers Hotel and pay the final bill. Go to the jewelry store. From there, onward to the exchange and have a telephone installed at the new house. Return books to the Paradise Carnegie Library. Tidy, organize my study. Unpack rest of clothes. Stop at Smoke Truby's for a haircut. Check at the haberdashery about my wedding suit. Take second-best suit to King's Dry Cleaners, which promised that "We Give You the Royal Treatment". On second and third thought, all that amounted to at least three day's work. More than I wanted to tackle.

And what a bore.

If this were what retirement was like, then I would rather die at my desk with my fingers curled in a death grip around the typewriter keys. My last keystrokes would be -30-, the way every newspaper writer tagged the end of a story.

Death would occur, preferably, no earlier than the ripe of old age of one-hundred three. I did the arithmetic – that would be in 2010, a new century, a new millennium. I could not imagine myself that far into the future or wrap my mind around all the possible changes the world would have seen in that time. My grandparents were born in an age before electric lights, indoor plumbing, running water, refrigerators, telephones and automobiles. What was next? A personal aeroplane in every driveway?

Ah, come to think of it, there was something interesting I could do on a lazy day. I could drive to Muncie and check out that address Barney had given me as a potential hideout on the Gangland Underground Railroad. Maybe I could even talk someone into going with me. So much had happened since the trip to Chicago that I had not had the time or the inclination to follow up on it. No hard exertion, no stress, just a leisurely Friday excursion, foot on the accelerator, windows open, fresh breeze blowing the cobwebs out of my slightly damaged brain, a small cigar. Maybe I would stop for a quick restorative at Henry's on Wabash Street, my favorite Muncie speak. I would be home in time for supper.

Perfect.

I crossed out everything on the list except *pick up pay* and *go to bank.*

I ended up going alone. Doc would not complain too much, especially if he never found out. After all, what could happen on a leisurely afternoon drive?

With a full tank of gas in the Buick, I turned onto State Road 27 and headed southwest on the brand-new, two-lane concrete highway that connected Paradise to Muncie, twenty-eight miles away. Eight years ago, when I left home for Muncie State Teachers College, the road was a part gravel, part dirt track that wound all over lower creation. The state engineers had straightened parts of it, but Dead Man's Curve was still there – a sharp, almost ninety-degree hard turn to the left that had been the last earthly sight of numerous inattentive or inebriated motorists. I counted seven tiny, white crosses there, clustered at the berm like a bouquet of strange flowers, a reminder of man's folly and man's ultimate fate.

Muncie was a miniature Chicago in some respects. It was, or used to be, heavily industrial. Many shops would never reopen, but the glass factory, the region's largest employer, had fired up its furnaces and put men back on its payroll at the first of the year. Muncie also boasted the largest slaughterhouse and meat-packing plant between Chicago and Pittsburgh. As I passed the city limit sign and crossed the railroad tracks, the unmistakable odor invaded my nostrils – part raw blood, part decomposing pork, entirely nauseating and altogether profitable.

And it was reputed to be an open city, a place where gangsters could come for a vacation from the attentions of the law. This bustling small city of about forty-five thousand was not in the same league as Joplin, Missouri, or St. Paul, Minnesota, or the queen of crime resorts, Hot Springs, Arkansas. But Muncie certainly held its own in that felonious geography.

An understanding – and consequently rich – chief of police saw to it that the hard men were welcome. In exchange for avoiding murder, rape, kidnapping, bank robbery and other unacceptable mayhem, the visiting lords of crime received referrals to friendly boarding houses and could roam at will with few checks on their behavior. This covert industry also mass-produced crap games, speakeasies and prostitution. The city fathers rationalized that otherwise upstanding citizens participated in those activities, too.

Barney O'Malley's information consisted of few hard facts, but many tantalizing hints that the Gangland Underground Railroad was run largely by a sophisticated group specializing mostly in legitimate deals and handling only the hottest bad guys who were on the run and needed a quiet place to get away from it all for a few weeks. These criminals were at the top of the most-wanted list, the ones with the biggest photographs in the Post Office, the ones even the casually corrupt city officials were afraid to touch. That meant Muncie was a star in that constellation of crime – a tarnished star, but a star, nonetheless.

I thought I knew my way around this compact little city, but it took much twisting, turning and two round trips across the Miami

River before I found Hastings Street. Judging from the number of vehicles and the dogs snuffling about, Hastings Street appeared to be the main drag of a care-worn neighborhood tucked away on the southeast side of downtown. I cruised through a barren streetscape comprised mainly of small, two-story, wood-frame houses crowded roof to eave. It was as if one sagging structure were expected to effectively brace the one next door like two drunks propping one another up on the long walk home.

This pocket-sized area, confined by railroad tracks on one side and a smelly creek on the other, was about four or five blocks long and three blocks wide. The back yards were short and narrow, sporting scraggly vegetable patches, trash barrels, clotheslines and the occasional shed or one-car garage. The front lawns, so called, were given over mostly to bare earth. The houses all displayed varying stages of flaking paint and despair. At one time in the not-so-distant past, the inhabitants had been among the working poor. Now they were just poor.

While the rest of Muncie might be bustling, Hastings Street was quiet as a graveyard. Two things struck me as out of place – the number of new or nearly new automobiles parked alongside the crumbling curbs and the number of hard-eyed men sitting in porch shade. Most wore shirts with the sleeves rolled up in the heat or had stripped down to their undershirts. Hats or soft caps had been pulled down to their eyebrows. This was, I speculated, more for concealment than protection from the sun. I counted at least three men who openly sported pistols in shoulder holsters or tucked into the waistbands of their trousers. These men might have been out-of-work homeowners or visiting relatives, but I somehow doubted it.

I parked in the 1100 block. The residents might not want a reporter nosing into their business, but nobody could fault a guy for trying to make a buck. Right?

Right.

I needed a good pretense for snooping. Preacher? Salesman? Lost traveler? I looked around for a prop. The black grip on the back seat, not yet put away from moving, would serve. Very well, a door-to-door salesman I would be. But what to sell? I rejected brushes, encyclopedias and raffle tickets. I rummaged through the grip and found the oversized, leather-bound, ornately illustrated Bible that had come down to me from my father. Adele and I, sentimental fools that we were, planned to use it during the wedding ceremony. I now remembered placing it in the bag and putting the bag into the car, where I had thought I could not possibly forget it. The blow to my head must have thoroughly red-penciled that memory.

I hoped the rest of my missing memories were bad ones I would never get back. Forget where I put my hat? Not a big deal. Forget the first time I kissed Adele? Never. It was August 24, 1924, at the Lincoln County Fair behind the Home Economics Building. We were seventeen. She tasted like spun sugar.

The next question was which house to begin with? Definitely not one of the houses with armed men on the front porch. I was parked opposite 1126, Barney's target house. No way in Hades was I going there first. On my side of the street was a vacant lot and a shack with weeds four-feet tall in the yard and boarded-up windows. Nothing happening there.

The next house, at 1123, was different from all the others. It had a neatly tended green lawn with flower beds tucked behind a white-washed fence. The porch did not sag, and the shutters were newly painted a crisp black. While I watched, an elderly woman wearing a clean cotton housedress stepped out onto the porch and peered down the street. She fanned herself with an apron with red flowers embroidered on it and let out a small sigh. I figured she was wondering why the afternoon mail was late.

Tie snugged tight, hat tipped to a jaunty angle and satchel in my hand, I was ready to sell the nice old lady. A loud creak caught my attention. A man stood at the top of the crooked steps of the house I had thought abandoned. He squinted, perhaps at the bright sun, perhaps at me. He was about my age and wore work muscles like a tight suit of clothes. He hefted a cement block in each hand as if they were bags of feathers.

Think inoffensive. Think unthreatening.

"Afternoon, brother," I said.

"Waddaya want?" He dropped the blocks and scratched the back of his neck. The movement revealed the outline of a small handgun concealed in his right pants pocket.

"Why, nothing, sir, unless you'd like to, uh, hear the word of the Lord. I have some superior Bibles right here. The ink, the very ink was blessed by the, uh, High Bishop of the Sanctuary of the Divine Resurrection in Jesus's own Holy Land. Says so, right here on the inside flap." I could not tell whether he was buying my spiel or not. "It's only one skinny dollar down and ten cents a week for one year. Salvation is cheap at any price. Isn't that right?"

"Ain't interested, *brother*. Move along." His accent was pure Noo Yawk, and his look vaguely Mediterranean. His attitude was all mean.

"Yes sir, yes sir. Thank you. May the Lord be with you. Thank you." To myself, I added, also thank you for not shooting me right here on the sidewalk with my father's Bible in my hand. I moved along, as ordered.

The elderly woman had disappeared inside. I sniffed newly baked cookies and fresh coffee through the screen door. If Heaven had a smell, that would be it.

"Are you planning to stand there all day, young man? Are you dreaming, or just working up the courage to knock?"

I had conjured out of pure fantasy a little old lady who baked cookies and had a clichéd granny's sweet and gentle personality. Never assume anything. My first city editor had drilled that precept into my head: *assume* makes an ass out of you and me. He had been right. The real woman turned out to have a commanding presence and a steely voice to match, a combination of Ulysses S Grant and Eleanor Roosevelt. Perhaps I had been dreaming, or my brain had blanked for a few moments. It was that damn concussion, again.

"Yes, ma'am." That was all I could think to say.

"Yes, ma'am – *what?*"

"Uh – I'm here to interest you in the world's finest Bible." That was feeble, but better than no response at all. "Could I talk to you for a few minutes? I won't take much of your time."

She inspected me through the screen door, apparently concluded I was not an axe murderer on the prowl and invited me to take a seat on one of the wicker chairs on the porch. "I'll be right back," she said.

She returned bearing a tray with a pot of coffee and a plate of cookies. Again, she fixed me with a stare that made every lie I had ever told started to bubble to the surface like sulfurous gas from a swamp. For reasons I could not explain, I felt a desperate need to confess to this complete stranger. But I had begun this sham and could not think of a way to wriggle out of it without demonstrating that I was an even greater fool.

"Please help yourself." She gestured to the tray. "Since you appear to be the first traveling salesman I've ever met who's tongue-tied, I'll start the conversation. I'm Mrs. Alberta Rogers. I'm a widow. I was born and raised in Muncie. And, I should add, I already own two Bibles. And you are?"

"Uh, Francis Rumsey, ma'am. From Paradise, just down the road." That was the first name that came to mind.

"Yes, I know where Paradise is located." After a strained pause, she prompted, "And you were about to say?"

"Uh, yes. These cookies are delicious."

"Thank you. The Bible?"

I collected myself. "Yes Mrs. Rogers, what I have here is a leather-bound, gold-embossed Bible that I'm sure is nothing like either of the copies you now own. It's special. The ink it was printed with was blessed in the Holy Land. This is the kind of book you could pass down to the grandchildren and to generations after. It would become a family treasure, so to speak."

"And how much does this *family treasure* cost, young man?"

I was on a roll. "For the quality, it's very inexpensive, especially since all of Jesus's own words are printed in red so you can find them and take them into your heart right away when you open it."

"Price," she insisted.

"Just one dollar down and ten cents a week for one year."

"Hmm." She topped off her coffee and stirred in a teaspoon of sugar. "Mr. Rumsey – you said Rumsey, correct?"

I nodded.

"Did you happen to know a Miss Carlotta Lane from Paradise?"

Uh-oh. "Yes, Miss Lane was my eighth-grade English teacher. She passed away last year."

"Yes, I know. I went to her funeral at the Rumsey Funeral Parlor. There I met a thoroughly distasteful man named Francis Rumsey, the owner of the that establishment. He was patronizing, pretentious and phony."

That described him – and me, I suspected – perfectly, at least the phony part. And Mrs. Rogers knew it.

She continued. "Her casket was a cheap as one could go and still depart this world with a little respectability intact. I'm sure Lottie would never have picked that one. Chipped gilt paint on the outside and bright pink satin on the inside. Dreadful, just dreadful. If I weren't a charitable Christian woman, I would swear that awful Rumsey dug that coffin up, dumped out the original occupant and reused it. And I know for a fact she paid for her funeral expenses in advance and took care of all of the details. I wouldn't be surprised to find out that Mr. Rumsey pocketed the difference between the two caskets. Lottie's niece wouldn't have known the details, and I'm sure the mousy little thing was too shy and too grief-stricken to notice or complain. Do you happen to know *that* Francis Rumsey, but any chance?"

Should I fess up or brazen it out? Fortunately, she plowed right ahead and spared me the opportunity to tell more lies.

"May I suggest, young man, that if you're going to appropriate someone else's name, you choose a person who's a little more likable?"

I surrendered utterly and unconditionally. Mrs. Rogers's porch was my Appomattox Court House. I bowed my head. "How did you know?"

"What I did not tell you earlier is that I was a third-grade teacher at General Lew Wallace Elementary School for thirty-four years. I can spot a boy who's telling a lie even before the words are out of his mouth. Frankly, I've seen eight-year-olds who lie more convincingly than you. And Carlotta Lane and I took teacher training together at the Normal School and have kept in touch all these years. I've visited Paradise many times."

She handed back my Bible. "I could call the police right now and have you arrested for impersonating someone else and taking dimes from old ladies, not that the police ever come to this part of town. Not these days. Instead, perhaps you would like to tell me your story – the real one. I have lots of time with little to do except wait for the mail and talk to strangers. Let's start with who are you and what do you really want?"

"Like Scheherazade," I muttered to myself.

"Precisely," she said. "Tell me a good-enough story, and I'll let you live for another day, so to speak. I'm impressed. You obviously have some education."

"Yes, ma'am, two years at the Muncie State Teachers College that used to be the Normal School."

"Go on."

I gave in. I told her my real name, where I was from, my line of work and how much I hated Francis Rumsey. I told her what had brought me to Hastings Street and the encounter I had with the man with the concrete blocks. I may have mentioned Adele once or twice or three times. I offered to show her my driver's license, but she patted my knee and, with a twinkle in her eye, said that she believed me. A piece of paper from the State of Indiana was not going to make any difference to her.

And then I listened. She had quite a story to tell about her little neck of the woods – names, dates, people, places. Barney O'Malley had been right, in spades.

CHAPTER 20

Saturday, July 15, 1933

I awakened to a sunny Saturday with nothing much to do. I decided it was time to bite the bullet and have a serious talk with Ted Thompson whether he wanted to talk to me or not. Besides, I had heard there was a lot of traffic on his road these days. People driving by who were strangers to Thompson's neighbors. Flashy cars, out-of-state license plates, all times of the day and night, people said. Things like that got noticed. God bless gossip.

A personal inventory revealed that my pounding head and the assorted aches and pains had reduced from a boil to an annoying simmer. All my body parts moved with only minimal creaks and squeaks. I predicted a good and fruitful day ahead. There was only so much *nothing* I could abide. Give me work, any day.

After a leisurely bath, eggs, toast and a pint of strong, strong black coffee, I would be prepared to face a potentially unpleasant task. It was only ten o'clock, plenty of time to visit Thompson and see Adele later. Besides, Adele had ordered me out of the house for the day. She planned to decorate, sort, organize, put away. She had informed me, firmly, that I would be in the way.

If my hunch was correct, the Thompson place might be another stop on the Gangland Underground Railroad.

Ted Thompson's two-hundred-eighty-acre farm in Madison Township was about ten or twelve miles southeast of town. His house stood back from the road about fifty yards down a rutted, weed-infested lane. I had driven past his place more times than I could count but had never stopped in to visit. Rural Route 6 was a barely improved dirt road so narrow that automobiles had to pull off to the berm, and drivers prayed they would not tip into the ditch. They had to do this to allow tractors, harvesters and farm wagons to pass. It was an unwritten rule of rural life rarely violated: farmers possessed the right of way. And farmers were the economic lifeblood of the county. Besides, it was the courteous thing to do, and we prided ourselves on being thoughtful and polite. That is, until we were not.

The road eventually angled to meet the state highway that led to Muncie. The road weaved through the midpoint of Lincoln County's oil-and-gas boom of the turn of the century. Almost every other field still sported an oil pump. If you squinted, a pumper looked a bit like a dinosaur skeleton with its head slowly lifting and falling in a steady rhythm. The boom had been thirty years earlier. Today, most wells produced one or two barrels a week, at best.

Ted Thompson might not have been so cash-poor if his grandfather, Dale, had not been such a self-righteous, single-minded, unbending, misbegotten, short-sighted bastard. The salesmen, the oil prospectors, the drillers all had come to Dale's front door with hats and wads of folding money in their hands. They skedaddled after Dale poked a 12-gauge in their faces and told them to get off his land *now* if they wanted to live to see the next day. Or so the stories go. "I don't want those men and their dirty, noisy machinery in my fields, trampling my crops. I don't believe their promises, and I don't trust their smiles. This oil-and-gas thing is a flash in the pan, anyway," he said. Or words to that effect. With added expletives. And gunshots.

Dale's stubborn ferocity could not protect him from disease. He was in his eighties when he was struck down by a fever. Ted's father, Kirby, was badly mauled by a runaway tractor in 1926 and slowly wasted away. After Kirby died, Ted took over a property that had been neglected for years and was just starting to make a go of it again when the Depression and the baby's sickness drained his resources.

The farm occupied good bottom land for crops. Fifteen or twenty acres of woods produced firewood to heat the house and fuel the cook stove, plus a little lumber for a cash sale now and then. But there was not much joy there to plump the Thompson family purse. It was the Depression, and there had been no more than a dozen new houses built in Paradise since the 1929 Crash. There was not much call for lumber, these days. The farm had all the expected things – pasture for a couple of cows and some runty pigs, chickens for eggs and the frying pan, a large garden and a family cemetery on a low rise near the house. This farm was not particularly remarkable, but it meant everything to Thompson and his family. Ted would have punched me if he had heard me say this, but I pitied him. All that work, all that tradition, all that hope – and all of it snatched away after Rumsey snared him in the land-grab scheme.

I had just started to ease back onto the roadway after moving to the side to allow a horse-drawn cart to pass from the opposite direction, when I heard honking behind me. I swerved to the right just in time to avoid being side-swiped by a snazzy yellow Stutz with Illinois license plates and two men in the front seat. Thompson's place was about half a mile ahead of me on the left. I saw the yellow car turn into Thompson's lane. This was an interesting, if unexpected, development, I thought. Rather than turn in behind them, I kept going. I knew there was a road used now and then by hunters and loggers about two-hundred yards beyond, so I pulled in there and parked out of sight of the road. What now?

I was wearing my second-best suit. I folded the jacket and placed it on the seat. I started to take the car keys but decided to leave them in the ignition in case someone wanted access and needed to move the car. I figured if I cut through the woods, then skirted Thompson's open field by hugging the fence rows, I could make it to his place unseen. What I would do then was anybody's guess.

I made it to the top of the low ridge above Thompson's house by wriggling through thick underbrush. With my belly button pressed into the earth, I was almost completely concealed by a thorny bush, but I was only twenty feet from the house's front door. I could see and hear perfectly. The patch of ground that passed for a lawn held four automobiles – the yellow car that had passed me, two others I did not recognize and the well-waxed and shined Plymouth I knew belonged to Lawrence Farrell, one of Paradise's six lawyers. Why we needed that many lawyers, was anybody's guess. Five men, all strangers to me, were working in the Thompson family graveyard and passing a bottle back and forth. I had caught Farrell and Ted Thompson in mid-conversation.

"I'm sorry for you, uh, situation, Mr. Thompson, truly I am. But there's nothing I can do at this point. The law is an unkind mistress."

They stood at Thompson's front door. A toothpick-thin girl of five or six clung to big Ted Thompson, her arms wrapped tightly around him and her head resting on his hip. I was embarrassed. As a reporter, I had asked awkward and rude questions of all sorts of folks from stick-up men to society matrons to politicians of all stripes but eavesdropping on this conversation gave snooping a bad name. I willed a buzzing fly to move away and take his cousin, a mosquito, with him.

"It ain't right Mr. Farrell, it just ain't right." Thompson, a man given to parsimonious use of words, was positively talkative. His eyes cut to the men digging, sweating and drinking in the family's once-tidy cemetery. "This is my family's land, my land."

Farrell patted the air and made soothing noises. "As I said, I'm sorry, but there is nothing I can do. You might not own the land, now, but you're still here." Farrell seemed embarrassed, too.

"Yeah, somebody else said something like that not too long ago."

I suspected that somebody might have been me.

"See, I'm not the only one who thinks that way."

"Lord Almighty, don't you get it?" Thompson gulped in some air. "This here's my family's land, been so since great-grandpa Hector Thompson moved to Lincoln County from someplace in Pennsylvania. He was only nineteen years old, imagine that? And he made this farm what it is. That was in eighteen and thirty-seven. It says so in the front of our Bible, where all the children's names are written, when they were born and when they died. I don't give a damn what that thieving bastard Rumsey says, it ain't right."

"I'm sorry, Poppy," the little girl said, and squeezed her father tighter.

"Ain't your fault, Carol Ann. Go find your momma."

She stuck out her chin, a tiny feminine version of her father's, and gave Farrell a stare cold enough to stop a rampaging bull in its tracks. "Don't you dare be mean to my Poppy. Don't you dare," she said.

"Come, now. Shoo, little girl." Thompson watched her disappear into the house. "I'm --"

"Not to worry, Mr. Thompson, she's just a child and she loves her father. But we can't change the facts. You signed papers. You received cash and a decent funeral for the baby you lost. That, as you know very well, was in exchange for your land here. You're a tenant, now. There's nothing more I can do. There's nothing anyone can do." He thought for a moment. "I suppose you could try to buy this place back from the Chicago property firm that bought it. That's the only recourse I see."

"Buy it back? With what – my good looks? Hell's bells, I've got those boarders over there in the grave plot who don't pay me but a dollar or two, if they happen to remember. Where would I get the cash? Answer me that."

Farrell struggled and failed to find an answer.

"That's the way it is, I guess." Ted Thompson was not the kind of man given to weeping in public. He maintained a demeanor as stony as the granite slabs in the plot on the little hill on the other side of the lane. He looked Farrell straight in the eye. "Mark my words. I'll get it back. This is my place. I'll get it back, if it's the last thing I ever do. Tell Rumsey that. Tell those people in Chicago. I'll get my land back one way or another, and I'll get Rumsey, too, if that's what it takes."

"Threats, Mr. Thompson, are never a good idea. I will forget I heard that. I suggest you do, too."

Thompson did not reply; he had run out of words. Both men stood silent for a moment, then Farrell tipped his hat and stepped back to his Plymouth and drove off.

The defeated farmer sagged against the doorframe and watched until Farrell's car vanished in the humidity-laden haze. I dug my elbows into the soil and started to wriggle backward, but laughter from Thompson's boarders, if that was what they really were, caught my attention.

I could not make out everything they said, but what I did hear was disturbing.

"Poppy. Oh, Poppy." One affected a high-pitched voice. Getting a cheap laugh out of a child's distress was contemptible.

Another said "body." It could have been "hobby," or "poppy" again, but I did not think so.

"Too much work for me," one said clearly.

"Pass . . . you . . . damn . . . hold . . . bottle . . . son of a bitch." Some of the speaker's words were blown away by the breeze or lost in another spasm of laughter.

Suddenly, the man sitting closest to the lane stood, every fiber in his body alert. He swung his eyes from side to side, searching for something. He shushed his companions and gestured to where I was concealed. The others looked my way, too. I froze. Had I been seen? Questions cascaded through my brain: How far was it to my car? Could I make it there before the men caught up with me? How much time did I have? Did they have weapons?

"Look! Over there! In front of that big tree." The standing man took two steps, leaned over the ragged fence surrounding the grave plot and stared intently with one hand shading his eyes. I prayed he had not visited the eye doctor in a long, long time.

The brush rustled behind me. Something cold bumped against my cheek, and I jerked involuntarily. I twisted to the side and saw an old, grey-muzzled, spotted dog. "Shoo! Go away! Go, go!" I whispered. The dog stared at me dumbly for a long moment, then shook himself. What seemed like a year later, the dog came to the realization that I was not a threat, did not have any treats, and was not going to play with him. He trotted down the hill and turned to the house. The dog scratched at the door a couple of times, and little Carol Ann let him in.

The men instantly relaxed and more laughter ensued. I heard more fragments. "Dog . . . gun . . . shoot . . . damn . . . shows you, don't it . . . you worry." The standing man turned back to his companions, but I distinctly heard him shout, "Shut up. Just shut up!"

I had an opportunity while they were distracted, and I took it. I cautiously slid backward until I reached the tree line. I was a good thing I had worn old clothes. I had not counted on playing Boy Scout, sleuth and cowboys-and-Indians in the same day. An old, drooping elm and waist-high weeds provided ample cover. Twigs and thorns had pierced my palms, but the bleeding was minimal. One trouser knee was torn beyond repair and sweat had glued bits of leaves and dirt to my skin. The itching was nearly as intolerable as when I endured chicken pox as a kid. Straightening my spine to vertical sent a jolt of pain through the lump on my skull. It half-blinded me for a second, but it also cleared my brain. I realized that Farrell, too, may be involved in this – whatever *this* was. Not welcome news. I had known Farrell since I was in short pants. What now?

Sally Thompson, Ted's wife, came out of the house, wiping her hands on her apron, and shouted something. The men in the graveyard threw down their shovels. I checked my watch. It was quarter past noon. Dinner time.

CHAPTER 21

The Telegraph-Register
Wednesday, July 19, 1933

BANK ROBBERY!

Members of feared Dillinger Gang suspected in daring daylight heist of city's Lincoln National Bank

10 hostages taken on thrill ride, thousands of dollars snatched, one injured in well-planned job

Fake movie scout revealed as criminal mastermind Homer Van Meter of Fort Wayne

By Walter G. Pratt

The previous days had passed in a happy blur. My black eye had faded to a manageable yellow with green margins. I had completed all my pre-wedding assignments – new suit picked up, two suits and three shirts ordered to replace the ones I had ruined, rings collected, house and yard made presentable, car washed and partially packed for the honeymoon trip, haircut, study somewhat organized and Ocie placed in charge of checking the roof and making other repairs as needed.

I was not happy with having been shown to be a gullible fool. Homer Van Meter, whom I paraded all over Lincoln County as the movie scout Homer Vaughn, had tricked me into believing his cockamamie story about filming a movie in Paradise. My old copy desk chief had drilled the words *verify, verify, verify* into my ears, but I had ignored that advice. My embarrassment was topic number one in every barber shop, lodge meeting and cafe in a thirty-mile radius. Van Meter would have made a successful used-car salesman. He certainly sold me. All Jeff Heston said in that mild way of his was, "Don't let this happen, again."

Lightning flashed close by, followed by a crash of thunder. A passing cold front announced welcome relief from the high temperatures and much needed rain. I was very happy about that. The only better thing on the weather horizon would be if we had sunshine and less humidity for the wedding on Saturday.

I was also fairly happy with the way the robbery story had turned out. I was not at all happy with the man standing in front of my desk.

Federal Bureau of Investigation Special Agent George McMaster dropped The Telegraph-Register issue with the bank robbery story on my desk.

"Welcome to Paradise," I said.

"This isn't a social call," McMaster said.

"May I quote you?"

"Don't be a smart ass."

"Ah, but that's my stock in trade," I said.

"Not funny," he said, then pointed to the headline. "This isn't funny, either."

"No. You're absolutely correct – not funny at all."

I fingered the cryptic telegram Barney O'Malley had sent to me yesterday afternoon – EXPECT A VISITOR STOP TREAT HIM NICE STOP. I slid it into my center desk drawer.

"Take a seat. Let's start over."

I survived McMaster's adamantine stare.

"I'll play nice," I promised, and silently blessed Barney O'Malley for the heads-up. I only wished Barney had specified who *him* was so I could have been better prepared. Oh, well – coulda, woulda, shoulda.

McMaster settled into my visitor's chair, played with his watch fob, shook the rain drops from his hat and took a deep breath. It was obvious that he was working himself up to something.

"I need your help," he finally said.

"Sure. Anything. If I can."

"Your pal O'Malley filled me in on what you guys have been working on."

"Which *what* are you referring to?" It could have been one of a half dozen *whats* – the floating casino, Dixie's murder, the mysterious grave, the Gangland Underground Railroad, the bank robbery, the crooked land scheme, and other frauds and misdeeds too numerous to mention.

"Which?" McMaster actually appeared disconcerted, an uncommon experience for him.

The front door of the newsroom was darkened, not by storm clouds, but by the appearance of a large man carrying a bulging paper sack. He consulted a piece of paper but seemed uncertain of his bearings. No, it could not be *him*, I thought to myself.

"Excuse me," I said to McMasters, "I'll be right back. Finish reading the story."

"Don't take all day. This is urgent federal business."

"Keep your shirt on. This is newspaper business. Won't take a minute." Delores Mackey typed like a dog after a bloody bone, oblivious to the rest of the newsroom. Her head was buried in the wedding and engagement announcements that would appear in the Saturday edition. I pounded on her desk. "Hey, Delores, there's some guy standing in the entrance. He looks lost. Could you see what he wants? I'm kind of tied up."

"You're always tied up, Pratt. Don't try to shovel him off on me. You saw him first; you take care of him. I'm busy," she said.

"Miss?" McMaster spoke up. "Would you mind, please? I'm here on behalf of the United States government. I must speak with Mr. Pratt immediately."

"Oh, well, I guess that's different," Delores said. She let out a theatrical sigh and threw down her pencil. "You owe me, Walter."

Delores and the stranger chatted quietly for a minute or two. She nodded her head, looked at the slip of paper the man carried, and kept cutting her eyes back to me.

"Sorry, Walter, but that man insists that he speak with you. Only with you," Delores said. "Before you ask – no, he won't talk to anyone else. This is something personal, I think. And you still owe me." She punctuated that sentence with a hard poke in my shoulder.

I apologized to McMaster and said I would be right back.

The stranger in the doorway looked at me, then took another look at the note to make sure he had the name correct. "I was told to come here, come to the newspaper. I'm looking for someone called Walter Pratt. You know where I can find him? He's expecting me."

I shooed him back into the hallway out of McMaster's direct line of sight.

Big Jim Rypanski, for that was who he turned out to be, lived up to his billing. He was big – broad-shouldered, maybe six-foot-three and two-hundred-and-thirty pounds, all of it muscle. At a year or two shy of thirty, and with the little wave in his slicked-back blond hair, he resembled a beefier, less self-aware version of a young F. Scott Fitzgerald. As Adele remarked after she met him the first time, "Many men are handsome, but only a very few men are beautiful. Mr. Rypanski is a beautiful man." I took her word for it.

I did not have time to talk to him at that moment, and I certainly did not want McMaster to connect Rypanski to me. Damn Barney! Why couldn't he have just said whom to expect? I gave Big Jim directions to the Daisy Diner and told him I would meet him in half an hour. Rypanski shelved for the moment meant I still had to deal with McMasters.

And McMaster was growing more irritable by the second.

"Where were we?" I asked.

"*I* was trying to solve an important crime. *You* were farting around."

"Point taken, Agent McMaster. I'll help if I can. And this conversation is on the record. Is that understood."

"Okay, unless I say otherwise. Is *that* understood?"

We agreed to agree.

It turned out McMaster was investigating the Gangland Underground Railroad hoping to locate the gangsters' hiding places, coordinate a massive raid, and arrest as many as he could in one fell swoop. I gave him what I could, leaving out Ted Thompson's farm. McMaster was especially interested in the Muncie location, which he admitted had not been on his list. I told him to get in touch with Mrs. Alberta Rogers. I knew that tough but thoroughly delightful lady would be very happy to get rid of her unpleasant neighbors.

"What about this undertaker from your charming little town. O'Malley mentioned he might be connected to our investigation? Your reporter friend hinted that you have a history with him. We've been keeping an eye on that mortuary school for quite some time. From what we've learned, your friend Mr. Rumsey is somehow tied to the activities of Benny the Nose and his gang."

"Ah."

"Ah, what? Specifically."

"Ah, he's a piece of work is our Francis Tolliver Rumsey. And he's not my friend. Not by a long shot."

"Then what is he?"

"A lying, scheming crook."

I told McMaster most of what I knew about Rumsey – the suspicious burials, the cemetery outside Chicago, the land deals in Lincoln County that tied him to certain Chicago real estate transactions. I left out Dixie Lee and Big Jim Rypanski because I could not yet determine how they fit into the big picture.

"Is that enough to get you started?"

"It'll do, for now," McMaster conceded. "Stay in touch. Call or wire me immediately if you hear anything else."

"Yes, sir, always happy to help," I said as humbly as I could manage. I am a good little Boy Scout.

McMaster growled some words that might have included *thank you* and headed back to Chicago. I hoped he would stay far from Paradise and me. That was one unexpected visitor taken care of, now onward to the second.

Herb Daishell made a what's-going-on gesture with raised eyebrows and nodded toward my table in the window where Big Jim Rypanski sat huddled over a cup of coffee.

"Hello, Jim. May I call you Jim? Thanks for waiting."

"Sure. No problem." He fiddled with the cream and sugar containers on the table. "Uh, Mr. Pratt, I ain't stupid or nothing, but I still don't know why O'Malley sent me here to Indiana to talk to you. He even bought my train ticket. He said it was important, and it might be a good idea for me to get out of the city for a while. Cops, uh, you know what I mean?"

"Don't worry about that. Nobody in Paradise needs to know about your past. That was then; this is now."

"But I can't stay long," Rypanski insisted. "I gotta get back. My wife is missing. Nobody's seen her or her twin sister for months."

"I know where Dixie is. I'm sorry, Jim, but I don't have good news."

The big man crumbled before my eyes. I told him about the murder as gently as humanly possible. It did not seem to be that much of a surprise to him. I surmised that he already suspected the worst. I offered to take him to the cemetery to show him Dixie Lee's grave.

Weeds and grass had begun to colonize the heaped dirt over her burial place. Big Jim's tears watered them.

My mind whirled. An identical twin sister named Trixie? That was new news. It also explained why there were two graves, as well as a possible explanation as to how the mortuary school gangsters, assuming they were the people responsible for the sister's death, and Francis Rumsey had mixed up their identities.

I settled Rypanski and his one suitcase at the Travelers Hotel. He got the room two doors down from mine on the third floor. It was only four o'clock. We had time for a few other disagreeable tasks.

First stop – Sheriff Hoyt Peterson's office. Rypanski paled a bit when he saw that he was entering a jail, but squared his shoulders and marched in. It did not take long for him to identify Dixie Lee's effects – the purse, the distinctive yellow dress.

"I'm sorry for your loss, Mr. Rypanski," the sheriff said. "But I need to ask you: do you know why your late wife come here to Paradise? You got any idea who mighta wanted to kill her – and why?"

"No," Rypanski said. "She was real sweet, real pretty. Everybody liked her."

The sheriff dumped out the contents of her purse on his desk. "Any of this mean anything to you?" he asked.

"Ain't nothing to me," Rypanski said. "Just purse junk. Lady stuff."

When the sheriff turned his back for a moment, I palmed one of the slips of paper.

"I'm kinda tired, Mr. Pratt. It's been a long day – the train, Dixie, you know."

"Sorry, Jim, but we have just one more place to visit."

We caught Mort Walker at the train depot sweeping the platform before closing for the night.

"Hey, Mort, got a minute?"

"Sure, Walter, what's up?"

I showed the station master the slip of paper I had purloined.

"Yeah, that's one of ours. It's under lock and key in the storage room," Walker said. "I've had to move it several times. You picking it up? Hope so. I could sure use the room."

Walker brought out the valise with the matching half of the receipt still intact, had Rypanski sign for it and handed it over.

I had a good idea what was in it.

It turned out I was right.

Big Jim opened the valise and let out a grunt of shock and surprise. "What the fucking Hell?"

The valise was stuffed with cash – about $40,000 worth, I guessed.

I told Rypanski about the missing money that had been stolen from the floating casino.

"I don't want no part of this," Rypanski said. "This money killed my Dixie. Don't belong to me, anyhow. You take it."

He shoved the valise onto my lap.

"Are you sure about this? That's a lot of money. You could have a good life. Start over."

He buried his face in his hands. "No way. No."

"Tell you what – I'll hold onto it for a little while. If or when you want it, you can have it back. That okay with you?"

He shook his head again. "Keep it, just keep it."

I pulled out five-hundred dollars in twenties and tens and folded them into his breast pocket. "You're going to need some walking-around money. You'll need to pay for rent, food, whatever you need so you can get back on your feet. Think of this as Dixie's last gift to you."

He stared straight ahead with tears streaming down his cheeks once again.

CHAPTER 22

Friday, July 21, 1933

At 3 o'clock Friday afternoon, I was counting the hours before my wedding – twenty to be exact. The paper already had gone to press, and I had nothing to do, except hold the fort. I was thinking more about the joys and responsibilities of married life than news when the phone rang. I let Hattie Webster pick it up. Adele had given me another list. This drill was rapidly turning into a customary practice – something else to get used to. I planned to sneak out of work early to get my Sunday suit from the dry cleaners. I had to stop at the bank. I needed cash to pay the reverend, buy our train tickets, honeymoon expenses and –

"Mr. Pratt." Hattie Webster's shrill was the vocal equivalent of bumping into a shark in a swimming pool – absolutely guaranteed to jerk you back to reality pretty damn quick. "Mr. Pratt! Pick up the line, please. Central says somebody wants to talk to the newspaper. It's urgent. Since Mr. Heston isn't here, you'll have to take the call."

Delores Mackey leaned across her desk and whispered, "Better you than me."

All I needed right now was a call from Mrs. Biddy Fussbudget, and there were at least a dozen of that ilk who called regularly. It was always urgent. Their stories usually went something like this: Mittens the cat had gotten herself trapped at the top of the neighbor's maple-apple-oak-mulberry tree, and would I please, please bring a photographer and tell the story of Mittens' harrowing ordeal?

Today, it was not one of the biddies.

"Jeff?"

"No, Herb, it's Walter."

"Walt, thank God! Sorry to bother you, but there's something fishy going on. By the way, Madonna and I will be there tomorrow with bells on."

"Thanks. But what's going on? Why the call?"

"I'd go myself, but Reba Witherspoon dropped a glass and cut her hand pretty bad. I've got to run her over to Doc Joplin's place to get a couple of stitches."

"Herb, slow down. Go where? Do what?"

"Well, maybe it's nothing, but – "

"Herb, just spit it out. I've got a million things to do before eleven o'clock tomorrow morning."

"Yes. Well. There's this smell. I wouldn't bother you, but I've smelled this before. In France, in the trenches. It's pretty bad."

And would I come over and find out what was going on?

I yelled loud enough to Hattie to hear, "I won't be back."

She looked at me sternly over the rims of her spectacles and waggled a finger. "Be sure to stand up straight tomorrow. It's disrespectful when a bridegroom slumps. I'll be watching." She may even have offered a hint of a smile. I would think about that later.

Delores Mackey gave me a thumbs-up. "See you tomorrow. Don't be late."

It was ninety-three degrees in the shade, the sky was a moldy green and a thunderstorm threatened from the west. I tried to ignore the sweat trickling down my neck as I followed Herb Daishell's tip and my nose to the alley between Rumsey's Funeral Parlor and Mortuary and the Daisy Diner. A sign reading "Closed – Please Call Again" h hung on Rumsey's front door since Tuesday. Odd, maybe, but I had not given it much thought. Only one person – Flossie Williams from Damascus, a wide spot in the road eight miles south of town – had died of natural causes in the past week, and the Williams family always used Miller's establishment.

That did not count Ralph Gardner, of course. But his death had been far from natural.

As soon as I took five steps into the alley, I knew what Herb had meant about the odor. Imagine a dead mouse in the wall multiplied by twenty thousand. The clouds of flies made the shadows noisy as well as darker – a live, buzzy storm cloud.

I sat on one of the Daisy Diner's ash cans and lit a cigar, party to combat the aroma and partly to gain some time. I needed to figure out what to do. I could call the city cops, but Chief Thurl Gaskins was about as much help in an emergency as a knife at a gunfight. I would not trust Officer Snooky Slack to be able to find his shoes if they were on his feet. Sheriff Hoyt Peterson was a strong possibility, but who knew where he was or how long it would take before he got here. Jeff Heston was out of the office on a secret mission that I suspected had something to do with the wedding. Herb Daishell was at Doc's place. That left me.

Doing nothing was a valid choice, just not my style. Besides, this promised to be one Hell of a story.

I had walked through this alley dozens, maybe hundreds, of times, but never really paid it much attention. It was just wide enough for Rumsey's hearse to pass without scraping the garbage cans lining both sides. A few weeds poked though the brick pavers. Except for the kitchen door, the diner's wall was blank clapboard. It needed a coat of paint. Rumsey's wall was solid brick, except for the last twenty feet. Attached to the main building was a wooden garage and what I guessed was the entrance to the upstairs living quarters. Thunder boomed, and a few seconds later a burst of blessedly cold rain bit into my face. I hugged the wall under Rumsey's eaves to avoid what was rapidly becoming a downpour. Three tall, narrow windows overlooked the alley at the rear of the original, brick portion of the building. They were dark and appeared shut tight.

I was not alone. Ginger Binchley crawled out from behind one of the diner's garbage cans with a half-eaten slice of pie in his hand. Herb often put out leftover food for Binchley, a homeless man and the town drunk. Most people simply ignored him. He was harmless. He took one look at me and scurried away.

Rumsey's trash cans provided a convenient step up. I scraped the palms of my hands on the brick, but I managed to hoist myself high enough to peer into the first window. But I could not see a damn thing. The windows were shut tight and appeared to be covered by heavy black drapes.

The smell was worse next to the window. A strange sound, a loud, insistent hum, came from inside Rumsey's. I cocked my head and listened. I could not place the noise, but it sounded a bit like the buzz or crackle of an electrical appliance on the fritz.

I found a wooden box in the alley and picked up a loose paving brick. Placing the box on top of the garbage can boosted me high enough so that my shoulders and chest cleared the window sill. I checked to make sure nobody could see me, then heaved the brick through the window. Fortunately, the drapes deadened the sound of the breaking glass.

Once I crawled inside, the buzzing became louder and more intense, and the smell was worse. The handkerchief I clapped over my mouth and nose did little to lessen the stench. It took all my willpower to keep from gagging. No lights were on, and the interior of the building was as dark as the bottom of an abandoned coal mine. I groped along the wall to my left, bumping into tables and chairs, in the process knocking over something that made a metallic clatter when it hit the floor. Eventually, my fingers touched a light switch, and I pushed the buttons.

The room flooded with strong electric light from the high-intensity fixtures in the ceiling. I guessed it was Rumsey's embalming room. Along the rear wall, medical-looking equipment dominated the stripped-down décor – hoses, industrial-sized drums of chemicals, cosmetic supplies. Saws, knives and other tools of one sort or another cluttered shelves along the wall. Where I stood, there was a desk piled high with papers, what looked like a freight elevator with a closed metal screen covering the opening and a wooden door a little farther along. This appeared to be the common wall shared with the pretty parts of the funeral parlor. Opposite me, the third wall held sinks and a wringer washer. The windows occupied the fourth wall. Three metal tables stood in the center of the room. They were almost invisible through the cloud of black flies that swirled over them. I grabbed a sheet from a stack near the door and waved it to scatter the flies.

The meatloaf I ate for lunch landed on the floor. I stared. Three naked, bloated corpses, their features distorted by death and decay, were laid out on the tables. One I recognized as old Jed Bailey, who had gone downhill fast in the weeks since he lost his Ruby and his farm. The second was a youngish man who had a large hole in his chest. I had never seen him before, I think. It was that difficult to tell. There was no doubt as to the last. It was Mrs. Francis Tolliver Rumsey. Louise Rumsey had two bullet holes in her chest and one in her face. The bullet to the face was for spite, Doc Joplin said later. That shot came post mortem, well after the first two bullets had done their work.

Louise Rumsey was a stout middle-aged lady with the intelligence of the average rabbit and the sex appeal of a cast-iron stove, but she had not deserved to die like this. No one did.

"Nooooooooo!"

This wail cut through my stunned stupor. I heard two thumps. When I turned toward the door, Rumsey stood there with a shocked expression on his face, and a valise and a large suitcase at his feet. I can still see the him in my mind's eye. The man slowly turned to me and it took a second or two for the recognition to register.

"You? You! You again. No. No. No. You're not supposed to be in here. Nobody's supposed to be in here. No. No. No." He kept saying *no-no-no* over and over as if the sing-song syllables would make me – and the three corpses -- magically disappear. "This isn't what it looks like."

"Not what it looks like? Really, Francis? *Really?*" I gestured at the bodies. "Those aren't mosquito bites. Those are bullet holes."

"Yes. I guess so. They might be that."

Rumsey's entire body was taut, as if he were frozen in place while simultaneously wishing himself somewhere else. Twenty seconds ticked by like twenty hours. Then he swung his gaze to me, and the filmy, far-away look in his eyes cleared. This abrupt shift in attitude was accompanied by a growl that began in his gut and twisted past his vocal cords as a piercing shriek.

Before I could move, react, or speak, Rumsey charged. Head down, one hand bunched into a fist, the other hand wrapped around a small pistol, Rumsey rushed straight at me. He was not young and he was not in tip-top physical condition, but he was strong and fueled by bullish anger and the primal need for self-preservation. And he was only six feet away.

I stood near the center of the room in the midst of the embalming tables. I carefully scooted step by slow step to my left, trying not to make any sudden moves. I had thought to make it to the broken window and jump. But Rumsey must have seen my eyes dart in that direction, and he slipped over to cut off that escape route. It appeared as though he had completely forgotten the gun in his hand. Instead, Rumsey seemed intent on crushing me with his bare hands. Perhaps he wanted a very personal, skin-on-skin act of revenge for all the ill-intentions and evil acts my entire clan and I had inflicted upon him. It did not matter whether those acts were actual or imagined. To him, they were real.

I made it to the wall and slipped along it while trying to maintain eye contact with Rumsey. My hand touched a small table with some objects on it. I did not even look. I just picked up anything I could touch and threw them at him – an empty jar, an enamel basin, an ashtray, a small table radio. Rumsey bobbed and weaved, and none of my impromptu weapons touched him. He lowered his head for another charge, but after just two steps, his foot slipped in the greenish-yellow liquid that had spilled from the container I knocked over when I first entered Rumsey's embalming room. The fall jarred the gun out of his hand, and it skittered across the floor, stopping eventually in the open doorway, far away from both of us.

This opened a chance for me, a small chance, but a small chance was better than no chance at all.

"C'mon, Francis. Let's stop this nonsense. We're both grown men. We can come up with a solution to this mess that's good for both of us," I said. "Let's just walk out of here. And we can forget everything that's happened." I gestured to the three corpses.

He grunted and growled like a cornered beast, shook his head from side to side and glared. Spittle flew from his mouth as he spoke.

"Forget? *Nonononononono!* I hate you. I hate all the Pratts. And everything you stand for. Growing up on the right side of the tracks, never a worry about where your next meal was coming from. You think you're better than me. Your mother did, too. Well, I'm smarter than you, and I have a lot more money than you'll ever see." *Hahahahahaha.* He laughed a crazy, out-of-control laugh that I had believed only bad actors in bad movies laughed.

Then he stooped and picked up a knife that had fallen to the floor during our mêlée. It must have been a tool he used in his embalming, but I did not give a fart about its intended purpose. I knew Rumsey's sole objective was to kill me with it. It was a death tool, pure and simple. It was bigger than a butcher knife but smaller than a machete, and light glinted off the sharply honed edge. We circled halfway around the room, and all the while Rumsey held that knife steady and firm in his hand. Rumsey maintained a grim silence that was more frightening than his previous rant.

I heard a gasp from the doorway behind me. I turned, and while I was momentarily distracted, Rumsey lunged.

Bang! Pause. *Bang! Bang! Bang!*

Rumsey halted mid-step while a look of utter surprise spread across his doughy face, then tilted and slowly slumped to the floor. Two of the four shots had hit him, one to the heart and the other in the neck. He was dead. After all the death and drama and violence, now he was only a fresh meal for the flies.

Behind me, the sound of hoarse, ragged breathing filled the aural space left after the gunshot echoes receded. Julia Porter was pale and swaying from shock. Rumsey's gun was still in her right hand and her bucket of cleaning supplies was in her left. I, too, felt shocky, limp and dizzy, with the adrenaline streaming out of my system.

"Julia, are you okay?"

She shook herself out of her trance and slowly turned to me.

"Am I okay? Yes, I think so. A little shaky, maybe. I hated that bastard. I'm not sorry he's dead." She looked at me, then at what was left of Rumsey. "He *is* dead, isn't he? Please tell me he's dead."

"Yes."

"Are you alright? It looked like he was trying to kill you."

"I'm okay, and, yes, he was trying to kill me."

"Why?"

"Because I knew his secrets."

"Good." She closed her eyes for a moment, then straightened her spine to stand tall. "People call Johnnie a bastard, but Rumsey was the real bastard. I'm glad he's dead. I think I'm happier right now than I have been my whole life. Good riddance. I'm glad he's dead."

Shouts from the street interrupted Julia. Passersby must have heard the shots. I took the gun out of her hand and tossed it next to Rumsey.

"C'mon, Julia, we've got to get out of here." She continued to stare impassively at Rumsey's corpse.

"Now! Take your bucket. We have to make it look like you were never here."

I started to shove her toward the doorway and, in the process, managed to stumble over Rumsey's valise. The clasp popped open to display not pajamas or a shaving kit or underwear, but money, lots of money, bound tightly with rubber bands. On impulse, I picked it up, grasped Julia's arm and hustled her down the stairs.

"Julia, you know this place. Is there a rear door? An exit we could use without being seen?"

She nodded.

"Show me. Now."

"This way. Through the garage," she said.

Back outside, the storm had passed and we stood in fresh cool air and sunshine, I was happy to escape the stench of gunpower and death. I heard sirens, but all the commotion seemed to be at the front of Rumsey's funeral parlor. I remembered to close the valise before I led Julia over to Doc Joplin's back door. He asked no questions. A quick glance betrayed we were shaken, disheveled and looking nervously over our shoulders. In other words, we needed help. Julia trembled like a plucked string, and her eyes revealed she had begun to awaken to the knowledge that she had just killed a fellow human being, albeit a despicable one. She gripped my arm so tightly I knew I would have bruises. Doc gave her half a sleeping pill and ordered her to lie down on the sofa in his office. He handed me a restorative stiff drink from his precious stock of bootleg genuine Canadian. I took him aside and gave him the condensed version of the afternoon's events. He agreed to hold Rumsey's valise for safekeeping. I also told him to expect a phone call from the local constabulary.

"Don't let her talk to anybody. I need a little time to figure out a way to keep her out of this mess. Take her home with you and keep her for the night. If you can, stop by her house and pick up Johnnie on your way. The county prosecutor dropped all the charges yesterday, so he's home, now. I know this is a lot to ask, but --"

"Not a problem. We'll take care of her. If we need a cover story, we'll say she came out to help with a massive house cleaning. But it might not come to that. We'll see." He laid a gentle hand on my shoulder and looked me straight in the eye. "And how are you holding up? Do I need to worry about you, too?"

"I'm doing okay, considering a raving maniac tried to kill me, and a man died at my feet. I'll be all right, really," I said, then added, "I think."

Doc shook his head, not entirely convinced. The phone rang. "Told you," I said. He winced.

I glanced at my watch. The events in that gory crucible – what had happened to Julia, to Rumsey, to me – had lasted less than a quarter of an hour. It was not yet four o'clock. And I still had things to do.

Uncle Adolphus had been right. One day I would have to choose between doing the correct, the socially acceptable thing, or answer to a higher order of correctness, make a decision to do the morally right thing. This was that day. I had already broken at least a dozen laws. If the fuzzy ideas I was thinking were realized, I would break a few more before the day was over.

The Mueller heritage won; Grandmama Pratt lost.

Doc and I hastily concocted a story that, if we were lucky and no one with the power to imprison us looked too closely, might explain the events in that embalming room. We could always fill in the details later.

Meanwhile, I had things to do and people to see.

EPILOGUE

Friday, August 24, 1934

Adele and I were married at 11 a.m., on Saturday, July 22, 1933, as planned. I might have been a little paler than I would have been otherwise, given the circumstances. I had fully expected a tongue-lashing from Hattie Webster for my slumping posture, but she just smiled and hugged me. I sagged at the front of the First Methodist Church of Paradise with Barney, Jeff and Doc standing beside me. Doc had wanted to gift-wrap me in bandages, but I refused, despite feeling as if my entire being had been reduced to the square root of zero.

Jeff was just as wrung out as I was. Neither of us had gotten a minute's sleep. We had spent all night putting the Rumsey story together, and it would appear in this afternoon's newspaper. We had more-than-a-little help from Barney O'Malley, and the bags under my Chicago friend's eyes were proof positive of the work he had put into it. The headline said it all:

KILLER REVEALED!

Francis Rumsey murdered mystery woman, committed suicide on eve of arrest

Wife, two others found dead in funeral home

'I killed Dixie,' dying undertaker confessed

Sheriff investigates Rumsey business deals; Chicago gangland connections suspected

Adele's cream-colored dress with hundreds of tiny pearls sewn all over was a corker, as promised. We honeymooned in Wisconsin and even caught a fish or two when not otherwise occupied.

Jeff Heston was right. I had found the material for my big book. The novel was not finished. I needed to change the names to protect the guilty and add a literary flourish here and there. But it was nearly done, and I was proud of it. Adele even approved of my grammar and punctuation. I admit I had to use my imagination in places, but that was only to fill in the gaps in Dixie's story. Otherwise, the narrative is factual. I checked everything I could.

Mose Truby consulted his brother railroad conductors and was able to piece together much of her movements around the Midwest during the weeks after she fled Chicago. That yellow dress was unforgettable.

Mort Walker finagled a railroad pass for me, so I was able to travel. It took months of searching, but in December, I found Dixie's mother in Hog Bend, West Virginia. It was no wonder why Dixie left home. Mrs. McGraw had not a shred of mother love. "Good riddance," she said. "Them girls was nothing but trouble."

Dixie had six brothers and a sister still at home, all with handsome faces, red hair and freckles. You could have plopped any one of them onto a street in Dublin, Ireland, and they would have been indistinguishable from the crowds surrounding them. LuEllen, at fifteen, was an underfed, unpolished ringer for her sister. I now knew how Dixie's green eyes must have looked in life.

"How far is Paradise?" LuEllen asked me with a catch in her voice. "And you seen Trixie? That's my other sister, Dixie's twin. We ain't heard from her, neither." It broke my heart to have to tell her she had lost both her sisters.

My buddies in Chicago put me in touch with a couple of gangsters – currently semi-retired courtesy of the Illinois prison system – who filled me in on what happened that night in the back room of the Cook County College of Mortuary Science. A rival gang robbed The Red-Headed League's casino and a gunfight followed. Dixie and her sister disappeared in the mêlée, along with the $42,000 in cash. Francis Rumsey was there losing money, as usual. Benny "The Nose" Green and his pals desperately tried to locate Dixie and the missing cash. Thugs from Atlantic City to Sacramento had been alerted to be on the lookout for her.

A few weeks later, Francis Rumsey spotted Dixie on his sidewalk in Paradise.

The rest of the story came out after auditors finished tidying Rumsey's estate. Francis would have been a very rich man with more than $270,000 in cash. He had cleaned out all the business and family bank accounts, sold or mortgaged every stitch of property he owned, and hauled away anything that would bring a fast buck. This pure speculation, but we think he planned to kill his wife, change his identity and skedaddle to Terra Incognita. It all was solidly premeditated.

Much has happened in Paradise and the wider world in the past year.

Herb Daishell inveigled the men's Sunday school class at the Methodist Church to chip in, and we were able to ship Dixie's fake tombstone from that bleak cemetery outside Chicago that Hans and I had visited. The Illinois authorities were not particularly cooperative, but Herb had been a supply sergeant in the World War, and he knew how to get things done. Dixie's grave in Greenlawn Memorial Cemetery was nameless no longer. Herb also got the inhabitant of that Illinois grave, whom Doc Joplin believes could be Dixie's sister, exhumed and shipped to Paradise. Dixie and Trixie were together again in the womb of the earth.

Jeff and Rosemary Heston had a baby girl the first week of May. Little Arlie was as pink as a rosebud, and Jeff was all puffed up with pride.

Adele and I have decided to wait before we start a family, but not too long. I have caught Adele standing in the doorway of our spare room just staring. That will be the baby's room. I have gone there, too, usually in the middle of the night after I have awakened from a nightmare. That happened less often, now, but often enough. It was the flies. I would hear them in the dreams that left me drenched in sweat. They choked my throat, crawled into my lungs, buzzed in my brain. I would wake with a pounding heart and with a silent scream filling my ears. Then I would pour myself a cold drink of water, or maybe something a little stronger, and visit the baby's room.

Francis Rumsey's death, and the events that led up to it, were so shocking they had made headlines as far away as New York City and San Francisco. The dailies in Cleveland, Indianapolis, Denver and Philadelphia made job offers. I turned them all down. Jeff Heston breathed a sigh of relief, gave me a ra and named me managing editor. I was performing basically the same work, except that I would have to fill in for Jeff and run things when he was out on the golf course, but the title – and the extra money – were more than welcome.

Louise Rumsey's nephew, Fred Grun, quit his job at a Terre Haute funeral parlor after inheriting the mortuary. He had to change the name because no one in Lincoln County would have crossed the threshold of any establishment with the Rumsey moniker on it. It was now the Grun Mortuary Chapel. Rumor has it that the new owner was thinking about adding a furniture showroom to bring in extra cash between the burials. One of the first things Grun did was to install iron bars over the embalming room windows. I wished him well.

Julia Porter and Johnnie moved away. I heard they were living with an aunt somewhere in Michigan. At least they would have enough money to provide for a secure future. Lawyer Rowland Shuster put together a trust for Johnnie, so he would be taken care of for life. The trust was financed by a gift from an anonymous friend.

The same anonymous friend bought back Ted Thompson's farm from the Chicago real estate company after the federal authorities had finished their investigation. The stoic Thompson wept when lawyer Shuster presented him with the deed free and clear, with all debts and taxes paid, plus enough cash to make improvements.

After a few other anonymous disbursements to Rumsey's victims, the Prattsburg Lending Library and to development of that unfinished downtown city park, all of the money was gone. I burned Rumsey's valise.

Jeff Heston was understandably reluctant, but my first act as managing editor was to hire Big Jim Rypanski. All those muscles came in handy in the press room, where he was now Ed Jones's apprentice. Jim was courting Winnie Arbuckle, and it looked as though he was going to make an honest woman of her. He seemed relieved to have left his old life behind. Jim visited Dixie's grave from time to time. I know because I see him there when I, too, come to pay my respects. I opened a bank account in Rypanski's name and deposited the $41,280 from Dixie's valise into it. He has a nest egg, now, whether he wants it or not.

Uncle Adolphus Mueller and Greta Hauptmann got married in June. I was best man and Adele was matron of honor. Aunt Greta finally gave into convention. As Barney O'Malley said when he toasted the bride and groom, "Who'd a-thunk it?"

Barney's big story was a five-parter that ran Page One above the fold. Paradise even had a small role in it – small in Chicago terms, enormous to us. That Chicago real estate company, Copper Beeches Property Management, Inc., turned out to be ninety percent legitimate. Hidden in the other ten percent were the houses and farms of the Gangland Underground Railroad, including the Thompson place in Lincoln County. Ted Thompson escaped prosecution because the authorities understood his role was as a victim, not a perpetrator. The gangsters had kept Ted's children home as hostages whenever the farmer went to town. Rumsey, as vice president of the company, was in it up to his eyeballs. Benny Green was the real boss. Barney got another story out of the casino. FBI Agent McMaster, and the feds rolled up the operation, even arresting two Chicago police captains.

There was also sad news in our small world.

Hattie Webster caught pneumonia and died the week after Christmas. I am thoroughly convinced that she is happily following Mrs. Arletha Heston around Heaven collecting dimes from the other angels. Mrs. Heston had died two months earlier.

And Homer Van Meter. We just received word that police in St. Paul, Minnesota, had shot him to death earlier this week. There were twenty-seven bullet holes in his back. What a great guy. What a waste of brains, looks and talent. I am pondering his life. There might be a novel about Homer, or a man who bore an uncanny resemblance to him, in bookstores someday. The working title is *Gone Bad.*

Doc Joplin did a little detective work. He identified the unknown man found with Louise Rumsey and Jed Bailey on the embalming tables. Doc did not need modern science, fingerprints or dental records. He went through the corpse's pockets, something Thurl Gaskins forgot to do. We knew his name, but nothing else. My best guess? He was one of Rumsey's gangster connections who had landed in the wrong place at the wrong time. More we would never know.

Doc also committed a couple of felonies for a good cause. When he was called to the embalming room that awful day, he surreptitiously tossed my brick out the broken window. Fortunately, no one seemed to have noticed that all the broken glass was on the *inside* of the room. He claimed to have heard Rumsey's dying confession stating that the undertaker had murdered Dixie. Doc also managed to convince a skeptical Sheriff Hoyt Peterson that Rumsey had committed suicide, despite all evidence and common sense to the contrary. I believed the sheriff had closed his eyes to the obvious and had chosen justice over the strict imposition of the law.

I knew a few other things.

I knew I would never set foot in another funeral parlor as long as I lived. Adele was not particularly happy about this, but she understood.

I also knew that Francis Tolliver Rumsey, may he rot in Hell, was one cold customer.

* * *

Where to, now? I was headed to the fairgrounds to follow up on a tip. Mrs. Viola DeWinter was convinced that there was cheating in the annual cake-baking contest. This was one of the highlights of the Lincoln County Fair. She had a big stake in the outcome. Her devil's food cake had won five out of the past six years. This was not as exciting as a murder, perhaps, but it was an important thread in the fabric of life in Paradise.

As it was written in Ecclesiastes: "Better is the end of a thing than the beginning thereof," but I thought that you would still like to see how it all began.

Or as Doc might say: *Mihi permitte tibi dicere quod faciam . . .*

* * *

In the meantime, here's a glimpse into Dixie's story. You will find it in bookstores come November.

THE GIRL IN THE YELLOW DRESS

By Walter G. Pratt

Dixie Lee Rypanski, née McGraw, stepped off the northbound New York Central train at 3:23 p.m. It was the afternoon of July 3, 1933. It was bright and hot, and she shaded her green eyes against the glare with a gloved hand. The two stately American elms guarding either end of the depot's narrow platform bowed their limbs in obedience to the heat of a Hoosier summer's day.

She had seen dozens of train stations in the past month. Some were grand affairs. These called attention to themselves with stone arches, laughing monsters and curly carvings. Some were shabby, little more than telegraph shacks with sagging porches where the occasional passenger could wait. She had seen hundreds of towns and cities from train windows. This one, that one, no, maybe. She catalogued them as the train sped by at a steady fifty miles an hour.

Sometimes she debarked and stayed for a day or two. There were always rooming houses or salesman's hotels near the train stations in the larger towns. She walked the streets past the grand houses of the business class and the humble homes of the workers. She wandered the shops, trying on hats or fingering the dresses. She checked the prices of coffee and dressed chickens, listened to the local gossip. She went to church one Sunday morning the previous week or the week before, somewhere in Ohio. The worshippers offered up loud prayers, hard stares and a pamphlet asking "Are You Saved?" Her mother would have howled at that one. Dixie's bones remembered every beating she had endured for skipping Sunday school to play by the river with Trixie.

She drew attention. Maybe it was her bottle-blonde hair with the wide wave that dipped over her forehead to touch her eyebrow just so. Maybe it was her clothing, which was a little too tight or too big city in style. Maybe it was her habit of standing perfectly still in shadows, of peering around corners, of walking a little too fast across open spaces. Maybe it was that shiver she could not suppress whenever she saw a fedora tilted at a certain angle.

And there was that one time in Altoona. Or was it Warren? Or Akron? It was one of those red-brick, hard-working towns where coal soot turned everything grey, even in summer. She had gone to the picture show, some film about tap dancing with a pretty brunette in it. Behind her, she heard a familiar cough and knuckles being cracked – *pop, pop,* pause, *pop.* She rushed to the aisle without so much as an *excuse me* to the patrons whose knees and feet stumbled against and tripped over. *Pop, pop,* pause, *pop.* There it was again. Electric sparkles danced before her eyes and she fell. When she came to in the theater's office, the usherettes handed her a cup of sweet hot tea.

"It's nothing," she lied. "I forgot to eat today. Thank you, kindly."

The usherettes shook their heads and tried to talk her out of it but let her out the back door. She had managed to plaster a sweet smile on her face and force the fear from her voice. But that was weeks ago.

During the long stretches when she rode the trains aimlessly from town to town, her mind drifted back to the places and events that had set her trek in motion. Trixie talked to her from time to time. Dixie saw her in the reflection that stared back from the railroad car window. Trixie whispered to the rhythm of the train wheels: *Be strong. Remember Mamaw. If we could run away from her, we can run away from this. I'm okay. I'm okay.*

But Trixie was not okay. She would never be okay. Trixie was dead.

She had no idea where Jim had gone. Her husband could have been anywhere, could even be dead. She hoped he was still in the relative safety of jail. She had not dared to write to him or send a telegram. *Jim, Jim, Jim – be safe, my love.* That was a close as she could come to uttering a prayer. All the deities seemed to have abandoned her.

Trixie was dead. It all had begun so innocently.

Dixie and Trixie were harmonizing on the final chorus of their featured number, a syncopated version of a bouncy Irving Berlin tune, when the band came to a ragged halt. Some of the drunker patrons booed, but then they heard shots, and a lot of big men with big guns and handkerchiefs covering their faces burst through the doors. Trixie grabbed Dixie's arm and dragged her behind the bandstand. More gunshots. Dixie wished Jim were here. He would know what to do.

"Come on, sister. Let's get out of here," Trixie said.

There was a door straight ahead. They ran for it. The door opened onto a hallway. It was dim and narrow, just a walled-in path that led from where they had been to wherever they were going. Neither of the McGraw sisters had been in this section of the casino. They had been instructed to stay with the band at all times and not wander. Dixie had sneaked a smoke one time out on the loading dock and had gotten royally chewed out. The hall ended at an office that was little more than a wider spot in the corridor. No one there. They caught their breath.

"Where are we?" Dixie asked.

"We're where there ain't no shooting," Trixie replied. "That's the only thing that counts."

Beyond the tiny office was another larger room lit only by a single overhead lamp. Four men wearing tuxedos huddled over a table, stuffing money hurriedly into a cheap wooden casket. Dixie and Trixie recognized the men. They ran the floating casino. The middle-sized man with the skinny moustache was Benny Green, the man who had hired them.

Heavy footsteps behind them pounded down the hall they had just vacated – at least three or four men by the sound of it. There was nowhere to hide in the office. The sisters tiptoed into the larger room and found shelter behind a screen of boxes and hid with their arms wrapped around one another.

"That's the best we can do, boys," Green said. "Nail it."

"Gotcha, Nose. Give it up." The chasers had entered the room with guns drawn. "Hand over the money. That's all we want."

One of Green's men reached for his gun, and the bullets began to fly. The sisters crouched as low as they could. Dixie felt something warm spread down her forearm where it was wrapped around Trixie's shoulder. *I've been shot!* – that was her first thought. But she felt no pain. It was like that in the movies, but she had seen animals shot when her father went hunting. If the first shot was not true, the animals screamed in pain until put out of their misery. Then Trixie slumped against her. Dixie put her hand over Trixie's mouth. She was still breathing. The crack of gunshots eventually stopped.

"We got 'em," a man shouted. "Stop the damn shooting."

"Better check 'em," another man said.

"There might be more, Carmine. Look down the hall."

One of Bennie Green's tuxedoed thugs stepped past the women's hiding place and peered into the adjoining office. "I don't see nobody," he said.

"Let's scram," Green said. "That bunch ain't looking here."

A thickly accented voice came from the hallway. "Don't shoot. It's me, Paulie."

"Get in here," Green said. "What going on in the main room?"

"It's under control. The hoods, I think they were DiSanto's guys, got the money on the tables, some of the customers' jewelry and wallets. I couple of our guys got sapped. The customers are pretty nervous, making call-the-cops noises."

"Give 'em free drinks. That'll shut 'em up for a while. I'll be out in a minute."

"Hey, Benny, listen," one of the gangsters said. "Sirens. You hear 'em?"

"Shit! Let's get out of here," Green ordered. "You okay, Francis? You been hit?"

"No," a shaky voice answered. "But what about --"

"The bodies? Leave 'em. They ain't going nowhere. We'll clean up tomorrow. That'll be your job, Francis, making our new friends disappear for good. I gotta clean up and make nice. Gotta calm down the customers and find out what kind of damage we got out front."

The sirens receded.

"Hear that? The cops are looking at least two blocks away. I think we're in the clear," Green said.

The men shuffled out. A door slammed in the distance. Dixie held her breath and counted to ten. Trixie moaned. She was coming to. *Thank the great God Almighty who rules the heavens and the earth,* Dixie prayed. Mamaw would have been proud of her.

"C'mon, Trixie, get on your feet. We gotta get out of here," Dixie said and pulled her sister into the light. "Oh my God, you're shot." Blood gushed from a wound in her neck.

"Ain't nothing, sister. Mamaw's whippings was worse." Trixie tried to laugh. "I don't feel so good. I can make it, though." Her laughed turned into a deep cough. Blood trickled out of the corner of her mouth. "Ain't it funny, I get hurt, and I start sounding like Hog Bend. Cain't git it out of our system, can we, sister? Think of all that money we spent on them elocution lessons so we'd sound high class."

"Shut up. We gotta move," Dixie said.

"Which way?"

"Back where we came from. I can find where I parked the car from there. I got to get you to a doctor."

"Did you see all that cash?" Trixie asked between coughs. She was trembling.

"Yes. Let's go."

"I'm getting me some. They owe us for what we've been through tonight. Gotta pay the doctor, too."

"Oh, Trixie."

"I'm older, and you gotta do what I say."

"Three minutes don't count," Dixie said.

"I ain't leaving without the money."

"Okay, okay."

Dixie stepped over the dead men on the sprawled on the floor. One had a satchel about the size of a doctor's bag. She could use that. Green's men only had time to put one or two nails into the top of the coffin. She gave a hard tug and the lid gave way. It was heavy, and Dixie could not control it. The lid fell to the floor with a crash. She held her breath.

"Hurry up!" Trixie said. "I'm getting dizzy."

Dixie scooped wads of money – some loose, some rolled, some banded – into the bag. Most were twenties and hundreds. There were thousands of dollars. She let out a little yelp. She had found the bottom of the money. It rested on the naked corpse of a man with bullet holes in him. She could not distinguish whether the hole had been made earlier and killed, or whether they were the result of the recent gun battle.

"There's a girl in here!"

Dixie turned and saw a man in the shadows. He sounded like the one with the shaky voice who had been afraid. She could not make out his face. Dixie grabbed her sister's elbow and dragged her through the little office. The light switch caught her eye, so she hit it in passing. They were in complete darkness, now, but she knew where they were going. Trixie stumbled beside her, slower at every step.

Backstage was a door with a big red sign: EXIT ONLY. Dixie pulled her sister through it. No alarm went off. That was good news. The air outside felt cool and fresh, but Dixie did not have time to appreciate it. Trixie's breathing was growing more and more ragged. Dixie sat Trixie down on the steps to the loading dock.

"Stay here. I'll bring the car around."

"I don't think I'll make it, sister," Trixie said.

"Yes, you will. We're twins. We're half of each other. I won't let you die. Stay put and stay quiet. I'll be right back."

The car, Jim's 1932 Chevy, was about a hundred feet away, parked in an alley across the street. Dixie kicked off her high-heeled shoes and ran barefoot. She was faster and quieter unshod, as she was as a skinny child racing across the hills with her brothers and sisters. She had just reached the opening in the fence, thankfully unlocked, when a voice stopped her cold.

"Got her!" a man said. "Francis, over here. This the broad you saw?"

Dixie held her breath. A flashlight beam cut through the dark, and she ducked behind the wheel well of a truck. The light was focused on Trixie, who had slumped onto her side.

"That's her," said the man with the shaky voice. "She's dead."

"Let me see. Get the fuck out of the way," ordered Benny Green, the boss. "Aw, crap. It's one of those McGraw twins, the singers. Couldn't sing worth a damn, but they looked good. Customers liked them. Give me the light."

He focused the flashlight closer on Trixie's face. "Which one is it? Any of you got a clue?"

"What's that?" one said.

"You mean the necklace? What's that got – oh! D-I-X-I-E. That's what it spells. That's her, then."

Dixie fingered the matching necklace she wore that spelled T-R-I-X-I-E. The trinkets were supposed to be their good-luck charms. They had them made at a booth at the World's Fair and wore them for one another.

"Yeah, boss. That's her, but where's the other girl? And where's the money?"

Dixie did not wait to wipe the silent tears streaming down her cheeks. She ran like a cat afire, found Jim's car and drove as far and as fast as possible.

But that was weeks ago.

Here was yet another little town, somewhere in Indiana. To her left, she saw rows of neat wood-framed houses, with fresh paint and well-tended lawns. To her right, she could catch just a slice of downtown, where the Oolitic limestone courthouse butted the sky at four stories tall, counting the dome that was painted gold to rival the sun. It was a friendly town, she guessed, modest and clean except for the summer dust that lay on everything like nature's mantilla. It was the kind of place that nobody had ever heard of or cared about, except the people who lived there. She stepped onto the platform, uncertain of what she would do next.

"All aboard for Elkhart, Gary, Chicago and points west," sang out Mose Truby, the conductor on the afternoon New York Central train.

She turned to him, picked up the scuffed cardboard suitcase at her feet, checked the knots in the twine that tied it together. A valise and her purse were in her other hand. She took a hesitant half step toward the passenger car, then stopped.

"You coming, miss? This train don't stop long. We got seventeen minutes to make up and track to cover, if we're going to make it to Chicago on time."

Just then, a soft breeze sprang up and swirled the dust, make green waves float through the elms and cool the sweat that clung to her body like wet bandages. A board dangled from the side of the train depot. The rusty chains holding it creaked when the wind tugged at it.

She looked up.

PARADISE

It was a sign.

* * *

Mort Walker, the station master, remembered her walking into the depot to cash in the remainder of her ticket – $4.40. She wore a perky yellow hat, straw the color of dried field corn, with a tiny net veil. Yellow gloves matched the hat. She had a soft voice with a little accent that sounded funny in his ears. Southern maybe, he thought, not magnolia Southern nor quite hard-scrabble Southern, but definitely from somewhere south of here. He gave her directions to the best places to eat, nice places where a lady alone would feel comfortable, where the menu would not be too hard on the pocketbook or the digestion.

When the station master turned to another customer, the woman started to leave but hung back, checking the clasp on her valise. "You need some help, miss?" asked Mickey Remick, the station's jack of all trades. Remick swept, helped load baggage, and filled in for Mort Walker when the station master took a rare day off.

"I've got to walk a few blocks, and it's so hot. Can I leave one of my bags here?" she asked. "It has to be someplace safe. With good locks? Just for a day or two." She held up the valise. "It's small, won't take up much space."

"Sure, miss. The baggage room is padlocked day and night. Nobody goes in there except the station master and me."

"Guess that'll do. Thank you, kindly."

"I'll get a tag, and we'll put your name on it. It'll be safe, I promise. You can pick it up anytime you like."

She borrowed a pen from Mickey, then hesitated for a moment before putting the nib to the cardboard tag to fill in the blanks. Then she quickly wrote MRS. JAMES RYPANSKI and a Chicago address. Mickey added HOLD FOR LATER PICKUP and the day's date. Her eyes followed Mickey as he obtained a large ring of keys from the busy station master, who did not look up. Mickey unlocked the storage area and placed the bag inside.

She offered him a quarter tip, but Mickey turned her down. "Uncle Sam'll be paying me come Wednesday morning. I'm joining the Navy. Always liked the water."

She laughed. "See the world and all that?"

"Yes, ma'am, that's exactly what I intend to do."

Jack Myer glanced out the window of Myer's Drug Emporium and saw the flash of her yellow dress as she walked by. She must have sensed him looking at her or perhaps she startled herself by catching her own reflection in his just-washed front window, because she jumped. She frowned slightly, probably from the sun in her eyes, then caught sight of the pharmacist in his starched apron. She smiled at him. He thought he might have detected a little wave from her gloved hand. And what a smile! How sweet she was, he thought, yessir, sweet as sunshine.

Mrs. Margie Hopkins had just parked her Ford on the north side of the Courthouse Square to keep in the relative cool of the afternoon shadows. She caught a glimpse of yellow across the street and squinted. A girl, she thought at first. No, a young woman, twenty-two or twenty-three years old, Mrs. Hopkins decided, all decked out to beat the band. A stranger. Nobody she knew and she, by Heaven, knew everybody. After teaching fifth grade for twenty-five years, two-plus generations of Paradisans had passed before her stern, grey eyes. But that dress! Far too flashy for Paradise. Cottons and gabardines were what everybody wore in summer, except for Miss Mary Kitchens and Miss Vesta Martin, those old maids who ran a little chicken farm and thought nothing of being seen in public wearing men's trousers. How much had that yellow dress cost? And where had it come from? Some big-city department store, no doubt. Yes, indeed, that was a store-bought dress. She would buy lemons, that's what she would do. The dress was the exact color of lemon meringue pie.

Just past the courthouse, Francis Rumsey swept the sidewalk in front of his funeral parlor. He scraped the broom across the concrete up to the alley and not one inch beyond. The Daisy Diner was on the other side of the alley. Herb Daishell could take care of his own. None of his business. Dirt in front of his establishment was another matter. Appearances counted. Business was business. He picked up a wilted flower left from the Urcyl Dandarelle funeral that afternoon. Good turnout. Cash money already in the bank. He started to flick the red carnation into the street but was stopped by a discreet cough.

"Excuse me, sir."

"Ma'am." Rumsey automatically tipped his hat to the lady and stepped back. Then he stared.

The woman floated past him. She was a yellow cloud propelled by two tiny feet. The full skirt that grazed her calves had a deep ruffle at the low neckline and at the end of the elbow-length sleeves. The gauzy fabric was printed with flowers, a whole field of yellow flowers. She glanced over her shoulder and nodded her thanks. For less than a second their eyes met. Then she smiled, shifted her suitcase to her other hand and walked on.

Francis Rumsey felt sweat crawl down the inside of his stiff shirt collar. The sweat was not all from the heat.

Herb Daishell, owner and chief cook of the Daisy Diner, first noticed the scuffed suitcase. It was little better than a cardboard box with pretentions and wrapped around a half-dozen times with rough twine. He was bent over, sweeping a broken water glass into a dust pan and silently cursing Reba Witherspoon's arthritic fingers. Reba made the best pies in the county, and the customers liked the grandmotherly way she treated them. But, dangit, he thought, the woman could not hold onto a handkerchief if her life depended on it. Next to the suitcase were feet in flat-heeled shoes that his wife, Madonna, would have described as sensible, except for their color, a yellow somewhere between the color of egg yolks and butter. Connected to the shoes were trim ankles crossed over one another followed by the curve of shapely calves that disappeared under the hem of her yellow dress.

"Hey, Herb, quit your day dreaming. You have any more of that swamp water you call coffee hiding over there?"

"Sure, Walter, if you've got the greenbacks to pay for it."

Walter G. Pratt capped his fountain pen and laid it next to the child's schoolwork tablet lying open beside his right elbow. It was a fat thing with pale blue lines on thin, buff-colored paper. He pushed the remains of the meatloaf special around on his plate and took a long look at the woman who had just come into the diner.

She was perhaps twenty-one, not an inch taller than five-foot-three, with round cheeks, round bosom, round everywhere she should be round, and a mouth wider than fashion dictated. High, thin eyebrows penciled into an exaggerated line gave her an expression as if she were always on the verge of asking an important question. She possessed the kind of prettiness that old age would never destroy, only mellow. That was provided disappointment, booze, a man with ready fists, too many babies too young or permanent hunger did not destroy that lovely face.

Who was she, he wondered, this stranger in the small universe of Paradise, Indiana?

Bright as the first dawn, the girl in the yellow dress lit a cigarette, leaned her head back on a neck too slender to bear such a weight of beauty and laughed. Her laugh was merry enough but there was something secret in her eyes. She was afraid. She hid it well.

That was what he wrote. Those four sentences would haunt him for a long, long time.

THE END

Made in the USA
Lexington, KY
16 November 2018